THE PITFALLS OF POLITE SOCIETY

At first Charlotte behaved as was expected of any well-bred young lady.

When she heard that the man she loved had left her forever, she promptly fell into a swoon and lay abed with a broken heart for weeks.

When her stern father and sensible mother commanded her to re-enter society and find a suitable husband, she dutifully obeyed.

When George Beresford made his proposal of marriage in his bored voice, she said yes as expected.

But as her wedding day drew near, Charlotte realized she was about to lose all chance of happiness—unless she forgot her fine manners and fought for what she wanted . . .

Lady
Charlotte's Ruse

ROMANTIC ENCOUNTERS

- ☐ MARIAN'S CHRISTMAS WISH by Carla Kelly   (163311—$3.50)
- ☐ QUEEN OF THE MAY by Emily Hendrickson   (164881—$3.50)
- ☐ DUNRAVEN'S FOLLY by Dawn Lindsey   (163346—$3.50)
- ☐ THE GENEROUS EARL by Catherine Coulter   (163354—$3.50)
- ☐ CAROUSEL OF HEARTS by Mary Jo Putney   (162676—$3.50)
- ☐ THE GALLANT LORD IVES by Emily Hendrickson   (164202—$3.50)
- ☐ MARRIAGE BY CONSENT by Elizabeth Hewitt   (162706—$3.50)
- ☐ LORD HARRY'S FOLLY by Catherine Coulter   (162714—$3.50)
- ☐ NEWMARKET MATCH by Anita Mills   (161017—$3.50)
- ☐ THE PARAGON BRIDE by Leigh Haskell   (162234—$3.50)
- ☐ THE PILFERED PLUME by Sandra Heath   (162242—$3.50)
- ☐ THE AUTUMN COUNTESS by Catherine Coulter   (162269—$3.50)
- ☐ THE ROSE DOMINO by Sheila Walsh   (163826—$3.50)
- ☐ A DOUBLE DECEPTION by Joan Wolf   (158083—$3.50)

Prices slightly higher in Canada

Buy them at your local bookstore or use this convenient coupon for ordering.

NEW AMERICAN LIBRARY
P.O. Box 999, Bergenfield, New Jersey 07621

Please send me the books I have checked above. I am enclosing $_____
(please add $1.00 to this order to cover postage and handling). Send check or
money order—no cash or C.O.D.'s. Prices and numbers are subject to change
without notice.

Name_____

Address_____

City _____ State _____ Zip Code _____
Allow 4-6 weeks for delivery.
This offer is subject to withdrawal without notice.

Lady Charlotte's Ruse

by
Judith Harkness

A SIGNET BOOK

SIGNET
Published by the Penguin Group
Penguin Books USA Inc., 375 Hudson Street,
New York, New York 10014, U.S.A.
Penguin Books Ltd, 27 Wrights Lane,
London W8 5TZ, England
Penguin Books Australia Ltd, Ringwood,
Victoria, Australia
Penguin Books Canada Ltd, 2801 John Street,
Markham, Ontario, Canada L3R 1B4
Penguin Books (N.Z.) Ltd, 182-190 Wairau Road,
Auckland 10, New Zealand

Penguin Books Ltd, Registered Offices:
Harmondsworth, Middlesex, England

Published by Signet, an imprint of New American Library,
a division of Penguin Books USA Inc.

First Printing, August, 1982
13   12   11   10   9   8   7   6   5

Copyright © 1982 by Judith Harkness
All rights reserved

REGISTERED TRADEMARK—MARCA REGISTRADA

Printed in the United States of America

BOOKS ARE AVAILABLE AT QUANTITY DISCOUNTS WHEN USED TO PROMOTE PRODUCTS OR SERVICES.
FOR INFORMATION PLEASE WRITE TO PREMIUM MARKETING DIVISION, PENGUIN BOOKS USA INC.,
375 HUDSON STREET, NEW YORK, NEW YORK 10014.

Chapter 1

The sudden heat of June had struck London, after a cold and rainy spring, like the blast of a smithy's furnace. Everywhere the dust was raised and people's tempers short. Even the hawkers lifted their singsong voices without much conviction, pressing upon the irritable populace their various Spanish oranges, wilted violets and damp muffins in a lackadaisical manner, then rushing for the shade of the nearest doorway when no one was about. The crush at the gates of Hyde Park was denser than ever, for added to the usual swarm of fashionable carriages and dandies was what seemed like every nanny in the Metropolis, shepherding her charges into the promising coolness of green grass and green trees. In the City, clerks haggled over their ledgers, whilst even the normally cool-tempered men of business in the sanctum sanctorums of Rothschild, Meyer and Salomon pressed kerchiefs to their dripping brows.

Issuing from the offices of his father's solicitors in the Poultry, Gerald Stanis Kirkland staggered a little from the sudden blaze of light and drew forth his watch. Four o'clock! With a muffled oath he turned his steps in the direction of Milk Street, striding like a man who would much rather run. Four o'clock! That fellow would talk forever if you let him. And what cared Gerald for the price of timber, old or new, legal boundaries and the marketability of arable land when poor Charlotte was waiting for him in this heat? Poor angel! The thought of her made him stride on more briskly than ever, whistling a faint tune into the glare of the afternoon.

Gerald's way led through a tangle of small twisting streets, the underbelly of the great City's life, where much of its money and nearly all of its laws were made, but which was so removed from the elegant bustle of the fashionable districts that those who profited from its daily din might hardly have known of its existence. The streets and alleys were crowded, but not with the tonnish ladies and gentlemen who mobbed St. James and Bond Streets. The masses in evidence were chiefly men and women whose business it was to ease the lives of the aristocracy: maidservants and menservants, clerks, tradesmen, shipping officials, lawyers and merchants, and mixed in with them a generous dash of sad creatures begging ha'pennies at the corners, turning organs or merely lolling, too sick or drunk to care, in the shadow of a doorway.

In such a menagerie of human existence, Gerald must have seemed like a being from another world. His tall, strong frame was clothed meticulously, from the immaculate coat of pale-grey superfine molded to his shoulders by one of the premier tailors of Pall Mall to the dovelike softness of his kid gloves and the gleaming Hessians that encased his long and muscular calves. His face, too, well sculpted and refined, attested to the long line of privilege from which he was descended. A lucky trick of fate had given him those keen and twinkling blue eyes with their faint air of surprise; those cheekbones, which seemed to have been fashioned after the best of the Greeks' many gods; that strong clefted chin and vigorous mouth; but the expression of sad shock that overcame those features after glimpsing a poor deformed female offering him a hot trotter could only have been formed in the elite schools in which he had been tutored. He was not the only one of his family to have attended Eton and Cambridge: eleven generations of "gentlemen"—men to the very literal manor born—had preceded him. He was destined to be the twelfth baronet, when fate and his father's health should judge fitting.

Having come from a conference which had made him feel, if anything, that he had been born under an unlucky star, this brief immersion in London's netherworld gave Gerald a sense of unjustified good fortune. He was not aware of the eyes that followed his speedy progress towards the corners of Lyman Road and the Highway. His nostrils flared, despite himself, at the sight of a cripple turning an organ whilst a monkey, done up in petticoats and a bonnet, danced. And yet all the while his conscious mind was engaged upon another sight altogether: a sight of such tranquillity and elegance, a face so gifted with beauty and serene understanding, that a glimpse of it would surely have made one of the sad creatures about him stare. Nevertheless, part of his mind was reciting, "You lucky brute! To have been born in good health with strong limbs and a heritage that ensured your welfare! Why, beside all these unfortunates, should you feel yourself deprived for having inherited, as well, an estate entailed away by high living?"

Arriving at his intermediate destination, Gerald glanced up and down the street for a hansom cab, but there was none to be seen. He set off at a half gallop down Lyman Road, determining to hire a mount at the posting house around the corner. Just as he turned into the little alleyway leading into the commercial stables, however, his eye lit upon a hansom putting down its passengers. In one sprint across the cobblestones he nabbed it and, with a breathless command to the driver, leapt up.

"Hyde Park, guv'nor, half a flash" was promised him, and in a moment they were jolting wildly in the direction of the West End. It was that time of day, however, when London lets forth its working population and when the other half—that half which either does not work or works at night—is setting out for the evening. The streets were jammed with vehicles and people, and that great crossroads leading from the City of London into the West End Highway was a veritable knot of confusion. Leaning back against the cab's moth-eaten cushion, Gerald watched coldly the inevitable crush of yelling humanity, his gloved fingers playing an irritable tattoo upon the carriage's scarred rim. What had shortly before served as a balm to his impatience—the thought of Charlotte waiting for him in the cool green of the Park—now made him mutter a stream of less than flattering epithets at the crowd. That she should have to wait upon this mob's stupidity! Or perhaps—and the thought made Gerald momentarily cease his drumming—she had not waited after all.

The idea had barely crossed his mind when the carriage gave a sudden jolt and started forward. It was just at that

moment, as his neck was jerked back by the sudden movement and his head turned a fraction to the right, that he
caught sight of the figure in the crowd. That fellow!

The change in Gerald's face was instantaneous, as was
the one in his heart. His cheeks were drained of colour,
and his blue eyes seemed to turn a leaden grey. That fellow!

His eye had not lit upon him for above an instant, and
yet it was sufficient. That long and graceful slouch, rather
like the posture of a cat about to leap, the tall hat set rak-
ishly askew, the famous cane—needed less for walking
than for the occasional refreshment of its owner, for it
was common knowledge that the cane was hollow only in
the morning when it was filled up anew with port—all this
was unmistakable. Gerald had no need to glimpse the features hidden from view by the fawn velum of the hat's rim
even had he the desire to see them. He would have known
by half of what he had observed who the fellow was. That
slouch, that arrogant saunter, even the hand, half cupped
about the cane's head with the little finger preposterously
thrust out—all were emblazoned upon his memory with
the clarity which only bitter hatred can give. That that
hatred was in no small part due to envy did nothing to
lessen it.

It is an amazing fact of life, but nonetheless a fact, that
no man, however fortunate, has not somewhere on earth
his better, whether in looks or education or wealth or
some less obvious manifestation of nature's bounty. Even a
king will begrudge his fellow monarch a thousand acres of
land if that is all that stands between them to make them
equal, while amongst his subjects, who can say how many
causes there may not be for envy? A kitchen maid envies
her upstairs counterpart, a footman envies a valet, a coal
scuttle envies a chimney sweep—or vice versa. The damsel
born with golden hair thinks she is too pale and wishes to
be her brunette sister. A commoner longs to be a baronet,
and a baronet thinks he ought to have been a viscount, at
least. Up and down the pyramid of life the game is
played, sometimes with more bitterness than others. And
though much of this is vanity, and all of it folly, who can
blame the man who envies another, not for himself, but
for the benefit of one even more dear to him than life?

Such was the case with Gerald, who, from looks and

manner, seemed to have everything fortune can give a
man. Certainly those poor creatures he had passed in Milk
Street would have been astonished to discover that he was
not the very epitome of gilded youth. How amazed that
pitiful beggar woman would have been to see him, only
minutes after she had received half a sovereign from his
gloved hand, nearly green with envy at the sight of one
who, to her, must have seemed his twin.

For a brief second, that very thought flitted through the
young man's mind, even as he turned away, pale and flinty
eyed. The idea brought an ironic half smile to his lips. He
was not immune to envy, not least when it reflected his
fear of losing his greatest wish, but he was not a cad, either. He knew perfectly well how frivolous his envy might
appear to anyone with even half his advantages. He was
not like the fair-haired girl enraged at the idea that some
gentleman might prefer her brunette sister. Gerald was a
fair man, and an honest one, even with regard to his own
weaknesses.

At the moment, however, his weaknesses obtained the
upper hand, for he was in a particularly vulnerable mood,
and the half smile soon gave way to the original scowl. He
had just come, as we have said, from the office of Mr.
Bantree, and that gentleman had regaled him with news
not entirely agreeable to a young man who hopes soon to
propose matrimony. It seemed his father's affairs, which
had for some time been in a state of disarray, were beginning to look black indeed. The year before, Sir James had
been forced to sell the best corner of his Devonshire estate. Now it appeared another parcel might have to be put
upon the market, and Gerald, the baronet's only son, had
been sent to consult with the solicitor. But Mr. Bantree
had bleakly informed Gerald that the only remaining piece
of the estate which could command a reasonable sum was
that very piece upon which the baronet's income most depended. The money was needed to settle an alarming number of debts, but to raise the amount required would be to
all but abolish the baronet's present income—and therefore his heir's future one. The possibility had next been
raised that timber should be sold in place of land. Mr.
Bantree had not been optimistic as to the feasibility of
this. A great deal of timber, at the day's declining rates,
would have to be sold. Nevertheless, he had promised to

look into the matter and to inform his client of the outcome of his investigations. Thus was the matter left, and Gerald had gone to keep his rendezvous.

Towards this meeting Gerald now hastened—the hansom cabbie having been driving at full tilt since they had left the intersection of the Highway—intending to offer himself to Charlotte. Such as he was, he had reason to believe she loved him sufficiently to compensate for his limited prospects. It had not occurred to him, even after the daunting interview with Bantree, to postpone his declaration. Charlotte would wait—she had said so before in all but words—until at least such time as he could secure a foothold in some profession if the estate could not be made to produce an income sufficient for the needs of both him and his father. Charlotte would wait—was not she an angel?—but ought she to?

Such was the doubt that began to creep up on Gerald after that one fatal glimpse of the man in the Highway. Why such a brief glimpse, or any glimpse at all of a third party, should cause these forebodings in his hitherto optimistic thinking is a question which must wait to be answered. For at this moment the hansom cab drew up at Hyde Park Corner, and in the business of climbing down and paying the cabbie, Gerald was forced out of his reverie.

Even at this hour—somewhat past the apex of the fashionable time for driving in the Park—the gates were crowded with stylish chariots and strollers. Dandies and fashionably frocked ladies, the grandest of which drove their own little pony-carts and landaus, vied for the attention of the public at large. Phaetons, barouches and the occasional full-rigged carriage jammed together to obtain access to the cool greenery within. The chief business of most was as much to be seen as to avoid the heat of the streets, but Gerald had no wish to be observed by anyone. Keeping his head well down, he quickly forced through the tonnish mob towards a corner of the Park well away from their elegant noise. It was a little dell shunned by fashion but much favored by lovers and children, a place for secret meetings that he and Charlotte had discovered one day in early spring. Glimpsing the familiar avenue of elm and lime trees which screened it from the view of the rest of the Park, Gerald's pace slackened. His expression grew troubled again as he was overcome once more by doubt. Moving stealthily, he paused behind the great trunk of an ancient lime and quite silently stared at the scene which greeted his eyes.

Chapter 2

It was a charming sight. At the edge of a small green, thickly carpeted with grass and shaded from the still scorching sun by an overhanging bower of copper beech, stood a small stone nymph with a look of pleased surprise watching the water trickle through her fingers. Beside the fountain and a little in front of it was a stone bench. Upon this bench sat a young woman of about nineteen or twenty. She was dressed in lilac, a shade so pretty that, even though her head was turned away and covered in any case by a double thickness of tulle, she gave at once the impression of great loveliness. Upon her head, which was propped at an angle, her chin resting upon a small lace-mittened fist, was a straw bonnet of the latest Paris design. Her slippers, lilac satin with small velvet bows, peeped out prettily from beneath her lilac underslip. But the most striking thing about her was not one thing in particular but rather the atmosphere created by the whole. She seemed a picture of dainty, feminine contemplation, and watching her, Gerald was seized anew with wonder at the innocent elegance which had first amazed him so many years before. Even as a child she had possessed the same miraculous combination of naïveté and womanliness, and now, as a woman, she retained a childlike quality even more seductive.

And yet it was this same childlike quality, a vulnerability far surpassing the sentimental hysteria of vogue amongst most young women of fashion, which now made him frown. She was so slight, so fragile! Surely she might be blown down by the merest puff of hardship!

A twig cracked beneath his foot, making him start and Charlotte whirl around.

"Oh!"

"Dearest Charlotte—I am so sorry!" he exclaimed, stepping into the little clearing with a slight feeling of guilt. "I'm afraid I have been spying upon you. You made such a surpassingly pretty picture, I couldn't help myself."

The veil beneath the bonnet seemed to quiver for a moment, and then a tinkling laugh issued from it.

"Really? I wonder it was very pretty, for I was just beginning to feel quite angry and neglected. I thought perhaps you had forgotten our appointment."

"Forgotten it! My dear Lady Charlotte, do you think me such a cad? That fellow Bantree kept me above two hours, and then I could not find a hansom cab."

"And then, of course, there was the dreadful traffic at the crossroads," continued Charlotte, keeping up the same tone of formal apology, in a chiding manner, but holding out her small hand to be kissed nonetheless. She snatched it back at once, however, after Gerald had made his exaggerated bow.

"You know it is quite improper, Mr. Kirkland, to kiss the hand of an unmarried lady, especially a young one."

Looking properly taken aback, Gerald muttered his apology, adding, "But you know that rule was invented by all the old married hags who cannot bear the idea that we poor men should get any pleasure out of life."

"Shame upon you, sir!"

By now the veil had been drawn back to reveal a set of features quite as entrancing as had been promised by the lovely pose of a moment before. They were small and dainty, as indeed was everything about Charlotte, but with nothing of the china doll about them. True, her complexion was a pale peach and cream, and her cheeks and forehead, nose and mouth, were delicately modelled. But in the eyes, which were large and almond shaped and coloured a changeful hazel, was a candour of expression wholly amazing to anyone who, meeting her for the first time, might have expected something quite demure and unchallenging. Perhaps more astonishing even than this, in an age when young unmarried ladies were not permitted

to dream of what their elder matron sisters freely indulged
in reality, was the quite apparent sensuality lurking about
the corners of that face. In the slight flare of the delicate
nostrils, the full, generous contours of that lovely mouth,
was to be seen a taste for pleasures not altogether spiritual. It was a contradiction as delightful as that between
her teasing laugh and the sincere welcome in her look as
she greeted Gerald. It was, as well, a source of continuing
fascination and wonder to that gentleman, who felt, when
watching her, the same sort of delicious intoxication which
one feels upon walking out of a hot and stuffy room, full
of the same old acquaintances reciting the same old cant,
into the crystalline night air.

"Well, and was there not a traffic jam?" she inquired of
him as she moved over slightly to make a place for him to
sit next to her.

"There was," replied he solemnly, meeting her mockery
with a little of his own. "And a dreadful one at that. I
thought you might have gone away. I nearly ran across the
Park."

"But halted long enough to spy upon me! Fie, sir! Are
you quite sure you have not been dallying over some
pretty bit of muslin in Milk Street?"

"I have been dallying over a most unprepossessing bit of
paper, if you must know the truth."

"Ah, poor dear! Then I shall give you something to
make up for your miserable afternoon."

And then, with a gesture quite unexpected, Charlotte
tilted back her head and closed her eyes. It was an offer
which could hardly be refused by Gerald. He kissed her
long and lingeringly, and in that kiss was all the hunger
and confusion in his heart.

Charlotte gave a little sigh. "I do think that ought to be
allowed, don't you? Although I ought probably to exact a
proposal of marriage from you before I allowed it, I suppose." She glanced sideways at him, with a look not altogether teasing, and saw that he was staring straight ahead
of him with a slight frown. "Dear me! I suppose you
didn't like it as much as I did!"

Her hand was still in the crook of his arm and now she
began to draw it away, but Gerald, glancing sharply back,
held onto it with his own strong fingers. "You oughtn't to
let me kiss you like that," he mumbled.

He was suddenly overcome with emotion and had to look away. That he should allow this sort of thing himself when their future was so uncertain! For a moment he could not bear to look at her, to see the confusion which he knew must be in her eyes or the accusation which he must read into her look, whether or not it was really there. With a brusqueness born purely out of a feeling of frustration, he stood up and walked to the edge of the little clearing. He expected some sort of protestation from Charlotte, but there was none.

She was staring at his back, biting her lip. It was not the first time she had seen her lover thus. In recent weeks he had betrayed more of his inner state of mind than he had been willing to admit to in words. Charlotte, though only twenty, possessed an understanding of the human heart which many women twice her age had not attained. Her natural ability to read people's real feelings in their looks and gestures was aided in this case by a love which had been born many years before.

As a child, when Gerald's father had kept a hunting lodge in Scotland adjacent to that of her own father, Lord Harrington, Charlotte had been used to following Gerald about the moors and hills like a faithful puppy. Even at twelve, Gerald had been strong, tall for his age, and the most fascinating creature she had ever seen. He was also—and to a little girl of seven, an only child, much cosseted and spoiled, this was the greatest wonder of all—marvellously, vibrantly masculine. He would take her little hand and lead her over the rough places, and when she fell down or grazed an elbow on a stone, he would sit down next to her and comfort her with stories of medieval knights and ladies. Those ramblings of theirs, which had come to an abrupt end when Sir James had been forced to sell his Scottish manor house, had constituted the greatest adventures of her life. She had worshipped Gerald as only a child of seven can worship a child of twelve. He had seemed to her then, as he did now, quite as wonderful for his gentleness as for his strength.

In the long years following that idyllic time, during all of her pampered and rather lonely growing up at the country seat in Yorkshire that was the Earl's chief residence, she had dreamt of those days and of that boy who had seemed as much at ease on the craggy Scottish hills as her mother did sitting at her dressing table. It was not until she was eighteen, however, and brought to London to achieve that final apex of her education—her presentation at Court and at Almack's—that Lady Charlotte Harrington, by then a fully grown woman, had realized the extent of her passion for Gerald.

At twenty-three, he had been a dashing young man about town for some years already. Eton and Cambridge had refined his manners and polished his mind, but he remained to her the same hero of rock and woods who had captured her imagination at seven. Never, never, would she forget that fateful evening upon which, still awestruck by the glittering world of fashionable London, she had turned round in the midst of the Duchess Devonshire's crowded ballroom to see Gerald's amused smile as he requested her hand in a country dance. She had fallen deeply and irretrievably in love during those succeeding hours, and not in all of the following two years, during which she herself had become one of the most sought after young ladies in the *ton*, had that devotion slackened for one moment. For him she had deceived her parents, who would have been shocked to discover their frequent secret meetings and who firmly believed that Gerald was merely another one of the suitors who customarily flocked about her in the ballrooms and supper rooms of London. They would have been shocked, not only at the impropriety of their innocent daughter, but at the idea that she, for whom they had planned great things, was deeply in love with the only son of an impoverished baronet.

Now, watching Gerald's broad back as he stood motionless at the edge of the little clearing, a number of emotions battled within her. First, she could not but be pained by the fact that her lover was so obviously troubled and feel some disquietude over the source of that trouble. Well she knew of Sir James's monetary troubles, though Gerald seldom discussed them with her. She knew that of all the difficulties standing in the way of their joint future this was the greatest, though by no means the only, one. She had attempted, by the subtle ruses which are at the disposal of a woman, to let him know that poverty did not frighten her if it was to be the only burden they would bear. Perhaps with a romanticism born from an existence which had known nothing of hardship or sacrifice, she had envisioned a life wherein she would be permitted to do those things for her husband's comfort which richer women cannot, because they need not, do. She imagined many children and a small house, a hearth made warm by the presence of love if not adorned by the luxuries of wealth. She dreamt of the toil with which she would prove, day after day, her enduring devotion to her knight, and of the evenings when, the day's work done, she could rest blissfully in his strong arms, comforted by the dear sound of his voice and strengthened by his love. Of mending and cooking and caring for a house she knew nothing, and yet she would learn, and oh! with what happiness! Such were the kinds of fancies entertained by Lady Charlotte Harrington, daughter of Lord Harrington, granddaughter of the Duke of Keynes.

Had Charlotte been quite sure that Gerald was troubled by nothing greater than his lack of fortune, she would have rested easy in the knowledge that she could erase such qualms from his mind. But she was not only a brave young woman—far braver than her doting parents could ever have imagined—she was, after all was said and done, a woman. As certain as she was of her own love for Gerald, Gerald's love for her, though amply and continually demonstrated, was never a source of utter security. And for whom is such the case? Let there be ever so strong an attachment between a man and woman, if they have not exchanged those vows by which their lives and hearts and destinies are tied together forever, some flickers of doubt, of human vanity and jealousy will remain. For all her trust in Gerald, for all her certainty of her own love for him, such a flicker still remained in Charlotte's bosom. Though she could hardly admit it even to herself, a cold dread passed over her heart, as she watched him, that the recent change in his disposition was caused, not by any fear of penury, but by a loss of his love for her.

Charlotte was too generous to suppose anything of the kind without some evidence, just as she was too humble to take his love for granted. Having no evidence, she pushed such doubt out of her mind. It had been, after all, only the slightest ripple of a doubt.

She ventured very timidly, "Was it so very dreadful with Mr. Bantree?"

Gerald, who had been scowling off into the bushes,

started at the question, as he had become lost in his own thoughts. "Dreadful?" he repeated, turning around with what he intended to be a perfectly bright smile. "No, not dreadful. No more dreadful than usual, in any case. But let us talk about something more interesting than that dour old fellow. Come, shall we walk in the avenue? It is a little cooler now, I think, and there is a breeze."

But Charlotte, though she stood up and took his arm and accompanied him very demurely into the avenue ancient limes, would not be put off so easily. "I think," she said, after a moment's silence, "that you ought to trust me more, Gerald."

"Trust you? And whom do you suppose I trust as much, dear girl?"

Charlotte, gazing up into his smiling blue eyes, felt instantly reassured. That moment of cold dread, of awful doubt, was completely vanquished by the long look they shared, and she felt a little throb of happiness in her bosom.

"Well then, you ought to tell me what occurred this afternoon," she persisted.

"Very well," said Gerald with a sigh, "but only if it is the sole manner in which I can convince you of my unfaltering trust."

Charlotte assured him that it was and with the cheerfulness which only a woman can display when, sure of her lover's devotion, she prepares to comfort him in his distress, she commenced interrogating him about the interview. It was not long before the cause of his ill temper was clear to her, though Gerald did not repeat every, nor even the worst, parts of his meeting with the solicitor. Indeed, she read between his words even more hopelessness than Gerald, in his somewhat elliptical account, left out. It seemed to her, in fact, at the end of about ten minutes, that Sir James and Gerald both would soon be in the poorhouse if things continued as they were.

"Dear Heaven," she said at last with a little intake of her breath, "it sounds very bad indeed. And is there no other method of settling your father's debts than that of selling land?"

"One can always sell timber, of course," replied Gerald, with one of those matter-of-fact, worldly expressions which are always fascinating to women, "but the price of it is very low these days."

"So you should have to sell a great deal?"

"If we had a great deal to sell, that is what we should have to do. Unfortunately, the land at Kirkwood—which, if ever I knew one, is a poorly named place—is scarcely timbered. We have got a little over three hundred acres of forest in the Park, but, of course, Papa won't be persuaded to sell *that*. I am afraid we must rest on the mercy of Mr. Bantree to come up with some more propitious manner of settling our debts."

Charlotte, upon hearing this news, grew silent for a while. Her small hand drew itself deeper into the crook of Gerald's arm, as if that pressure might in some way allay his troubles. Glancing up at the overhanging bower of branches, to the leaves rustling in the balmy afternoon breeze, she heaved a little sigh. It must be a terrible sin, she thought, to be as perfectly content as she was at that moment whilst Gerald was so obviously labouring under distress. She, too, of course, felt perfectly horrible—but to know that she *shared* his unhappiness made it seem almost a blessing! How odd, she thought, are the hearts of women.

Suddenly Gerald, following her own glance, inquired sharply if it was not approaching the time when he ought to send her home.

"Oh, no!" she responded quite firmly, "I shan't leave you until we have resolved upon a plan to solve your problems. They are, after all, mine as well—or so I should hope!"

He gave her a strange little sideways glance and then seemed to accept her resolve. Again there was a silence as they walked on, turning at the end of the avenue, from where some small figures could be seen promenading upon the gravelled paths in the distance.

"I have been thinking," ventured Gerald after some moments, "that I ought really to be looking into some career or other. It has occurred to me that the Diplomatic Service shouldn't be too bad a thing. I've always been rather restless, and my father knows Lord Asqyuthe pretty well. He might give me an *entrée*. What are your thoughts about that?"

Charlotte, at this sudden mention of so new an idea,

and the invitation to offer her own opinion concerning a decision affecting Gerald's future, was quite taken aback. Her first reaction was to blush deeply; her next, to blanch slightly.

"Why!" she exclaimed faintly. "Why! Is it—what you most wish?"

Gerald looked down to see the blush and also the blanch. His feelings upon seeing both were so mixed, so confused, that he did not know exactly what to say. Quite misinterpreting both, he leapt instantly to the conclusion that Charlotte detested the idea. Foolish man! Had he the slightest speck of understanding of the female heart, he should have gone on at once to what he wished to say, which was, could she find it in her heart to be his wife even if he was to be a diplomatist? This question had been upon the tip of his tongue all afternoon. It was what, with a moody look, he had been rehearsing to himself in the carriage at the moment he had seen that fellow, the fellow who made him rethink everything. He had rehearsed it again as he stood watching her in the clearing and yet again when she had offered her lips to be kissed, But now, just when he ought to have said it, when the re-sounding answer would most certainly have been a heart-felt Yes! he construed her blush to be caused by some-thing the very opposite of encouragement. In fact, he considered it to be born of fear. Therefore he said, with all of that superb repression of honest feeling which is so characteristic of the male sex, "Ah! I see you don't ap-prove of the idea. Well, it was only an idea, after all."

"What!" cried a bewildered Charlotte, who had been ex-pecting—and, oh, so happily!—just that proposal of mar-riage which did not come. "Why, I think it would be wonderful—that is—wonderful if you wished it!"

"Ah! Well, as I say, it was only an idea."

There are moments, turning points in history or merely in the mood of an afternoon, when everything seems to change all at once and for no apparent reason. The mood, that phantasmagorical illusion by which most of our lives are lived, dips from a crescendo of optimism to a veritable thundercloud of disenchantment. Such moments, caused by whatever look or word, an allusion misunderstood, an exclamation misconstrued, have been known to set nations a-battling and lovers a-quarrelling. Such a moment was this one. Though Charlotte and Gerald most certainly did not quarrel (they kept a perfect silence for some seconds, in fact, each contemplating his own distress), they might as well have. And, where a quarrel may sometimes discover the misunderstanding which has caused it by the airing of grievances from both sides, thereby opening the way to a reconciliation, silence broods upon itself and exaggerates all injuries in the mind.

It may appear that these young people had nothing to quarrel about; they were in love, and though restrained by the traditions in which they had been raised from articulating their love in any kind of coherent way, they had managed very well without words. Had they not, perhaps, been under so much constraint, both that of society and of their own shyness, they might have done still better. But young lovers very rarely tell each other all, and some people feel that it is largely owing to this lack of openness that young love is so intoxicating. It is a continuous guessing game, a charade in which each acts out for the other much of his or her real feelings but still leaves a doubt in the other's mind.

Charlotte, for her part, still retained a suspicion of envy. Not that she was an envious girl: far from it! But so passionately in love was she, and so godlike did she consider Gerald, that she assumed every other female upon Earth must find him so. Not being a particularly vain young woman, she assumed Gerald was not unaware of the many beauties in London, even if he did not become infatuated with them all. Though certain of his love for her, she could not be sure it might not evaporate all at once some fateful evening when he espied one of these creatures more pleasing than herself. Thus did every ball became a small torture for her, every theatre party or *fête champêtre* another minute bit of Hell. She assumed now, as she seemed bent upon doing at every note of coldness from his lips or slight aloofness in his manner, that the fateful moment had arrived. Surely he had fallen in love with another woman! Surely his mention of the Diplomatic Service was merely an invention keyed to shake her off! She had prayed for and indeed expected a proposal of marriage this afternoon, for Gerald had made some rather broad hints when last they had met. Instead, he seemed reserved, changeful, altogether not himself! With a sinking heart, her mind flitted desperately over the past few entertainments at which they both had been present and which had occurred since their last private meeting. Who could it be?

Gerald, on the other hand, who had indeed intended to make his declaration that afternoon, had very different reasons for his anguish, for anguish it really was. He had emerged from the office of his solicitors in a subdued, but not pessimistic, mood. He had been made aware at last of the irrevocable nature of his father's, and therefore of his own, near penury. It had been at that moment that the idea of the Diplomatic Service, an idea which had in truth long been at the back of his mind, had come to the fore. He had determined to question Charlotte about it in such a way as to allow her true reaction to show itself. He felt really that it was about the only way in which he could afford to marry her, and if she disliked the idea, which he must instantly tell, then their marriage could not take place, at least not so soon as he would have wished. Even if she was enraptured by the thought of being a diplomatist's wife, their wedding would have to wait upon his getting a good posting. He knew the Earl would not like the thought of his only daughter marrying anyone who was not ten times as rich as he and with a title to match. But the Earl could always be wrapped about Charlotte's finger, if Charlotte dearly wished a thing. It was not the Earl's reaction which had worried him, but Charlotte's. And now he saw—at one small glance, he saw clearly—what an idiot he had been! To suppose she could love him sufficiently to live far from her family and friends only for the sake of living with him! Clearly she was aghast at the idea, if too polite to say as much. Again he glanced down at the fragile figure walking beside him and felt the smallness of the hand tucked into the crook of his elbow. What a presumptuous cad he was, to be sure! To suppose she would like anything only because *he* liked it!

And now again the thought of that other gentleman he had seen from the window of the hansom cab flashed across his mind. George, Marquis of Beresford—the very name caused a tremor in his stomach just as it caused tremors in the bosoms of nearly every unmarried young lady in London, though for very different causes. George Beresford, his old schoolmate at Eton if not exactly his bosom chum,

Charlotte's cousin, and heir to one of the greatest fortunes in the kingdom, the man her father would have loved her to marry and had thrown in her way at every possible moment! The odious, pompous, selfish, evil—for Gerald truly believed him to be so—worldly and fashionable George Beresford! Charlotte laughed whenever his name was mentioned, but was she right to do so? And moreover, was her laughter all that it seemed? Again he glanced down and saw the slightly averted profile beneath its lovely bonnet, but he could not read her expression. What was she thinking?

"It is getting very late," said he at last, turning them once more in the direction of the gates. "I had better see you into a carriage."

Charlotte did not demur. Her heart was too full. She was suddenly overcome by a desire to weep, for she felt that somehow, in those last moments, everything had been lost. She kept her head down and followed him like an obedient puppy.

They arrived at the Park gates in time to hear the chimes of Big Ben strike six o'clock. It was late indeed. Realizing all at once what she had so completely forgotten during their hour in the Park—that she was expected—she climbed nervously into the hansom cab that Gerald hailed.

"Where is your maid?" he enquired, searching the street with his eye.

"Over yonder, beneath the lamp post. She always waits for me there."

"Ah! So she does!" And his long legs carried him over to the spot where, again conversing briefly with the plainly dressed, kind-faced young woman, Charlotte saw him hand something stealthily over. A piece of gold! When he had so few! Charlotte felt that her heart would burst.

"Well, then, driver," said Gerald to the coachman upon his return, "you shall deliver these ladies to the corner of Grosvenor and Mount Streets, will you? There's a good fellow!" And then another piece of gold changed hands, and Charlotte was staring out of the window, with her gloved hand pressed against the glass, at his retreating back.

Chapter 3

Just at the moment upon which Gerald was learning from
his solicitor the true state of his financial ruin, Lord Harrington was making his way through the heated City
streets. His pace was rather slow, as he was getting on in
years, but he still retained a jaunty, upright stride. He had
been a famous dandy in his day, although they didn't call
them dandies then. His had been a finer day altogether, as
he was fond of telling Lady Harrington, who already
knew. The modern young people were rather spoiled and
had no sense of humour. They liked to go about with
those absurd high collars, which got in the way of a man
more than the old-fashioned ones. It was Brummel's fault,
all of these high jigs and stiff bowish mouths—men smirk-
ing at one another, as if their lips might crack if they
showed any sign of emotion. The frocks were rather fine,
though, he thought, as he cast an approving glance at a
neatly turned ankle preceding him down St. James' Street.
Rather fine—though, of course, he shouldn't like to see *his*
wife in one of those wetted-down gowns the fashionables
wore. She was set too much ahead of herself, was Lady
Harrington, rather too heavily developed at the waist. In
fact, it was rather a good thing for her that the waists of
gowns had moved up so much. It looked a comfortable
enough *habillement* for a female getting on in years.

Lord Harrington stepped past the entrances of Boodles
and White's with a little sniff. Not what they used to be,
certainly! They were almost purely gaming establishments
now, and the rules had certainly deteriorated with time! In

his youth young men had had some sense about how much
they could squander at cards between dinner and breakfast. To be sure they had squandered quite enough, but
nothing like these young pups! He had heard that brat of
Devonshire's had cost his father five hundred pounds the
other night. Mighty onerous, if one were to ask him!

But, of course, thought the Earl, pausing before the
doorway of a high marble building with a maroon carpet
running down the steps of its porticoed entrance, no one
ever did ask him. Not even Charlotte, the darling of his
old age! A sigh quivered out of his long throat and seemed
to settle into the handsome, angular lines of his face. His
thick grey eyebrows, which looked even bushier now that
half the hair had fallen off the top of his head, ruffled im-
perceptibly as he scowled up at the edifice before him.

"Humph! The Solarium Club, indeed! Newfangled bit
of rubbish, I should think!"

But up those carpet-covered steps he marched, nonetheless, and, with an imperious nod, greeted the doorman,
shrugged off his cloak, handed over his silver-handled
walking stick and dispensed with his hat and gloves.

"Sir James Kirkland?" he growled.

"I believe he may be found in the Reading Room, your
lordship. Shall I inquire?"

"Send in my card, if you'll be so good," returned Lord
Harrington and turned abruptly to peruse a rather old,
bad, and dirty portrait of somebody or other upon the opposite wall.

In a moment the footman reappeared. "Sir James is ex-
pecting you, my lord. You shall find him through the second door on the left."

As the Earl passed down half the length of the corridor,
wincing at the wine-red tapestries upon the wall, he
amused himself with thinking that footmen invariably
called one "your lordship" when they were unsure of your
title, but only progressed to "my lord" when they knew it.

The door at the left appeared to open into a sort of
done-over Reading Room, one in which just about everything went on except the perusal of books and journals.
Two fireplaces (not lit, thank heaven—these clubs so seldom seemed aware of the weather outside their doors),
half a dozen ormolu tables, and as many of those pleasant
commodious chairs that were the sole saving grace of

gentlemen's clubs made up the furnishings. His lordship was relieved to see that only two of them were occupied: one, by an angular, dozing creature in the corner, and the other, by Sir James.

"Well, well! If it isn't my old friend Harrington!" exclaimed the latter, rising with some difficulty (for the baronet had not retained the agility of his youth any more than his former slenderness). "I dare say I haven't seen you in—in a dog's age!"

"Rather more than that," replied the Earl coolly, ignoring the baronet's extended hand and drawing up the nearest chair.

"Well, I say, Harrington! It couldn't be *much* more, heh, heh! We are *both* of us old dogs, now, I expect! But I must say this is an—how d'you call it? Unexpected pleasure, or somethin'."

"You may dispense with the formalities, my dear Sir James," responded the Earl evenly, glowering from beneath his eyebrows at his old neighbour.

"And how are the hounds, eh, Harrington?" continued the jovial baronet, who seemed bent upon maintaining the cordiality of this meeting against all odds. He was, reflected the Earl, a most irritating fellow—always had been. Continually spouting rubbish of one sort or another, larking about Town, whilst his land and estates went to rack and ruin. Was not that why he had to give up the hunting place in Scotland—and sold it, moreover, down the river to the damn Slocum fellow? As if he wished to claim neighbourliness with some merchant or other, however well to do!

"Jupiter is still making his courses very well, thank'ee. And I've got another brood, out of Henshaw, coming along. They promise good things for the coming autumn."

"Not feeling the pinch a bit, are you, old boy?" demanded the fellow impertinently, raising—or trying to—one of his grizzled eyebrows. The baronet's face faintly resembled a plum pudding. Its colouring was very like, and the great pits beneath his eyes might well have been raisins, thought the Earl. It all came from trying to keep up a style of life unfitting for his age and pocketbook. Ever since the death of Lady Kirkland, he had gone from bad to worse. Gallivanting here, gallivanting there—always the aging rake, and with his poor son to pay for it!

Which brought the Earl round to the subject about which he had in fact come.

"Eh-humph! Not while I have any say in it, old man! I've had to sell a bit of timber from the western side, but that is about the extent of it. I shan't get rid of my pups."

"No, no!" guffawed the baronet, "Heaven help us, I should think not! Harrington part with one of the pups—No! No!"

Lord Harrington eyed his old neighbour coldly as the latter continued to vent his mirth and, when this offensive spectacle seemed to have subsided, dove in. "What I have come about, Sir James, in point of fact has nothing whatever to do with pups."

"What, eh? Not pups?"

"Not pups," returned the Earl definitely. "Most certainly not pups. At least—not mine. It has something to do with a pup of yours, however."

"A pup of mine!" echoed the baronet, nearly choking on a sudden renewal of his mirth. "But my dear fellow, I haven't any pups, as well you know! I haven't had any pups for eons. Not since I gave up Lackamoor, in fact. But *you* know that." Suddenly the baronet turned upon his companion a look of immense suspicion, as if the Earl had just accused him of purloining his wife. Lord Harrington chalked it up to the meanderings of a port-soaked brain.

"I am quite aware of that, Kirkland. Dear me, will you kindly stop interruptin'?"

The baronet suddenly sobered and stared biliously at the Earl. He had in fact consumed a great deal of port the night before, a thing for which he was acutely sorry this afternoon. The only thing he desperately longed for was another bottle, for he thought only thus would he be able to overcome the desperate throbbing in his brain. "I say, shall we have bottle of claret?"

"I do not wish for any, but if you must—"

It appeared the baronet must, for he promptly rang for a footman, who hastened off in search of the requisite wine. When this was fetched and duly dispensed and handed round, the Earl drew a deep breath and attempted a renewal of the conversation.

"The fact is, Kirkland," he recommenced in the threatening tones with which he was accustomed to upbraid his stableboys, "I wish to call off that boy of yours."

The baronet, who had leaned rather heavily into his glass of port, began to sputter. "Gerald? D'you mean Gerald? Why, what has he done?"

"Nothing much so far. But he may, you know. These young chaps do, and behind one's back." The Earl breathed a heavy sigh and went on to elucidate this somewhat ambiguous accusation. "He has been hanging round my Charlotte of late, rather too much. I suppose he thinks I don't pay any notice to these things, but I do, you know. I can still tell the bloodhound in the pack, despite my aching joints. I saw them whispering together behind some palms at Lady Demlot's the other evening. Charlotte has her fill of beaux, to be sure, but I don't see any of the *others* whispering in her ear behind the palms."

Sir James's eyes had been popping since the beginning of this little speech, but now he closed those protruding portions of his physiognomy and, putting back his largish head, let out a terrifying guffaw. "Oh, my dear fellow!" he sputtered between wiping his eyes and howling again. "My dear, dear fellow!"

"Don't dear fellow me, sir! I have come upon a matter of very grave consequence to myself and Lady Harrington."

"I thought you was goin' to say Gerald had eloped with her or something!"

The Earl gave a slight gasp. "Eloped! Good Heaven, man! It's bad enough their whispering behind palms, don't you think?"

"Of course," went on Sir James, drawing out his lace kerchief and dabbing at his eyes. "The boy never was all that quick. *I* should have eloped with her long ago, if I'd wished to."

"Dear me!" whispered the Earl, "Dear me!" He was too amazed by the outrageous conduct of his old *bête noire* to say any more for the moment. He gagged slightly and stared in a most nonplussed fashion.

"He's sweet on her, is he? Don't blame him myself. They always did like each other, even as children," went on Sir James seeming to fail to grasp the outrageousness of what he was saying. "*I* should be sweet on her, too, if I was eight-and-twenty instead of eight-and-fifty; I should indeed!"

"I haven't any doubt of it," growled Lord Harrington,

"though you may be sure that even at eight-and-twenty, she would never have given you a second glance."

Sir James looked deeply offended. "Oh, I don't know about that, Harrington old thing. I had my share of petticoats in my day, as you did also, if memory serves me."

"Well, I didn't come to argue about your past excesses, Kirkland. I came to make you call off your young pup. I shan't have it, I tell you! Charlotte is meant for better things."

At this, the baronet's eyes grew round again. He seemed to swell up a little, and his cheeks puffed slightly. He did his best to glower but was not greatly successful.

"I *beg* your pardon, my lord! I shan't be ordered about like some young kennel-keeper! And if my boy has taken a fondness to your girl, *I* certainly shan't be the one to throw the damper over it! Good luck to him, says I! And pretty pickings, too! It's about time one of my family got some good out of one of yours after all these years."

Now, if the Earl had been outraged before, here was fuel to make him burn twice as hot. His cheeks jerked, his great shaggy eyebrows did a little dance upon his bony forehead, and his large ears turned very pink. But some god must have been looking after him, for, instead of bursting forth in venomous outrage, he was struck by a thought that made his cheeks and eyebrows quiet down and his flushed face regain its normal colour.

Obviously this state of affairs did not do much to please his friend, who was waiting in joyous anticipation for the coming battle. Sir James saw the change in his old comrade-at-arms' features and eyed him disbelievingly.

The Earl's brain, meanwhile, was ticking over rather faster than was its wont. His bony proboscis lifted just a trifle as he sized up the opposition, not unlike the manner of one of his own hounds calculating the resistance of a fox. He heaved a deep sigh and made a motion as if to rise.

"Very well, Kirkland, if you must be so stubborn. Poor fellow, you always did stick in your tracks, and I suppose nothing I can say could possibly avert even the greatest calamity once you are set upon a course."

"Why, what?" muttered the baronet, blinking rapidly. "Here, here, old chap, don't go! What are you saying?"

"Only—" enunciated the Earl, regaining his seat with

perhaps just a touch too much rapidity, "only that whatever pickings Gerald may get shall be mighty slim. I don't know what they shall live upon, in fact, if they insist upon being so foolish." Lord Harrington paused long enough to get a glimpse of Sir James's astonished face, a sight which filled him with a pleasant warmth.

"What, shall you disinherit the poor child? By Jove, Harrington," declared the baronet with infinite disgust, "you are a deuced fine fellow! Disinheriting your only child only because she likes to whisper behind palms!"

"It is not a question of disinheritance," replied the Earl deliberately. "I am afraid, my old friend, that *that* is not the case at all."

Now it is possible that Sir James ought to have put up his guard on being so cordially addressed by a man who had never bothered to be civil to him before. He would have, had he not been too intrigued by the preceding remarks. "What? Are you saying you could give her nothing? Good God, Harrington, have you run through everything?"

"Well, there is a little left," admitted the Earl sadly, "but only a very little. There is the house and land, of course—the three houses, to be exact. But as to ready money, or even my own income, my dear fellow, I am afraid there is precious little of that. Hardly enough to be worth mentioning. As a matter of fact I was informed by my own steward just a fortnight ago that I shall probably have to sell some land in the autumn. It is a deuced state of affairs, I can assure you!"

For the moment forgetting that his own situation was hardly any better and that his son was at that very moment conferring over precisely the same sort of matter with his own solicitor, Sir James stared at his old acquaintance with disgust. "R-really, my dear Harrington!" he muttered, "R-really! How could you possibly have been so foolish?"

"Oh," replied the Earl, with a wave of his hand. (He was getting rather fond of his little charade.) "It was quite simple, really. What with one thing and another, you know—well, *you* know!"

The baronet squirmed slightly in his chair, thus reminded of his own embarrassment of funds. "Yes, yes!" exclaimed he quickly, "It is very easily done, I know. Well, this *is* a surprise, by Jove! I certainly shall not encourage the match, in that case. To be sure, it wouldn't do for Gerald to marry—"

"A penniless girl," Lord Harrington finished for him. "Yes, I thought you might see it like that. Just as I am not eager to throw my child into a state of utter paupery by marrying—"

"A penniless young man. My dear fellow, of course not! And how right you were to consult me, after all. It would never do, never do."

"Particularly," went on the Earl, now smiling with great cheerfulness, "as they are neither of them fit to save a penny."

"Both idle and spoiled, to be sure. Well, then, what *are* we to do? You say you saw them whispering behind a palm tree? Well, it may not be the end of the world, after all. They *may* have only been playing, don't you know."

Lord Harrington, whilst quick to point out that whispering behind a palm was not as grave an offense for a young man as for a young lady, agreed to this point. But something, as he told Sir James, still gave him the uncomfortable sensation that they were more intimate than they were letting on. He went on to remark that his own favourite for his daughter's hand, the Marquis of Beresford, whom he had encouraged openly and who had been quick to take that encouragement to heart, had complained to him bitterly the other day that Charlotte did not seem quite as eager as she should be for his attentions. The girl herself could not be questioned—she was altogether a headstrong bit of muslin for all her dulcet temper—and he had taken to watching her with some closeness at the last few salons they had frequented together. It had become obvious to him, despite Charlotte's declarations to the contrary, that she was not only avoiding Beresford but finding every possible opportunity to speak to, dance with and whisper to young Kirkland.

"I don't like it, I tell you!" he finished with another glower. "That girl is my precious possession, and I am determined to see her married well."

Sir James, taking some offense at this insinuation that marrying his son was not 'marrying well,' made several noises. "Well, well, old chap—I mean to say—that is—really! Gerald is quite good enough for any girl, I should think! Though I do wish he would find one a little richer!"

"Beresford is a brilliant match," continued the Earl, unmindful of this little interruption. "A marquis, soon to be a duke, and as rich as Croesus. I am not altogether averse, don't you know, to keeping the dukedom within the family, after all."

This was a reference, not particularly subtle, to the fact that Lord Harrington's wife was the daughter of Beresford's uncle, the Duke of Keynes, who had no sons and whose estate was entailed away to his nephew. During the course of his marriage, Lord Harrington had more or less adopted his wife's family and now considered the Duke to be one of his own kin.

"I daresay," mumbled the baronet. He did not take kindly to Lord Harrington's continual mention of His Grace as though he were but one of the prize hounds in his kennel. "Well, well," he continued with a renewal of cordiality brought about, most likely, by the freshly poured glass of wine which had just been handed him by the attentive footman, "be that as it may, Harrington, we most abolish this unseemly match."

"Yes, indeed."

And then those two great minds bent together and in little over half an hour had produced a plot most enterprising in its scope and most ingenious in its unusually subtle twists and turns.

Chapter 4

The Solarium Club, contrary to the view of Lord Harrington, was not a hotbed of modern vice. Of all the gentlemanly establishments along Gentlemen's Row, as St. James Street was sometimes called, the Solarium was perhaps the least vulnerable to accusations of that kind. Whilst White's and Boodles boasted a more elite membership—if to be rich, titled, and without any occupation at all was to be a member of the elite—the Solarium was nonetheless a very prestigious meeting place. Its members were not all titled, but they were all members of the aristocracy in one guise or another. Perhaps chiefly owing to the fact of the Club's having early on banned the use of its card rooms for gambling, its membership included some of those who (extraordinarily, in a time when gaming was the chief amusement of the male upper classes) distained the diminution of their wealth through so speedy and vacuous a medium. Some came there to dine, as the chef was considered far superior to those at White's and Boodles; some, to avoid the inevitable swarms of dandified hangers-on at the other establishments; and there were those who frequented the Solarium simply to enjoy the rarefied peace and quiet of a building inhabited solely by men wherein no female had ever dared set foot.

Such was the case with Fitzwilliam Canterby, a young man of remarkable resourcefulness, who had gained some little reputation for himself amongst the female population of London. Canterby was a comely young man, who, despite the slightness of his frame and the irregularity of

his somewhat swarthy features, was considered by a great
portion of the City's belles to be amongst the handsomest
young men in Town. Some part of his attraction may have
lain in the almost puckish character of his features, for his
eyes twinkled devilishly beneath their winglike brows and
his ears were slightly pointed at the top. Indeed, even his
nose and chin were pointed: one giggling miss, having
danced with him for the first time at Almack's, had pro-
claimed him "altogether the image of the Devil—but such
a delightful, funny devil!" But the chief source of his irre-
sistible attraction must certainly have been his manner,
which was quite as pointed, twinkling, and devilish as his
eyes and ears.

Young Canterby was the third son of Lord Canterby,
one of the chief bastions of the House of Lords. His leg-
acy to his third son was very slight, for his fortune had
been nearly all divided between his first born and his second, which allowed little for the maintenance of his
youngest male child. Fitzwilliam, or Fitz as he was known
to his friends, was not in any case the Viscount's favourite,
being, in his lordship's words, "a daffy, unreliable sort of
chap," which indeed he was. And yet young Canterby was
almost universally liked, for he was the happy possessor of
a most amiable, witty temperment, even if he could not always be counted upon. But in the ballrooms and club-
rooms of London, reliability was less at a premium than
quickness of wit and agility of repartee, both social talents
in which the young man excelled. He was perhaps held
not in quite so high esteem by some young ladies who had
foolishly expected his word to be as good as it was pleasing, and for this reason he had taken to seeking refuge in
the unremittingly masculine apartments of the Solarium
Club.

On this sparkling day in June—only two days after the
events of which we have spoken—Canterby had yet another reason for frequenting that establishment. It happened that on the previous afternoon as he had been
lurking by the front door reconnoitering the street to be
sure it was clear of certain females before he ventured
forth, he had been detained by Sir James Kirkland. A
most interesting interview had followed, one which had
quite tickled his funny bone. It was on account of this interview that Canterby now lay in wait for his old school-

friend, Gerald Kirkland, whose habit it was to pass an hour or two every afternoon in the Solarium when he was in Town.

Now, it must be said that Canterby, besides possessing a puckish physiognomy, also had a somewhat mischievous brain. The plot which had been proposed to him, besides adding a much needed padding to his pocketbook (something which had quite astounded him, for he had supposed the baronet to be as impoverished as himself) had appealed to his sense of fun. Practical jokes were very much the rage amongst the young fashionables, and Canterby was known to be one of that form's masters. Indeed, he had himself engineered some of the most spectacular practical jokes of the decade, or so he considered, and this one proposed by Sir James (another source of amazement, for he had never considered the old fool to have an ounce of wit) was a veritable dilly. He now pondered the little scheme and, with a little laugh, thought what fun it would be when Gerald found out the truth. It did not strike him for one moment as cruel; to be fair, if it had, the young man would certainly have given it a little more consideration, though perhaps in the end he might have gone ahead with it in any case. After all, the whole thing was so beautifully simple! And such a neat, witty way to earn a hundred pounds.

Gerald, as was his habit, came into the Club a little after three and, as was his custom, went at once into the second Reading Room, where, having requested a bottle of seltzer water and the *Times*, he prepared to ensconce himself in comfort.

But his thoughts were far from the latest development of the Enclosure Act. In vain did he attempt to concentrate upon a most ingenious evocation of the events at the Prince Regent's last great fête, for which the Regent had commissioned an immense copy of Carlton House to be erected in the Palace grounds, into which he had put one of every imaginable kind of beast, each dressed up to resemble one of the government's luminaries. It was a fabrication of course but so close to what was conceivable from that outlandish imagination that the caricaturist touched upon a number of hilarious possibilities. The pictures were certainly diverting, but Gerald was not to be diverted.

His thoughts were elsewhere, as far as from the Palace

grounds as they were from the room in which he sat. His last interview with Charlotte had plagued him ever since it had occurred. He had felt both guilt ridden for having disappointed her and relieved that he had managed to postpone the awful moment of decision yet a little longer. That relief, however, was so slight compared with the terrible weight of the decision itself which must surely now be faced that he had not felt a moment's lightheartedness since he had parted with her at the Park gates. How, he asked himself now, staring distractedly into the smoke-filled air of the room, was a man to decide which was the least of two evils: to break a young woman's heart (for he was vain enough to believe it might be broken by him) or to perhaps burden her for life with an existence in which she could find no happiness? Which was the more gallant, the more gentlemanly? To request her hand in marriage, knowing she would soon grow to detest that moment upon which she had succumbed to a temporary passion, or to remove himself and any possibility of his suit from her presence?

It was a question which had been revolving in his mind for whole days and nights, which had given him no rest nor allowed him a moment's peace of mind. It was a question which, furthermore, was made the more difficult, the more painful, by his own complicated state of mind. Would he, after all, come to resent the woman for whose sake he had sacrificed the only career which he could conceive of embarking upon which would save not only her, but himself, from penury? He had seen with one glance at her face that the idea of his entering the Diplomatic Service had frightened her, that she would be miserable away from her family and friends, and (what he ought to have considered long ago) that the same daintiness and delicacy which had entranced him would keep her from ever being the sort of woman who could easily pull up her roots and transplant them to some new piece of ground. This, after all, was the chief requirement of a diplomatist's family. Was it not too much to ask of so fragile and delicate a creature? Would she not, in fact, be happier in the long run married to a man who could spoil her as she deserved and on her own terrain? A man whom, though she might not think it at the moment, she would probably soon grow to love, if only for his strength and his ability to shield her from life's dangers?

He knew, of course, that Charlotte would have instantly contradicted him. He knew she would be heartbroken, at least for a time, were he to disappear from her life. But would she not, like every other creature, be healed with time? Could he deny that she was capable of loving another man?

Such was the confusion of Gerald's thoughts at that moment when he heard a familiar voice beside him. On looking up, he recognized the speaker as young Canterby, a fellow he had known at Cambridge, though never very intimately. He was amusing, however, and Gerald, exhausted by the mental tortures he had been enduring of late, welcomed the idea of a brief respite from solemnity.

"Hallo, Fitz! What brings you to this bastion of tranquillity? I presumed you did not grace these rooms any more, now that you have become a member of White's."

"Ah! Spare me the sound of that name, old chap!" replied Canterby, sighing with an exaggerated affectation of weariness and sinking into the armchair next to Gerald's. "It is the Devil's own stronghold, I assure you. Only last week I lost my allowance for the quarter to that brat of Devonshire's who certainly cannot need it as badly as I do!"

"Well then, spare *me* from an account of it, dear fellow. Poverty is a subject far from endearing to me at the moment."

Canterby cocked an eye at his old schoolmate in sympathy and heaved another sigh. "Is it not the truth, eh? Those damnable bits of gold, how fickle they are, don't you know? As fickle as any female I ever knew!"

"What?" inquired Gerald with an amused smile at the infamous breaker of hearts. "Don't tell me you have met your match, old thing? I don't suppose the Devil himself could devise a better revenge for you than to pit you against a woman as flirtatious as yourself! Have you been jilted?"

"Jilted, I?" retorted the young swell in amazement. But then he was suddenly overcome by a fit of coughing and glanced in much embarrassment at his friend. "Dear me! I didn't mean to broach the subject, I assure you, old man!

A thousand apologies and all that! By Jove, what a knack I have got for sticking my foot in it!"

Gerald, looking amazed, demanded what Canterby meant.

"Why, my poor, dear fellow!" exclaimed Canterby, now with a look of deep sympathy, as one man may regard another who has just lost his last guinea. "You needn't play the fool to me. I know all about it, I assure you."

"Know all about what?" demanded Gerald, now with some irritability.

"Why, about that fellow Beresford and all that!"

"What about him?" inquired Gerald coldly. "I assure you, there is no news you may give me about that fellow that will affect me in the least."

"Oh, to be sure!" muttered Canterby, nodding knowingly to himself. "Naturally not. I mean to say, how much more can it affect one, eh?"

"Now listen here, Canterby," began Gerald with some fierceness, "if you are trying to tell me something, you had better tell me at once and have done with it. What on earth can Beresford have done which could affect me in the slightest?"

Young Canterby turned upon his friend a look of real—or at least very well pretended amazement—and clapped a hand to his brow.

"Good God!" he protested, "Don't tell me you haven't heard? Why, I could have sworn—By Heaven, Kirkland, I do apologize! I mean to say, nothing on earth could have persuaded me to mention it if I hadn't thought you already *knew*!"

"*Knew what*, by God? Say it!" Gerald was really angry now, and he turned upon his companion a look of almost terrifying wrath.

Canterby nearly flinched upon seeing it and avoided his friend's eye as he mumbled into his shirtfront. "Why, about Beresford, you know. About his being engaged to Lady Charlotte Harrington, or as good as."

A dropping pin would certainly have sounded like an explosion in the silence which followed these words. Gerald stared in disbelief at the figure beside him, the colour draining out of his cheeks. At long last, he found some breath to speak. "Are you quite sure, Canterby? How in God's name did you discover this?"

Canterby still did not feel courageous enough to meet Gerald's piercing look and replied into the general atmosphere of the room, though keeping his voice low enough to be indistinct to the other occupants. "As it happened, I ran into Beresford myself only yesterday, and he was only too eager to let me know that his application to the Earl had been received with the greatest delight. He led me to believe the acceptance of the lady herself is a mere formality at this juncture and that he fully expects to be a happily married man in a year's time. But good God, man, I thought you knew! Most assuredly I should not have mentioned it otherwise! After all—your families are old friends, I knew what your expectations were—did she not have the heart to tell you herself?"

Gerald did not bother to reply to this, but his expression said all that was needed. He stared straight in front of him now, surveying the contents of that room with a stony glare through eyes which saw those familiar surroundings as if for the first time. "So," he muttered, almost to himself, "—so, the decision was not to be mine after all."

"I beg your pardon, my dear fellow?" inquired Canterby, who was rather awestruck at the effect this news had had upon his old schoolmate. To be sure he had known the man was paying court to Lady Charlotte—as were a dozen others. He had certainly never suspected the depth of Kirkland's attachment. He began to wonder uncomfortably if he had not breached that narrow margin of gentlemanly conduct by agreeing to this little joke. But then his mind flitted back to the fifty pounds he had received from Sir James's own hands and the fifty more which had been promised if he succeeded in the rest of his assignment.

"Where are you going?" he demanded suddenly as he saw Gerald begin to rise from his armchair.

"I am going to confirm the news myself," responded Gerald in a quiet voice.

"Oh! I shouldn't do that you know!" exclaimed Canterby hastily. "I shouldn't do that! It is not an accomplished fact as yet! I mean, it shouldn't be exactly delicate of you, do you think? Something may still go wrong, and I'm sure the lady—"

"The lady shall not be disturbed. I intend to apply to her father."

Fitz Canterby stared after his friend in some confusion. He was not at all sure that Lord Harrington was a safe man for Gerald to interrogate. Or was he? The peer's son reflected for an unhappy moment, fingering the heavy pieces of gold in his waistcoat pocket. At length a smile appeared upon his lips. Indeed! Had not Sir James said something to the effect of "Harrington shall make up the difference"? He was sure that he had. In any case, what had he to lose? Only what he had so easily and unexpectedly gained the day before. Still, he did not like the idea of being caught out by Gerald Kirkland.

Gerald strode rapidly down the length of St. James and, cutting across Piccadilly, dove into Berkeley Street. From thence it was a matter of but a few moments to the Earl's mansion on Mount Street. Staring up at the noble brick facade of the great place, he hesitated, absently counting the windows on the third floor until he reached the fifth from the left. That was Charlotte's suite of rooms—how often before had he glanced up at it with a kind of secret comprehension, as if she must know, wherever in the house she might happen to be, that he was upon the pavement, and thinking of her. A sudden stab of pain, so strong that it might have been physical, drove through him—what would she think if she knew he was there at this moment, trying desperately to resolve his state of mind? And yet how different was that resolve from the one he had envisioned making an hour before! And yet it was not even different—for had he not been upon the point of renouncing her himself, that she might seek a better fortune elsewhere? Only he had not been given the choice, for she had taken it out of his hands before he had the chance to prove his love.

His pride was far more wounded than he could easily admit, even to himself. He thought of what she had been like, only the other day in the park, of how much he had taken for granted. Yet even then, walking with her hand in his arm, had she not made her decision? Or had it been the affair of a moment, hardly contemplated before? He thought of her waking in the early dawn, with the decision ready formed in her mind: a decision taken, if not merely for herself, than for her family and friends. Most bitterly did his lips form themselves about the words of Donne, written so many years before, yet still so pertinent:

Go, and catch a falling star,
Get with child a mandrake root,
Tell me, where all past years are,
Or who cleft the Devil's foot . . .
And swear
No where
Lives a woman true, and fair.

He saw a figure move in the window and caught his breath. But then a plain-faced, eager-looking girl pressed her nose to the glass for a moment before drawing the curtain; he saw it was the servant girl, and his shoulders drooped. With a sigh he turned into the wrought-iron gate and walked up the circular carriage drive. He paused again before lifting his hand to the knocker. His knock was answered at once. The butler, recognizing him, bade him enter and sent in his card by a footman to the Earl.

"Exceeding warm for the time of year, is it not, Mr. Kirkland?" inquired the butler as they waited.

"Exceeding, Simpson," replied Gerald with that infallible cheerfulness reserved by the English upper classes for conversation with their servants, particularly at times of acute anguish to themselves.

"Ah, here is Thomas, sir. It appears my lord is at home and in the library. Would you follow me, please, sir?"

Gerald did as he was bid and soon found himself in a large, somber room, panelled in walnut, with four busts (presumably representing former Earls of Harrington) facing each other from opposing corners. The walls were lined with shelves, and the shelves filled with handsome morocco volumes, some of which seemed actually to have been perused. At the center a long mahogany table ran half the length of the room, and at one end of this table, looking rather small in this setting made for giants, sat the Earl.

"My dear Gerald," said he rising and extending his hand with an expression of great sympathy. "My dear Gerald, how good it is of you to come to see me. I am an old man, I am afraid, and few fellows of your age seem to think it worth their while—well, well. Sit down, sit down."

Again, Gerald did as he was bid, noticing for the first time how gloomy was this place where he had sat for many a happy hour with Charlotte looking up some poem or other or settling a dispute over historical fact. He took his place at the Earl's right hand and commenced at once.

"Your lordship, I am afraid I have not come upon a completely happy matter—that is, of course, to myself. I had better say it at once. It has just reached my ears that the hand of Lady Charlotte is in fact—is in fact—"

The Earl nodded pleasantly but made no move to aid the young man in his quandary.

Gerald stared at him for an anguished moment and then blurted it out. "—that you have in fact received an application for your daughter's hand from the Marquis of Beresford. Am I correct?"

"Yes, yes, dear boy, that is a fact, most certainly." Again the Earl nodded, looking, it seemed to Gerald, more content every moment, quite like a cat before a bowl of cream.

"And that you have—that is—that you *and* your daughter have accepted the application for her hand?"

The Earl's long chin sank into his throat, and he seemed to glare at the buttons upon his waistcoat for a time. At length, having passed his hand over his chin, having raised his great bushy eyebrows three or four times, and having coughed, he smiled pleasantly again. "Well, Kirkland, that is not a question I should like to answer to *anybody*, you know. In point of fact, were it not that you are an old friend's son, nearly as dear to me as one of my own children, I should think it damned impertinent of you. But as I have always had a soft spot in my heart for your father"—here the Earl was rather stretching his acting abilities—"and therefore for you, and as you are an old playmate of Charlotte's and must therefore be nearly as concerned about her future welfare as I am myself, I shall beg the gods' pardon for confiding in you before it is actually a *fait accompli*. The Marquis did apply, in fact, not two days ago, and I have, with much joy, accepted his application. Beresford is my wife's nephew and Charlotte's cousin. As I am certain you are aware, her mother and I have long held hopes that he should one day become an even nearer relation. He is, as you know, heir to the Duke, my father-in-law.

"However," continued Lord Harrington with yet another weighty sigh, "such matters no longer rest in the hands of fathers and mothers. You young people have

such independent spirits that it has gradually become clear
to us that we must, in the end, bow to your judgement
upon such matters, no matter how poorly you may be
prepared to undertake such kinds of decisions. Yes, my
dear boy—I see by your expression you are not altogether
pleased—*I* have accepted the Marquis, though my daughter has not, as yet."

"Has she received a proposal?" demanded Gerald
abruptly.

The Earl smiled patiently. "She has received *one* proposal and refused it—"

For a moment, Gerald's heart leapt.

"But she has confessed to her mother that she intends
accepting him at last. It was supposed to be a kind of test,
I think. You know how these young ladies are, my boy—
they like to make us dance a jig for our supper. I suppose
she thinks it will make him like her better! Though, to be
sure, *I* am perfectly assured of his devotion already!"

Gerald said nothing for a minute or two, merely staring
off into thin air as if he had seen a ghost there. Even
the Earl, observing him, felt a momentary twitch of guilt.
But it was only a twitch, and a few minutes later, when
Gerald, having bid the Earl adieu, ventured out again into
the lovely afternoon sunshine, he leaned back in his ornate-
ly carved ancestral armchair with a sigh of satisfaction.
"Well done, my lord!" he muttered to himself, with what
some may have considered a trifle too much respect for
his own title, "well done, indeed! Not too heavily managed, that is what I liked best."

Having smirked at the room at large for several minutes
and muttered some more interesting congratulations to
himself, he gathered his forces to go upstairs. Now the difficult part lay ahead of him.

The Earl did not look forward to it with much enthusiasm.

Chapter 5

Charlotte stood swaying slightly in the doorway of her mother's dressing room. "It cannot be!" she exclaimed for the fourth time. "It cannot be! He should have told me himself! I saw him but a few days ago; he should have told me then!"

"Well, my dear," came the philosophical voice of the Countess, "it is very probable he did not think you would mind."

"Not mind!" cried Charlotte in despair. "Not mind! He knows I love him! He made me believe he loved me, too! How could I not mind? How could he do such a thing?"

Lady Daphne Harrington turned upon her daughter a look of supreme astonishment and distress. "What are you saying, child? That you loved him and he, you?"

"Oh, is not it plain?" wailed Charlotte, falling into her mother's outstretched arms. "I ought to have told you long ago, but I did not! But now he is gone, and it is all for naught, all for naught!"

Here the poor young lady could bear no more, and her grief flooded out through her eyes, and great sobs began to wrack her slight frame until her mother thought she must die of heartache to watch her child so dreadfully hurt.

"There, there, my heart, go ahead and weep. It is best so. There, there—oh, my poor Charlotte! Why did not you ever tell me about this? I supposed he was no more to you than a dozen other young men, any one of whom might at any moment set off upon a journey."

"But to—to America!" moaned her daughter, whose

head was buried in her mother's bosom. "He shall not return, I know it!"

Now Lady Harrington cast an accusatory glance at the figure of her husband, who was standing awkwardly in the doorway. Her look said much, though her lips were silent, and the Earl, looking completely overcome, could only stare back, aghast, at the crumpled and pathetic figure of his daughter.

"Perhaps it is better so, my dear," he ventured at length in what was meant to be a compassionate voice. "It may be that one day you shall look back with relief at his going. Perhaps one day, you know, when you have daughters of your own, you shall think what a glad day this was in your life!"

To this unspeakable prediction Charlotte could make no reply but a great moan, which seemed to rise out of the pit of her stomach and grow and grow. "How could you say such a thing?" she demanded finally, staring through her tearstained eyes at the speaker. "How could you say so? I love him, I tell you! I shall never love another, not if I live to be a hundred!" And with this angry and desperate pronouncement, the young woman tore herself away from her mother's arms and, hastening past her father, fled with great sobbing to her own apartment.

After she had gone, a deep silence fell upon the room. The Earl and his lady regarded each other in great dismay, and Lady Harrington, who had had no part in her husband's plot, heaved a sigh of unhappiness. Witnessing her child's distress was nearly twice the anguish for her, and she supposed it must be nearly as bad for the Earl. She was, therefore, amazed at his callousness, when she heard him say, "Well, well! It is a very terrible thing, to be sure. But I suppose she shall get over it. Other young ladies have, you know. She is only unhappy because he did not tell her himself that he was going away and she was forced to learn the news from me. You'll see, she shall forget about it in no time and be singing a lark's song again, my dear!"

"Really, my lord, I can hardly credit what I hear!" Lady Harrington, a large, plump, handsome woman with a heart as tender as a custard but the fierce protectiveness of a lioness for her cub, glared at her husband.

The Earl commenced what must have been some form of an apology but was cut off.

"Pray, Desmond, let us have some little degree of compassion for her distress before we begin to spout forth maxims for her future well-being!"

The Earl realized he was trounced and, with real pity in his heart and even more remorse, slunk off to his study to think. He did not, however, continue in this guise long. Scarcely an hour after he had gone downstairs, he was thinking how much happier, in the long run, his daughter would be. How he should delight, some ten years hence when she was a duchess with a brood of her own, in telling her how he had contrived the dissolution of her unfortunate attachment to Gerald Kirkland. Indeed, he thought, propping his booted legs upon the desk top (a thing universally banned in every other apartment of the house), this abrupt departure ought in fact to lessen the grief, ought it not? For how could she continue a devotion (a devotion which, in truth, was far deeper than he had suspected) to a young man who had treated her so ill?

The condition upstairs was not so happy. The Countess waited some little while before going to her daughter, so as to allow the young woman to regain a bit of her composure. Lady Harrington, being a woman, had a clearer idea of what this sort of shock could do to a girl than did her husband, but even she was appalled at the state in which she found Charlotte an hour later. The young lady was lying prostrate upon her large canopied bed with one slender arm flung across her face, and her eyes, which bore a strange glassy look but were at least dry, focussed vaguely into the air above her.

She did not stir when her mother came tiptoeing into the large, airy and commodious apartment. She might have been counting the molded plaster garlands in the ceiling for all her attitude of absorption.

Lady Harrington was not alarmed by this; she had herself lain in such a state many, many years ago. She could hardly remember now the young man who had sent her into such an awful condition, but she very clearly recollected the days of agony which she had passed. Her ladyship sat down softly upon the bed beside her daughter and taking one of her child's hands in both of her own, began to stroke it gently.

"Poor Charlotte," she murmured when the girl, paying no heed, let her hand lie limply in her mother's. "Poor, dear, sweet little thing. My love, I know it is very hard to believe at this moment, but in a year's time you shall wonder at the grief that now torments you. You will say, perhaps, that I am only your mother, but, you know, I was once a young girl myself and thought I was in love once or twice before I knew your father. I have passed hours as cruel as the one you are now struggling through and remember clearly thinking that I should never wish to live again. But I did live and am very happy for it, now. Trust me, my sweet. I shall not pretend that what you are going through is pleasant or easy, but, believe me, my own dear heart—the pain shall very soon pass off."

Charlotte made no reply. Her blank eyes remained focussed on the ceiling, her limbs remained limp, and her flesh seemed to grow colder every moment. She scarcely heard her mother or was aware of what she said. Indeed, she hardly knew what was in her own mind. She seemed to have stopped feeling, as if a great numbness had set into her heart and brain, as if the only sensation she would ever know was this horrible chilliness all over her. At first she had wept, wept with such a relentless force that she had been sure her poor wrecked heart would break. She had fled—nearly hysterical—to her room, flung herself upon her bed and almost screamed with anguish. Now it was as if there was nothing left to feel, nor any way to express that feeling. She merely knew that what had been, a few hours previously, a beautiful golden world flooded with light, was now more dark and dank and hollow than the most ancient and decaying cellar. Never should she feel again, never think, never speak.

Her mother seemed to read all this in the pallor of her daughter's cheeks, and the cold touch of her skin. She heaved a very deep sigh, and said, "You know, my love, that a mother's affection is so great, that if I could discover a method by which I could bear the burden of your grief, I should do so most cheerfully so that you should cease to be afflicted. But I am afraid life gives each of us our burdens to bear, and we are doomed to bear them alone. Only believe, my dear, what I have said and know that your father and I love you very, very deeply. Whatever it is in our power to do to help allay this suffering shall be done. But now I shall leave you to sleep, for it is the best remedy in all the world for a poor, unhappy child. I shall come to you later."

So, drawing a satin coverlet over her child's body, she crept stealthily from the room. As she passed down the hall to her own chamber, she gave instructions to her maid to leave Lady Charlotte undisturbed but to let her know the moment the young lady spoke or made any sign of life.

Lady Harrington was a sensible woman, as well as being a devoted mother. Perhaps it was because the Countess had come to motherhood late after giving up all hope of bearing a child that she was now so fond and affectionate with her only child. But she was also the daughter of a duke and had been raised firmly in a tradition of *noblesse oblige* and self-discipline. She knew very well what her child was suffering, but she knew also that the only cure lay with Charlotte herself. They must expect a day or two of this kind of conduct before she began to recover. It might, indeed, be as much as a week. And in the meantime, Lady Harrington would keep a constant eye upon her, letting her alone if she seemed to desire it and bearing company if she wished that. When Charlotte was ready to confide in her mother, she would do so.

With a heavy but not a pessimistic heart did Lady Harrington go down to her husband to find out what more she could about this strange, unhappy affair.

The Earl, however, appeared to be as much in the dark as she was herself. Young Kirkland had come, said he, only the day before to pay his respects and say good-bye. He had said he was off to America and that he did not know exactly when he might return.

"How very odd! That he should come to bid *you* adieu, but not Charlotte! If they were as intimate as it now appears, if he indeed had led her on so far, why did not he say good-bye to her? Unless, of course, he did not dare."

The lady looked quite fierce upon saying this, and the Earl, meeting her eye, nodded eagerly. "That must have been the case, my dear. Indeed, I am very sure of it! Heartless young cad!"

"But then why in heaven did he come to the house at all? It appears very strange that, were he really trying to avoid Charlotte, he should have dared put his foot in at the door!"

"Very like, very like," muttered Harrington, feeling somewhat nonplussed. He did not know how exactly he should explain his little ruse to his wife, and now, seeing her so very fierce about the whole matter, he did not believe he should attempt it just yet. He had an idea she might not think it quite as good a scheme as he had thought it. No, no—better wait a while.

And yet Lord Harrington still did not regret his plot. He thought it a better one every moment, in fact, and that it would indeed have been perfect had not it upset Charlotte so. Still, what alternative had he? Now that he was sure there *had* been an understanding between his daughter and the young Kirkland, he was twice as pleased that it was now broken off. After all, had he simply forbidden her to see him again (and what chance, after all, was there of that when the whole of London was full of ballrooms and salons open to them both?), she would only have resented *him* for it. But as it was (oh, how clever they had been, to be sure—or rather, *he* had been clever, for Sir James had hardly produced one iota of the scheme), Charlotte must blame the young Kirkland, for had he not rushed off to America and deserted her?

It is very odd that Lord Harrington who would have been the first man in the world to knock the block off any man who dared dream of jilting his daughter should have produced the scheme whose very heart was to engineer such a desertion. To be sure, he had not suggested that Gerald go all the way to America—that, most luckily, had been the young man's own idea. In fact, Kirkland had mentioned it several days after their first interview when he had come to say his farewell and to entrust Lord Harrington with his letter to Charlotte. Lord Harrington thought America the best part of the whole plot and wished he had thought of it himself, though he would have been nearly as content with France or Italy or even Prussia. Indeed, it was the one great weakness of the plan that he and Sir James had made no provision for that dangerous time after they had each arranged to have his own child jilted by the other's. What if they should have met at some theatre party or in some ballroom? What if their paths should have crossed at Almack's? But here Sir James had made one of his few contributions, pointing out that it was not very likely that either one would wish to speak to the other after such events. And in the end they had been spared this final embarrassment in any case, for young Kirkland had very conveniently removed such a possibility from their concerns.

"You are not listening, my dear!" exclaimed Lady Harrington, interrupting his thoughts. To this the Earl protested very vehemently, and his wife continued, "As I have been saying, I think we ought to leave the poor girl alone for the remainder of today, though I shall certainly look in upon her every hour or so to see if she wants anything. I am sure we shall find her much more herself tomorrow."

"Oh, I am convinced of it!" replied his lordship. "She shall be fit as a fiddle and happy as a lark again!"

"I do heartily hope it shall be so."

With this, the Countess went off to attend to her other affairs and to order a light but savoury meal for her daughter's supper. The Earl watched her go and then, opening the top drawer of his beautifully inlaid desk, drew out a sealed envelope. Having perused it for some time, he fingered the wax seal with a thoughtful expression. It was a pity it was so neatly closed—impossible to remove the wax without Charlotte's suspecting anything! He dearly wished he could get a glimpse of the contents, for, if it did not give him away at all, it might be just the remedy needed for his daughter's grief.

"But," thought the Earl, pushing it back into the drawer between some merchants' bills, "if I cannot read it, then she mustn't. It might be just the thing to give us away."

And so the drawer was closed again, and the letter hidden. And in the days and weeks that passed, Lord Harrington forgot all about it for there were many other things to occupy him, not the least of which was his daughter's health.

For it was to be a good deal longer than a week before Charlotte rose from her unhappy bed.

Chapter 6

Fitzwilliam Canterby stood upon the bowsprit of the schooner *Half Moon* and stared in fascination at the approaching shoreline. Beside him, his hair and cloak blown backwards by the brisk westerly breeze, stood Gerald Kirkland. Clutching the rail with one hand, Canterby leaned into the wind, and his twinkling, devilish eyes lit up in delight.

"By Jove, Kirkland, this was a famous idea of mine! I feel already that we have come to the Promised Land. I believe we shall both be rich as Croesus within the fortnight, I do indeed. Wait and see if you do not thank me for dragging you along with me!"

Gerald smiled slightly at his friend, his blue eyes half shut from the effort of looking into the wind, but smiling, nevertheless, for practically the first time since he had embarked upon the vessel at Southampton. "I look forward to it, old chap, and I hope you are right. I shouldn't mind a bit being rich as Croesus, even should it take a little longer."

"Well it shan't, mark my words!" Canterby shouted back over the roar of wind and slapping lines. "I wager it takes half the time. By George, haven't you heard about the fortunes being made in the fur trade? There are said to be more millionaires already in New York than in half of England! And here they don't stand upon ceremony, no indeed! Just choose your musket and forge into the wilderness! One doesn't have to be a duke to get a fortune!"

Gerald smiled back at his friend but said nothing. For

the first time in three weeks, his heart felt almost light. At
this moment, sailing into New York Harbour, this jewel of
a natural landlocked haven, and watching the blue Atlantic rush past the clean lines of the great ship's hull, he was
mightily thankful that Canterby had suggested the journey.
At a time when nothing in England had the power to
please him, when all his native land must serve only to re-
mind him of the injury which had been done to him, there
could have been nothing more keyed to heal his wounded
heart and pride than distant shores. The more distant the
better, he now thought, squinting into the blinding sun of
the New World. And everything about this land already
pleased him.

The Harbour, for one thing. Something about the quality of the light here seemed different. It struck the water
like a shaft of pure gold, glinting upon the distant shores
of Manhattan and the great forested hills of Long Island
rising sharply out of the indigo sea. There was a clarity in
it, a luminosity, which he had never witnessed before, even
in the sunny climes of southern Italy. It made him feel in
that instant, leaning against the ship's rail, his whole being
buffeted by salty air and sunlight, that he had emerged
from a nightmare.

Shouts from the crew of the vessel began to grow
louder. Sailors were clambering like monkeys up the
masts, yanking down canvas. They were drawing every
moment closer to the shoreline, and craning forward, Gerald and Fitzwilliam managed to discern the shapes: docks,
and behind them, a row of low-slung buildings. Gerald
had expected he knew not what—perhaps some primitive
wasteland, peopled only by savages with an occasional out-
post of rudimentary society—but certainly not this. He
saw at once, upon their getting alongside the coastline,
that here was already a mighty port, not, at first glance,
very different from that which he had left behind some
weeks before. Only even here, amid the universal bustle
and commotion of a busy harbour, there was a difference.
Not, perhaps, in the outward turbulence of activity, nor
even in the kinds of shouts and oathes issuing from the
mouths of nearly everybody. And yet there *was* a difference—he was not to be able to define it for some weeks.

Their vessel, named after that famous Dutch ship which
had carried Henry Hudson into the mouth of this great es-

tuary, soon drew up beside a pier and was made fast to the immense cleats which lined the ramp. The gangplank was lowered, a general bustle ensued, and in their own haste to get to their staterooms and secure their trunks before the worst of the crush began, neither Gerald nor Canterby had time for more philosophy.

From the moment of his stepping foot upon that shore, from his first glimpse of the Customs House, before which was assembled an amazingly long trail of humanity seemingly from every nation of the Earth and from every walk of life, Gerald was seized with an ardent liking for this brave, new land. He felt, as Canterby had so deliriously put it, that "anything might be possible here." Only for an instant, as he made a grab for his valise and elbowed his way through the hurly-burley of disembarking passengers and cargo, endeavoring futiley to keep up with Canterby, did his thoughts linger over the vision of a small, fragile figure sitting in deep meditation in the midst of a clearing in Hyde Park. But with a briskness astonishing even to himself, he shook off the vision and hastened after his travelling companion.

Canterby, whose enterprising nature was amazing Gerald more every moment, had procured a fellow to carry their trunks within a moment of setting foot on America's soil. He had soon found them a hansom cab and, with a series of incomprehensible jabbers and smirks, established their good faith with the customs officials. Before Gerald had managed to find his land legs, Canterby had spotted a coffeehouse, wherein he suggested they now partake of some nourishment before venturing farther.

The establishment, crammed into a corner between two warehouses, was very plain, but it was clean, and the busy landlord was all pleasant hospitality on seeing that his new customers were two English gentlemen. Having served them plentifully with cold mutton and ale—for the pair had not breakfasted that morning, being too absorbed with the business of docking—he stood back and watched them attack the meal with obvious hunger.

"They don't give ye much to eat on those vessels, do they, gents?"

Amused and a little taken aback by this democratic form of address, Gerald and Canterby shook their heads. The proprietor of the little shop did not, as a shopkeeper

at home would have done, back off at once, leaving them
to their solitude. Instead, he loitered behind their chairs,
peering down every once and a while to see how their
meal was progressing. At first his solicitude was a little offensive, but at last the two young Englishmen grew used to
it and began to question their host about his homeland.

They soon discovered the fellow had a wealth of information, and, being of Scots descent, as eager as they to
put some questions. He supposed they had been to Edinburgh? Most assuredly, they had. And was it not the
greatest city upon God's Earth? With smiles they expressed
great enthusiasm for its beauties as well as for the great
educational institutions to be found there. Not so great as
New York, however, he assured them. Though it was not
nearly so old, nor did it possess such distinguished buildings, he wagered there was very little to touch it.

"Ye shall find, gentlemen," he declared, "that within
this City, there dwell more enterprising men than anywhere else in the world. You must walk up to Mr. Astor's
house when you have the time and see for yourselves what
a great fortune is. I'll wager there is little to touch it even
in England! And now where be you gentlemen staying
while you are in New York?"

Here was a point the gentlemen were pleased to have
brought up. They had had recommended to them before
they had left England a hotel in Gouverneur Street called
the George Washington. The name seemed promising
enough—giving them a sense at once of the patriotism of
this young nation, even in the names of its streets and
inns. But their genial host threw up his hands when he
heard it was where they planned to spend the duration of
their stay.

"No, sirs, if you'll pardon me, ye mustn't think of abid-
ing there, no indeed! The man who runs the place is a fellow of my acquaintance, and not, if ye take my meaning,
the most honest jape in the City. I must recommend you
to stay in Vesey Street which is a very pleasant part of
town. It is just a step away from the Astor Mansion,
moreover, so you shall be assured of seeing it. There is a
hotel quite next door, The Lion, where you shall be assured of getting your money's worth. It is quite as elegant
a place as the George Washington, mark my words—but
you shall fare better, and pay less."

Gerald and his companion were pleased to be given these instructions, as they were neither of them travelling with loaded pockets and wished to make their pennies last as long as possible. Here, in fact, was another problem, for when they presented the landlord with two silver shillings to pay their fare, he frowned at the coins and shook his head.

"No, sirs, you shall have to make an exchange of currency, which you may do any morning at one of the banks in Wall Street. I shall take your silver and give you back your change in kind. But you shall not find everyone in New York so willing to oblige."

The pair walked out of the tavern some minutes later, smiling at the idea that British coin, recognized the world over as the most reliable money in existence, should here be scorned. Even in Italy and France, Gerald recalled, they were perfectly happy to be given English silver. But not in America!

They soon found, however, that their first American acquaintance had done them valuable turns, both in his advice about currency and in his recommendation of a hotel. The Lion turned out indeed to be a very commodious establishment. Though not as grand as some of the hostelries they had visited in their native land, it was clean, their chambers light and airy, and the food, though simple, hearty and nourishing. They were soon made welcome in the place, having given the landlord the name of their Scots acquaintance and, after being supplied with one of the young male servants to act as valet for them both, began to feel quite at home.

They passed three days exploring the City, walking miles each day through the labyrinth of roads near Wall Street and City Hall, along Broadway with its great churches and houses (including that of John Jacob Astor, the merchant prince, who had indeed built himself a palatial establishment) and along the lovely Fifth Avenue lined with the impressive mansions of the earliest wealthy settlers in New York.

It was to one of these houses that, on the fourth evening of their residence at The Lion, they were invited. Gerald had been given several letters of introduction to American families before he left London by his father, who, during the time of the American colonies' revolt against England,

had become friendly with one or two of the prominent Tories who had fled to England. Amongst these was an introduction to one Frederic Van Cortlandt, whose uncle had
been a friend of Sir James's. Upon presenting the letter,
and his card, at the great Van Cortlandt Mansion, Gerald
had found himself welcomed very pleasantly by the
family, which consisted of the gentleman, his agreeable
wife and their six children. He and Canterby had at once
been invited to dine on the following Tuesday and were
promised that a small party should be got up in their
honour.

What the pair found, when they arrived at the massive
stone and marble townhouse, was hardly less elegance and
pomp than they might have expected at any English aris-
tocrat's entertainment. As they alighted from their carriage, they were struck by the profusion of lanterns and
coloured lights illuminating the vast porte cochère. The
lights were hung from columns and trees and held up by a
double row of liveried Negro servants lining the great
marble staircase. The Englishmen found themselves, upon
going in, amidst a crowd of fashionably dressed men and
women, and the glitter of jewels, the rustle of silks and
satins, and the vast array of light, laughter, and luxurious
accomodations made them feel instantly foolish for having
ever imagined that this nation was a provincial, plain, drab
place full of earnestness and Godliness.

There was, indeed, Godliness to be found at the Van
Cortlandts'—but it was hardly the sort Gerald had envisioned from the travel books he had read. He had met a
small number of Americans, indeed, but they had been put
at a disadvantage, perhaps, by the great distance from
their homeland and the awkwardness which every traveller
feels upon attempting to ingratiate himself into another society. Here at home, they struck him at once as a universally agreeable lot, an intelligent, well-spoken, cultured
group of people without any trace of that resentment
which he had imagined they might harbour against a visiting citizen of their old enemy, England. Their Godliness
was to be seen in the profound welcome they gave him, in
the general cordiality they showed each other, in the very
visible love they bore their families and friends. Perchance
they were a trifle more plainspoken than the English, and
they were a good deal set upon proving their democratic

way of life. And yet they aped the European ways—Gerald saw at once that there was scarcely a female in the room who was not dressed in the latest Paris fashions, nor a gesture which did not in some way recollect the mannerisms of a Madame Recamier. They seemed informed of every event which had occupied the political wags at home, and, what he found more impressive still, were so intelligently aware of every aspect of their own government, so concerned and articulately involved (for he soon saw groups of men form in discussion of the latest tariff bills, the institution of new reforms, the City and State legislatures), that he found himself embarrassed for the ignorance exhibited by many of his own peers in England.

He and Canterby were drawn into the gathering the moment they stepped into the great salon, whose walls and ceilings, gilded and embossed, resembled the best of the Adam brothers. His host, a genial, distinguished gentleman in the prime of his life, led him at once to a group of men and women standing and seated about the handsomely inlaid pianoforte. He soon found himself introduced and was immediately engaged in conversation by a young man of about his own age, a Mr. Brown. Here was none of the frigid formality which might have attended upon the presumptuous entrance of some foreigner into the heart of *English* society!

Mr. Brown and one of the young Van Cortlandts were, at the moment of Gerald's coming up, engaged in a heated disagreement over the merits of the Hudson River steamers. The former gentleman, a personable, tall and amiable-faced young man, soon appraised his English companion of the source of their disagreement. It appeared that Mr. Brown's father was a shipowner, and that one of his steamers had lately broken a speed record for the journey from Albany to New York. The Van Cortlandt youth, on the other hand, was staunchly defending the charm of the old sloops, whose last year of prominence upon that River had been a decade since, before Robert Fulton had made his first earthshaking voyage on the *Clermont*. Uninformed of the matter, save that he had heard of both Fulton and the river steamers (and was amazed by both), Gerald listened for some time in silence to their discussion.

"I say it ought to be left to the population of the Valley,

who shall have access and who shall not," declared Van
Cortlandt, an earnest-faced youth of the pale colouring of
all his family.

"Pshaw, Sewie," returned the older Mr. Brown, "you
know not what you say."

"I know," said the young man, sticking out his stub-
born-looking chin, "that it is ruining that part of the
River. There is scarce an inlet in Cortland County which
has not lost its charm for all the steam and dirt."

"And yet you receive your mail much faster than you
used to do, and every sort of merchandise from the cities."

"I would rather not," retorted Van Cortland. "I would
rather preserve the beauty of the place."

"Ah! You say so now, but you were not alive in the
time when a letter took a month to reach the upper sec-
tions of the Hudson Valley. You do not know what it is
like to be without news, your women without muslin, your
forges without metal."

"But I *was* alive!" cried Van Cortlandt indignantly.

"Well, then, you were very young," returned his friend.
"But, Mr. Kirkland, what is your opinion of this argument? Do you prefer beauty to efficiency? Young Van
Cortlandt here believes he could exist upon the aesthetic
pleasures of the world, whilst I must remonstrate; but
then, my father is in trade—as you English say—he lives
upon the profits of the river steamers, and as his son, so
do I."

"In that case," returned Gerald with a smile, "I should
say that if I had my home upon the River, I should infinitely prefer the old sloops, for I have heard that steamers
make a geat deal of unpleasant noise and let off a positive
mire of dirty smoke."

"Here, here!" cried the Van Cortlandt lad, clapping him
upon the back, "Here, here! D'you see, Brown, he sides
with me?"

"On the other hand," continued Gerald, smiling more
broadly, "were I dependent upon the speed of passage for
my livelihood, I should certainly prefer the steamers. And,
as I am unfortunately cursed with a great passion for
scientific discovery, I should probably prefer them in any
case."

It was now Mr. Brown's turn to congratulate the new-
comer upon his good sense, which he did whilst giving an

exaggerated wink of victory to young Seward Van Cortlandt, who, making a comical face at the older gentleman, subsided.

"I see our new visitor has a most happy turn of phrase," came a new voice from behind Gerald. Whirling round to see who had caught him out in his diplomatic stratagem, he was amazed to see that the owner of the musical voice was an extremely comely young lady.

"You must not mind Seward's bullying, nor yet my brother's, which is certainly worse," continued the young lady in a laughing manner, slipping her hand through Mr. Brown's arm. "If you allow yourself to be caught up in their nonsense, you shall regret it very heartily, I assure you!"

"Now hush, Chastity," responded her brother in a fond voice, "you mustn't give us all away at once. I shall readily give up the dignity of young Seward here, but not my own!"

"Pshaw!" returned Miss Brown in an irreverent tone. "I am far more likely to defend the dignity of Sewie, who is the only one of the two of you capable of appreciating the beauties of Nature. But, Harry, I hope you will give up your quarrel long enough to introduce your friend."

The introduction was made at once, and Gerald, bowing over the young lady's prettily gloved hand, met a pair of teasing brown eyes as he rose.

Miss Chastity Brown was of medium height and colouring, but in no other way was she ordinary. Her very pretty, agile figure was set off to an advantage by a gown of emerald silk, overlayed with ivory lace. A long and slender neck rose up from her shapely shoulders, completely revealed by the daring lines of the Parisian frock, as was a very fetching degree of bosom; her glossy dark curls were becomingly arranged *à la grecque*. Gerald, looking into those wide and sparklingly clear eyes, felt at once an affinity for the American form of playful flirtation which he saw dancing there. Miss Brown's was not an altogether a perfect kind of beauty; far from it, for a close inspection would reveal a nose a trifle short and a trifle uptilted at the end and (most extraordinarily!) a dash of freckles sprinkled over it, which had not been bleached nor hidden by powder. Her mouth was a bit wide, and her generous smile revealed a set of pearly teeth a trifle large.

Her bones were unremarkable, being fashioned more closely after the style of a wood nymph or sprite than that of a goddess. She was not, as Gerald saw at once, the exquisite beauty that Lady Charlotte Harrington was, and, rather than making him think less of her for it, the realization, on the contrary, had the effect of increasing his admiration.

Charlotte's beauty, was—as was everything about her—now connected in his mind with pain and wounded pride. Despite all his reminders to himself that he had been on the point of sacrificing his own claim to her affections in order to save her (or so he thought), he could not for a moment forgive her having outmaneuvered him. How ungrateful are the hearts of men, who, in their best moments, are moved by thoughts as martyrlike as any saint, but when confronted with an event which takes the nobility out of their own gestures, bear nothing but resentment against the one for whom, a moment before, they were ready to give up everything!

To all outward appearances, even to the watchful eyes of his traveling companion, Gerald seemed untouched by the events which had sent him hastening out of England. If he had been broodish during the voyage across the Atlantic, his first sight of America seemed to have dissipated the cloud in his heart. At night, in the solitude of his own bedchamber, he sometimes stood long by the window, watching the night sky with moody eyes, and, on some rare occasions, actually sat down at his writing table and, taking quill and ink, began to scribble; but there was no trace to be found, either of moodiness nor epistles on the following morning. The servant girl, whose task it was to clean his room, had sometimes wondered at the number of half-burnt pages she discovered every morning in the grate when she went to make up the fire, but even she could have no inkling of what had been written there.

Be that as it may, Miss Chastity Brown now saw before her a man exceedingly attractive by her measure (and Miss Brown had taken the measure of a good many gentlemen in her short life), made more attractive still by the very evident admiration for her in his eyes. Indeed, she was quite used to being admired, for she was far the most popular, and richest, marriageable young lady in New York. Her papa, who "made his living at sea" as she liked to put it, owned half the vessels in the nation and ruled a fast-growing empire of naval commerce between the New World and the Old. Her ancestors had first made their fortune in the slave trade, but now her papa was so modern that he had even freed his own slaves and, being amongst the first men in the state to do so, was looked upon with much wonder and not a little resentment by his neighbours on the Hudson. The affairs of the Brown family had often caused wonder and envy and sometimes anger in their neighbours, who were by and large conservative old families of either English or Dutch extraction and who had brought with them to America fortunes already large. The Browns, on the other hand, descended from a saddle-maker of unimpressive parentage who had worked his way across the ocean by sewing canvas instead of leather. That, however, had been in the year 1702, and since then his sons and his sons' sons had done considerably better for themselves.

All this was known to nearly everybody in New York, or at least anybody whose opinion was worth having, and though some still remembered to censure the whole family by reason of the irreverence of the first wealthy Browns, most had conveniently forgotten that their blood had come from the veins of a saddle-maker. In a city whose wealthiest inhabitants included not only the old aristocratic clans of Livingston, Van Cortlandt, and Van Rensselaer but the more recently moneyed families of Astor and Vanderbilt, in a nation founded upon rebellion against the supremacy of the European aristocracy, it was extraordinary that such a fact should even have deserved notice. It was, moreover, a sign that even in the greatest democracy on earth, the existence of a privileged class, with all its attendant snobberies, was inevitable.

Miss Brown, therefore, knew exactly her place in that strata of society and how she was regarded by most of it. She was used to being admired, as we have seen, but was not spoiled. On the contrary, she delighted afresh at every new set of admiring eyes directed toward her and was twice as pleased that this particular set should belong to a gentleman so agreeable, so dashing and so exotic.

Gerald, of course, knew only that the charming Miss Brown was one of the prettiest and most intriguing of his discoveries in America. Willingly did he allow himself to be monopolized by her and her very amiable brother until the dinner hour, and when, having escorted his hostess into the dining hall, he found himself seated between that lady and Miss Brown, he felt not the slightest objection.

Chapter 7

His first duty, of course, was to Mrs. Van Cortlandt, and towards her he turned with many commendations of her charming house, her elegant rooms and handsome table.

"You are very kind, Mr. Kirkland," said that amiable woman in reply. "I suppose you did not expect anything very much in America?"

"On the contrary," returned the smiling Gerald, "I expected a great deal, only none of it so exquisite. I suppose in a way I expected too little fashion from so daring a people."

"People who are daring in one way are usually daring in others as well, I find. But we are not attempting to rival the European *ton*, I assure you. On the whole we are a solid, comfortable citizenry, who enjoy our luxuries as much as anyone else."

The truth of these words, spoken plainly and without any pretence, was perfectly evidenced by everything and everyone in the Van Cortlandt's dining room. As Gerald looked about him at the vast polished mahogany table, the masses of fresh flowers arranged at intervals along it, the handsome China-import porcelain and the plain but exquisitely made American silver, he saw that everywhere was this same tasteful simplicity. But nowhere was it more in evidence than in the thirty-six faces seated around that table, some stout, some thin, but all with that clarity of gaze and inner energy of purpose that makes the homeliest face remarkable. Never in Gerald's memory had he found himself in a group whose sheer communal resolve could be

more keenly sensed. Once more he felt that same exhilaration which had swept over him as he stood upon the
Half Moon's bowsprit sailing into New York Harbour.

"I think," he said, turning back from his perusal of the
room, "that you are far too modest, madam. I never in my
life saw a people less comfortable, if by that word you
mean the complacency of spirit which I have all too often
censured in myself and in many of my English acquaintance."

"I suppose that comes of having fought so hard to win
our freedom," remarked the lady with a smile.

"And yet you do not seem to hold a grudge against the
English, which I find altogether admirable, seeing how you
must have felt abused by us."

"Oh, but not abused by *you*, sir!" retorted Mrs. Van
Cortlandt. "In fact, not abused by any *one* person, or even
the monarch. I believe that if your poor King George were
at this moment to walk into this room, he should be
greeted as civilly, and with as much respect, as you have
been. We do not harbour any grudge against anything but
the unfortunate confluence of circumstance. Indeed, there
are many of us who had rather we had *not* rebelled
against the King. My husband's uncle, as you know, fled
to England at the time."

"Yes," replied Gerald, and with great interest asked
whether a great many families were so divided by the
cause of freedom.

"More than ought to have been," said she. "It does us
no credit to think how many of these who had profited
most at the hands of the British now prosper from the
democratic process." As she said this, Mrs. Van Cortlandt's eye seemed to wander down the table to the other
end, where, seated next to Chancellor Livingston's wife, a
florid gentleman was attacking his lobster with energy.

Gerald's eye followed hers, and he inquired who the
man was.

"Why, do you not know?" demanded the lady with
some surprise. "It is Henry Philipse, the son of Adolph
Philipse. His father owned nearly all the land which is
now Manhattan before the War. Having secured one
Royal Grant, he so ingratiated himself with each succeeding monarch that he was continually the recipient of new
lands. He fled to England when the rebels threatened him,

and all his holdings were expropriated by the Patriots. But now his son has returned and insinuated himself so completely into the government at Philadelphia that one would think he had been a general himself in the War with Britain."

Gerald felt some surprise at this story together with an ironic amusement at the universality of certain forms of political intrigue. But he was amazed that this same Philipse (who did not appear a great favourite of Mrs. Van Cortlandt) should be welcomed at her table. He felt, however, that to enquire further into the matter would be ill-bred and so did not press his hostess, hoping that somehow the matter might be illuminated to him. Mrs. Van Cortlandt, moreover, had changed the subject to one more interesting in his view.

"Now Miss Brown, on the other hand," she was saying, glancing at the young lady on his right now engaged in an animated discussion with the distinguished Chancellor Livingston, "is descended from a very different kind of people altogether. The first Brown to set foot in America was a saddle-maker; her great-grandpapa somehow contrived to buy a ship, or get it built—I do not recollect which—and now her own papa owns one of the largest fleets of vessels in America. *He* did not flee to England, you may be sure. Instead, he built a goodly number of ships, and, at his own expense, managed the convoy of supplies up and down the Hudson."

"A most remarkable example of generous patriotism!" remarked Gerald, glancing with new interest at the lady on his right.

"Ah, the Browns are the stuff of which the best Americans are made," agreed Mrs. Van Cortlandt. "They have never pretended to hate power or wealth but by a judicious temperament and delight in doing good have made their own fortunes satisfy the needs of many." Mrs. Van Cortlandt smiled at her young guest and finished in motherly tone, "And Miss Brown, I think, is one of the prettiest girls in New York. Though my own daughters shan't forgive me for saying so, Mr. Kirkland."

Considering that the young Van Cortlandt ladies were indeed young—the eldest being hardly seventeen—they could not have taken their mother's remarks too hard, though they had all agreed that Mr. Kirkland and his

friend were by far the most interesting gentlemen to set
foot in their drawing room in heaven knows how long.
They had all, with the exception of Phillipa, who was only
eight and had not been allowed downstairs, gone to an in-
ordinate degree of trouble with their dress for the evening.
At that moment Joanna, who was the eldest, was making a
heady attempt at conversation with Mr. Canterby across
the way. Seeing his infamous schoolmate delighting the
young girl with extravagant compliments, Gerald returned,
"I don't suppose they have eyes for anyone but Canterby, in
any case. I must warn the young devil to suppress his
poetical nature in their presence, lest he endanger their
hearts with the extreme sweetness of his words."

Mrs. Van Cortlandt followed her guest's eye and smiled
maternally. "Oh, I do not think it shall do Joanna any
harm to be made much of for one evening. Girls do like
it, you know!"

Gerald wished he felt his hostess' complacency, but
seeing his friend was beginning to wax lyrical, he remembered the trail of broken hearts he had left behind him in
England. It would certainly not do to give their hosts in
America so ungracious a thank-you for their generosity.

The lobster plates were cleared away and followed by a
sorbet à framboises—a delicious confection culled, as Mrs.
Van Cortlandt informed him, from the raspberries of their
countryhouse in Cortlandville. The Manor was one of the
first erected on the banks of the Hudson, and having
expressed the hope that she and her husband might welcome their English friends there for a visit in the near future, Mrs. Van Cortlandt turned to address the gentlemen
at her left.

Now Gerald was free once more to speak to Miss
Brown, who had, as if by a secret signal, turned towards
him at the moment the sherbet was taken away.

"I have been hearing a good deal about your forebears,
Miss Brown. It appears General Washington was much in-
debted to the generosity of your father during the War."

"Oh, that!" exclaimed Miss Brown, gaily, "It was very
good of Papa, I am told, but he did no more good than
did General Van Cortlandt."

Gerald looked at the gentleman seated at the opposite
end of the table in some surprise. "Why! He hardly looks
old enough—" he began.

"That is because I was referring to his father," replied a laughing Miss Brown. "Old General Van Cortlandt was the first Governor of New York and during the Revolutionary War commanded a regiment on the Hudson. You see, we are all descended of great patriots here."

"Except Henry Philipse," Gerald put in.

Miss Brown looked surprised. "Ah! So Madame has been telling you of him, has she?"

"A little," replied Gerald. "She said only that his father had sought protection in England during the War but that his son had come back to claim his father's place."

"More than his father's place, I believe." Chastity Brown smiled enigmatically at her companion. "But that is not so interesting to me as what has brought *you* here. Surely it is more fashionable to take the Grand Tour of the Continent?"

"More ordinary, perhaps," returned a smiling Gerald, "but hardly more inspiring. I have felt a sense of keen exhilaration since stepping off the ship. Never in my life have I felt so keenly that I grew up in a cocoon as I have in the past four days."

"Oh yes, you find us very quaint and industrious," said Chastity with a teasing look. "But come now—for *I* cannot think of anything more wonderful than to tour England and France and Italy—are not the pleasures of Europe more grand, more—"

She seemed to search for a word.

But Gerald cut her off, "More grand, certainly; but I have yet to see in France or Italy, or even England—and *I* am a patriot, too, you know—anything so interesting as the life here. Even the monuments of Rome and Venice can hardly touch it, for I think living history far more impressive than dead."

Miss Brown regarded him for a moment with a smile. "I like that very well," said she, "very well indeed. Who would not? To be thought more interesting than the monuments of Rome—"

"You mistake my meaning, my dear lady!"

"Well, at least to be your 'dear lady' is something. I like *that* a great deal better than all your old history, living or dead. But pray tell me something, Mr. Kirkland—for I confess to the curiosity of all primitive peoples—what does a gentleman of your kind do in England?"

Gerald looked surprised, for indeed he did not know exactly what she meant. "Why, we eat, sleep, contrive to amuse ourselves—like any old relic!"

Miss Brown put back her head and laughed, and Gerald found himself unwillingly comparing the high, assured sound of Miss Brown's laughter to the soft, tinkling music of Charlotte's. The comparison was not unfavourable, but he was grateful when the young lady's mirth had ceased and she exclaimed, "Relic, indeed! I meant, what is your life's work? Or is that not a proper question to put to the son of a baronet? For I suppose you will say it is to learn to be a baronet, which will probably serve me right."

Gerald stared at her in silence for a moment, as if struck by something, and his silence moved Miss Brown to remark, "Now I have irritated you, and I did not wish to. I meant only to discover a little more about you, for you see"—this with a brilliant smile—"I am a little primitive!"

"Well, then," returned Gerald, "as one old relic to a little primitive, I must in all honesty confess that the question has never been put to me before, or not, at any rate, so beautifully."

"What!" exclaimed Chastity incredulously, "No one has ever asked you what you *do*? I suppose it is felt to be ill-mannered? And yet here in America, everyone does something. It would be ill-bred to assume otherwise. Even my papa, who is dreadfully rich, says one's life's work is always for one's own pleasure, and if no profession or trade is found to be interesting, then some employment is to be found in politics. Indeed, nearly everyone does that."

What he did was a question that had never been put to Gerald before, and as he explained to his new acquaintance that in England, unlike America, at least amongst his own acquaintance, hardly anyone worked, unless the heated pursuit of pleasure was thought to be work, which indeed it was, sometimes, it dawned upon him for the first time in his life what an idle and insipid practice that was. To live, to be brought up to live, only for the sake of existing from one supper party to the next, from balls to theatre parties and back again, struck him of a sudden as the ultimate of foolishness. Indeed, save for one or two of his friends from his Cambridge days who had gone into the Clergy, he had hardly an acquaintance who could have answered the question any better than he.

It struck him also, and this perhaps was the thing which made the greatest impression, that when he had considered entering the Diplomatic Service, it had been a thought as revolutionary to one of his class and education as if he had suddenly taken it into his head to turn somersaults down Piccadilly. He did know of some men who had become diplomatists by chance or fortune—Wellington was one—but none who had set out to make it a "life's work." He knew officers in the Navy, younger sons for the most part, but even these were rare. If a man needed money in Gerald's world, he married a wealthy girl, and if he needed none, then he did whatever he liked.

He could not have explained all this to Miss Brown, even if he had wished to. To have attempted it would have been like trying to explain why butterflies had many colours and moths were rather drab. He only knew that Miss Brown's innocent question had stirred up a tempest in his own mind.

Seeing his look of intent absorption, Miss Brown exclaimed, "I *have* made you angry! Dear me, whatever shall I do to make amends?"

Gerald smiled broadly. "On the contrary, you have made me thoughtful, and that cannot be accounted a bad thing. In answer to your question I must tell you truthfully that if I have ever had any life's work at all, it was to be a gentleman, and that goal now strikes me as rather paltry."

"Oh, I do not know about that," remarked Miss Chastity Brown. "It strikes *me* as delightful! Who could wish a man to be anything else?"

"True—if it is a means to an end, or a state of being whilst one does something else. But if it is, as you put it, one's life's work, it is rather hollow."

"But if one is a gentleman," returned the young lady, "one is never hollow. Is not that part of the meaning of gentlemanliness? I always thought it was; one must be thoughtful and kind and honourable, and—gentle!"

"But one may be all of those things and still improve the world around one, be it in ever so small a way."

Miss Brown regarded her new friend for a long moment, and then said, "Yes, of course—well, that is all part of it."

It now struck Gerald what the great difference was between the English and the Americans: that while he had

been brought up to think that one lived to preserve the already existing good and to improve upon it as much as
possible, Miss Brown came from a tradition, though a very
short tradition, the founding premise of which was that
good must be forged out of every possible sphere whether
it had existed before or not. It was that difference, he
thought, looking up to see a great saddle of mutton born
into the room by a footman, that had caused the exhilaration he had felt since his arrival in America.

The conversation did not continue long, however, over
such heady topics, though Gerald, as the evening
progressed, was increasingly struck by the headiness of all
conversations in America. Everywhere one heard men—
and women—discussing subjects which at home would
have been thought boorish. Where politics were only permitted in the best drawing rooms of England if they were
properly spiced with wit and sarcasm, here he saw men
hovering together in a genuine rage of argument, and as
he soon sensed, their arguments were often the roots of
real change. The men and women gathered in the Van
Cortlandts' dining room included some of the most influential figures in the nation. There was Chancellor Livingston of Clermont; and Mr. John Jay, Secretary of the
Treasury; Mr. Brown, whose ships dominated the trade
with Europe; and Commodore Vanderbilt, who had made
his fortune more recently in the heavy Hudson River traffic. Mrs. Van Rensselaer and Mrs. Roosevelt, neighbours
on the Hudson, were, like many of their friends, secondarily involved in the nation's legislature through sons and
sons-in-law. An elderly man now, Mr. James Lee had been
one of the most important figures in the formation of the
new government and had been one of the first signatories
of the Constitution. All of these great men and their wives,
who seemed no less formidable to the two young Englishmen, were intimates of the Van Cortlandts. It was an inspiration to be in one room with them.

Gerald, who had felt the force around him only through
conversation with one of the great men's daughters, was
drawn to the energy which seemed to animate them all.
Here indeed was a group of men and women worth emulating and whom he should be proud to say that he had
met. With what wonder did he recollect now how some of
his acquaintance had come away from America with tales

of boorishness and boredom, saying they had never yet
met people who knew less how to talk! But on second
thought, when he remembered the source of those testimo-
nies, he was forced to smile to himself: who more boorish,
who more vapid, than those same privileged youths, who
had never lifted their own hands to any occupation greater
than spending, with as much rapidity as possible, the inherited fortunes of their fathers? The thought humbled
him. The whole evening, in fact, had the effect of hum-
bling him, and he came away after having conversed with
a handful of his host's guests feeling that he could do far
worse than to be able to claim them as his acquaintances.

Chapter 8

The evening had as great, though a very different, effect upon Fitz Canterby. As has been oftentimes observed, it is nearly impossible for two men to derive the same impression from an event, though they stand side by side throughout it, though they be similar in mind and character. And where they are of dissimilar inclinations, how different may their impressions be!

Canterby had gone into the Van Cortlandt's mansion with a single-mindedness which Gerald might have envied, feeling as he had done for these last weeks rather like a fish floundering upon the shore. Canterby, who had put his hundred pounds upon the voyage to America with the same feeling he might have had, had he put it upon a horse at Ascot, had staked the little he possessed upon the promise of the New World.

He had hardly any choice. His father had already warned him that he was not to get another shilling until he learned to behave himself, and Fitz was almost constitutionally incapable of good behaviour. His character ruled him, and his character was so weak that he could not but look at a pretty woman without wishing to make love to her. That she was married or in some other way beyond his reach bothered him not at all; he felt himself compelled to pursue the fox until it was properly brought to rest or he would not sleep. A number of ladies had come near to losing their honour for him, and some few had gone beyond the mark. Canterby, when he had got his trophy, soon grew bored, and the lady was left to the unhappy meditations of her own conscience. Thus far Canterby had not, to do him justice, actually ruined a lady who deserved the name. He had broken several hearts and disturbed quite a few; he had gone the gamut with a few of his friends' wives, who had done the same before and thought it all a good joke; but he had never ruined a young girl's honour.

To be plain, he had never been tempted. He was irresistibly attracted to flirts, and flirts must depend upon their wits to defend themselves. Virtue did not tempt him. His father would not have blinked had he proposed to marry anybody, so long as she was capable of supporting him. But Canterby's heart always played him false, if one may take the liberty of calling that small unfeeling muscle in his bosom a heart. Ah! But that is unfair. Canterby had his weaknesses, as have we all; he adored money and knew how to spend it so well that had there been a profession which specialized in the spreading about the countryside of gold, he should have been its most eminent member. He adored pretty women, particularly witty ones, and had an enduring fondness for fine clothes. He possessed, what is more, a discerning eye. He could detect the original from the imitation in a moment's time where some experts might be baffled; and though this talent was often put to other than virtuous use, it had always served him well.

He had detected, for one thing, that the wealth and opulence everywhere in evidence at the Van Cortlandt mansion was absolutely genuine. Accustomed as he was to distinguishing the pretender to wealth from the genuine article (for had not he perfected the art?), he was not to be baffled. Here, only four days after setting foot in New York, to which he had come with an almost desperate desire to make his fortune as quickly and easily as possible, he was quite sure he had found it. The Van Cortlandts and all their guests seemed to him like gifts from Heaven. The amiable and maternal Madame Van Cortlandt, the hospitable, hearty gentleman of the house, their six blooming children, all as innocent and good-natured as their parents—where on Earth could he have struck upon a better solution to his problems? Young Miss Phillipa, to be sure, was hardly his idea of a prize. Miss Chastity

Brown, that delightful little vixen, much more nearly
suited his idea of what a woman ought to be. But Miss
Joanna was already half caught (her ogling had nearly
blinded him), and Miss Brown, little she-devil, had given
him the evil eye, and hightailed it off with Gerald. Well!
Canterby was not particular. He did not demand a wife
that was perfection, only one that was rich. If Miss Brown
would not have him for life, he was quite sure she would
have him for a little less.

Having selected two targets for his not inconsiderable
charm, Canterby would have felt quite satisfied, even had
there not been other rewards in the offing. But there were
two possibilities: First, Canterby was not known in New
York, which was the reason he had come here. Where in
London his reputation had unfortunately spread beyond
the dimly lit parlours he sometimes frequented, so that no
suitably virtuous, or suitably moneyed, young lady would
any longer have him; in New York he was but another of
those English gentlemen so much admired by the American young ladies. He had let it be known that his father
was a marquis which had done wonders for the regard in
which he was held especially since he had let it be known
further that Gerald's father was only a baronet. (He had
not gone into details *vis-à-vis* his place in line for the inheritance.) In the second place, should all else fail and he
be forced upon the mercy of his wits, he had had a most
interesting discussion with one Mr. Philipse who had told
him much that was of interest about the world of trade in
America and about the fur trade in particular. Canterby
had concluded, after only half an hour over cigars and
port with that gentleman, that there were fortunes to be
had in this country for the asking.

Canterby, however, disliked work and did not intend to
indulge in it unless it was absolutely necessary. His first
choice of stratagems was the young ladies; the second,
making his own fortune. But to succeed with either he felt
he must get up the Hudson River, for both Miss Van Cortlandt and the fur trade were shortly to be in residence
there.

On the morning following their dinner on Fifth Avenue,
therefore, Canterby brought forth his idea to Gerald. They
were breakfasting rather late, owing to the small hour at

which they had returned to The Lion on the previous evening. The meal was served in Gerald's small sitting room where the two had fallen into the habit of holding council before the day's activities. Fitz came in in his embroidered dressing gown, the valet having been accorded Gerald before breakfast. Gerald, Fitz was amazed to note, had risen long enough before to have been out riding in Battery Park and was now sitting down to table in his boots and coat.

"Fitz!" exclaimed he, "It's a deliriously lovely morning, is it not? I never saw the sky so blue, nor the Earth sparkle with so much greenery! I have been down riding by the River and have seen the most extraordinary thing! The salmon run is on—the whole River is a stream of golden fins. Mr. Van Cortlandt told me all about it last evening, but I could not believe him. They say the salmon keep it up well into October."

"Really?" inquired the still dazed Fitz, "how extraordinary of you!"

"How extraordinary of *me*? Why, no such thing. Nothing could be more ordinary. You're still asleep, Fitz. Why don't you go back to bed for an hour or two?"

"I should lo-love to," replied Fitz, yawning as he sat down and shook out the linen napkin over his lap, "only I have wo-work to do."

"Work? Now, *that* is extraordinary! But in point of fact, so do I. Actually, I am going to rush through this so that I may be on time."

"On time for what?" inquired a suspicious Fitz.

"On time to meet Mr. Harry Brown, who is going to take me to a shipyard to see a riverboat being built for his father. He promised I might see the place before he goes back to Garrison. Garrison is where they live, you know. It is quite a way up the Hudson. Actually, they invited us to visit them, so if you like—"

Suddenly Fitz was upon the alert. Somehow through the daze of sleep (for it was only eleven o'clock, practically dawn) he managed to comprehend Gerald's meaning. "I do indeed, my boy, I do indeed! When do we start?"

Gerald felt slightly taken aback. "Why, I suppose any time we like. It had occurred to me that we ought to stay in New York City for another week or two—"

"No time like the present! We have seen all there is to see of the City, I imagine. Besides, you mustn't keep poor Miss Brown waiting over long, d'you think? I say we go when they do."

Gerald smiled at his friend, but even Fitz noticed the slight reddening of his face. "Why, you're colouring like any bride, man," he remarked lazily, inserting the silver prongs of his fork into the tender underbelly of a small fish. "Has Miss Chastity Brown so profound an effect upon you? But I daresay she has—she looks a perfectly edible little morsel to me. It is just my luck she took a fancy to you first."

Gerald shook his head in an irritable manner and muttered something about his friend's unfortunate turns of phrase.

"Well, that ain't a subject to bother you, old boy," returned Fitz. "If I were you, I should catch hold of her at once before she darts off into the blue like one of your salmon. She was the prettiest girl by far at last evening's entertainment, and I'm told she was by far the richest. You could do much worse, don't you know?"

"Fitz, I shouldn't go any further, if I were you," remarked his friend. "I am not in the market for a bride, nor even for a fish, as you so prettily put it. Miss Brown and her brother were most cordial. I find them both extremely agreeable; there is no more to it than that. And while we are about it, you had better curb your manner a bit with Miss Van Cortlandt. She is only seventeen—I don't believe she has been fortunate enough to know anyone the likes of you before and so in all likelihood has not mastered the art of dampening the ardour of your addresses."

"Oh, come on, old boy," scoffed Fitz quite agreeably, "women are all born capable of defending themselves. I shouldn't wonder the little thing has already dissected my faults with her mama. But *you*, old boy—I should think you had better have a little of your own medicine, don't you? I never saw anything like the looks you were getting from Miss Chastity!"

"The subject, old man, is closed."

"Very well," sighed Fitz, inserting a piece of fish into his mouth and thoughtfully chewing it. "But I *am* heartened to see you making so swift a recovery from the heartless treatment of that lady who shall remain nameless."

Fitz seemed unaware of the cold stare accorded him upon saying this and continued the sensual mastication of his food. Watching him, Gerald was struck, really for the first time, by the thought that his amusing, seemingly Devil-may-care and childishly selfish travelling companion possessed more than a trace of actual cruelty in his dandified frame. It was but a thought, however, and was shrugged off as one of those exaggerated ideas one sometimes get after too many sleepless nights. The night before, in fact, had been about the first real rest he had got since that awful day, nearly six weeks since, when he had heard about Charlotte's betrayal. Betrayal! What a word—but had not he invited it? And for the first time in weeks, Gerald found himself able to think rationally about Charlotte, to wonder, even, if she were well and happy—and when she was to become Lady Beresford. The thought, indeed, gave him a brief stab of pain, but then he deliberately turned his mind to more pleasant topics.

The day's activities promised a good deal of pleasure. Gerald found himself most happily intrigued the evening before by the running of this new, and evidently great, nation. Never had he been so stimulated by anything, at least that he could remember. Never had he felt more admiration for a group of people or more desire to learn as much as possible about the energy which motivated them. He had been enthralled by the description Harry Brown had given him of the work at the shipyards, and when the young man discovered Gerald's keen desire to see the craft in progress, Harry quickly invited him to come along on the following day, when he intended to make a check on the construction of one of his father's ships.

Harry Brown greeted him from the seat of his little town gig, and Gerald, who had come out to the street to await his new friend, was surprised at the transformation in the American gentleman from the previous evening. Where at the Van Cortlandts' Mr. Brown had appeared as elegantly garbed as any young earl, with satin waistcoat, linen fob, very modish evening slippers and stockings, today he was quite plainly clothed and might have seemed a shipwright himself. His muslin blouse was open at the throat, his leather pantaloons well worn, and his riding coat, though certainly of good quality, much ravelled at the wrists. It was a day of brilliant sunshine, and the air, as Gerald had discovered earlier, came into the mouth with the sweetness of wine. But it was August, and August in New York was a good deal more tropical than it ever was in England. Not only was the temperature very high, but the air was heavy with moisture. As Gerald climbed into the gig, he glanced in dismay at his own Hessianed calves and felt the melton of his riding coat scratch unpleasantly through the fine cambric of his blouse.

Harry Brown grinned. "You shall be sorry you are so elegant, Mr. Kirkland. I am afraid the shine on those boots shall most certainly be dimmed after plodding through the mud on the riverbank. Never mind—I shall lend you a pair of clogs if you like. I find the old Dutch footgear far more practical in my line of work, at least when it gets messy as it has a tendency to do."

Gerald was not at all averse to this idea and, when they passed half an hour clambering over rocks and between the skeletal hulls of the great ships under construction, was glad enough to have left his riding boots in the little shack by the river. Indeed, it was not long, with the ever-increasing heat of the afternoon, before he had discarded his coat and, like Harry Brown, turned up the sleeves of his blouse.

The shipyard was a great place, covering some two or three acres of muddy bank along the Hudson down by Battery Park and the commercial centers of Wall Street. As they had driven up, they had been greeted by the owner of the place, a Mr. Thomas Cheeseman, son of the man of the same name whose great handiwork had helped to vanquish the British men o' war in the Revolution and whose own ships had sailed once more against Britain in the last War. Mr. Cheeseman was a gentleman slightly older than either Gerald or Mr. Brown, and as it soon appeared, was an intimate of the American's. He personally escorted them on a tour of the great yard, stopping now and then to confer with the master shipwrights in whose charge the actual construction of the vessels was progressing. Gerald, who had never seen anything of the kind at close range—his chief experience of the art of shipbuilding having been

limited to glimpses from the main piers of Bristol and
Portsmouth—was intrigued.

As they made their way between the immense structures, rigged up on vast wooden frames, Mr. Brown and
Mr. Cheeseman explained the process of the construction.
The first step in building a ship was to lay down the
frame, both the line of the keel and the gunwales, which
was a crucial and difficult task. The curves of these main
timbers would govern the final shape of the whole, and as
the ship's seaworthiness and speed depended almost entirely upon its shape, the timbers had to be bent to an exact degree. This was accomplished by soaking the wood
and quite literally bending it into the proper shape. Next,
using the same technique, the rest of the frame was laid in
until the skeleton was complete. Mr. Brown explained to
Gerald as they waited while Mr. Cheeseman conferred
with one of his shipwrights that while New York was not
yet the greatest of the seaports in America—Boston and
Philadelphia still exceeding it in numbers of ships built
each year and as centers of overseas trade—he had no
doubt but that New York would soon catch up. Trade
upon the Hudson, from which much of his family's wealth
had derived, had long depended upon the use of sloops for
the carrying of cargo. But since the great discovery of
Robert Fulton of the steam-powered engine, the whole
business had been revolutionized. Now cargo could be sent
from Albany and reach Manhattan Island within twenty-
eight hours, sometimes even less. The invention had not
only improved commerce along the Hudson River but had
cut to a fraction the long and often dangerous journeys of
passengers from one town to another, who had before
been dependent upon the winds and currents, or, much
worse, the rutted Albany Post Road. Mr. Brown went on
further to explain that his chief business today was to in-
spect the progress of a new river steamer, the *Firefly*,
named after one of the *Clermont*'s first rivals upon the
Hudson.

Gerald was eager to see the steam-powered vessel, although it was only half constructed, and Mr. Brown led
him away from the chief part of the shipyard, where only
large ocean-going vessels were constructed, to a separate
area where the *Firefly* and two other riverboats were being
built.

Instantly amazed at the revolutionary shapes of these barges—for they resembled that style of vessel more than any other he remembered seeing—he was enthusiastic upon being given a glimpse of the plans.

"I must confess my gratification at seeing you so astonished," remarked Mr. Brown with a smile, "for it gives me no end of pleasure to see an Englishman awed by an American invention. For three centuries you have been calling us primitives, but now we have outdone every nation in Europe with our modernity."

It was a statement of fact, and Gerald felt some embarrassment for his countrymen's long contempt of the American mentality. He expressed himself duly awed and said he was eager to get a glimpse of a functioning steamer upon the Hudson.

"My sister told me you might honour us with a visit at Garrison," said Mr. Brown and then, with what Gerald felt pleased to think was a real warmth of feeling, added, "I will be as glad as she, if it be true. I know my father will be equally pleased to know you, and, of course, Chastity has taken quite a shine to her new American acquaintance."

Gerald made as cordial a reply to the invitation as its warmth demanded. Indeed, he said he had already mentioned the matter to his companion, Fitzwilliam Canterby, who had expressed himself almost as eager as he to make the journey.

"Excellent!" exclaimed Harry Brown, clapping his new friend upon the back. "We shall all look forward to your arrival with great impatience. In point of fact, if you do not mind delaying the remainder of your explorations of New York till your return, I would be delighted if you will keep my sister and me company on our own journey. We sail tomorrow on the *Arcadia*. If you will allow me, I shall arrange for your passages as well."

Considering Canterby's inexplicable eagerness to get up the Hudson, Gerald had little choice but to accept this kind proposal even had he desired otherwise. But, on the contrary, he found himself every moment more fond of his new friend, more stimulated by the American's company and more desirous of being shown some other of the many wonders of this country. Even in his innermost heart he did not believe that the charming Miss Chastity Brown played a very great role in his enthusiasm, but he could not deny that to further his acquaintance with her would be a most pleasant side effect of the visit.

Chapter 9

Lady Harrington shut the door quietly behind her and, as had become her habit in the preceding weeks, tiptoed softly to her daughter's bedside. A look of extreme pain came over her features as she stared down at the small, listless figure, whose eyes, great, dark pools of sorrow, gazed unseeing at the ceiling. As usual, Charlotte gave no sign of recognition of her mother's presence or, indeed, anything else. It sometimes seemed to her frightened mama, who had taken to watching the invalid's progress day and night, that she hardly breathed. It was as if the very life had been drained out of her, as if the tiny, fragile candle which must burn somewhere inside that breast had been reduced to a mere flickering ghost of light.

"Charlotte, my darling," she murmured softly, passing her warm hand over the chilly brow, "Mattilda is bring up your luncheon. You must try to eat something, my dear. The doctor says you must. However are you to regain your old good cheer and strength if you do not?"

No answer came, but then, none was expected. The Countess had made a habit of speaking thus to her daughter, although hardly a word had passed those pale lips for many weeks. Charlotte did, from time to time, murmur something, and she sat up in the most mechanical of manners when she was called upon to take some nourishment and dazedly partook of a sip or two of broth, but otherwise, hardly any sign of life had animated her since that day in June when she had been told of Gerald Kirkland's sudden departure for America. That afternoon she had wept and cried out and been visibly hysterical, and her mother, practical as she could be under the circumstances, had prayed that she would stop. Now she prayed for any sign of normal human life, hysterical or otherwise.

With a heavy sigh, Lady Harrington sank into the small armchair by the bed which had been installed a few days after that fateful afternoon. Taking up her needlework, she commenced to embroider a tiny turquoise bird upon the already intricate design. It was to be a pillow for the sofa before the fire when Charlotte should recover sufficiently to be moved.

In a few moments a knock came at the door, and the servant girl Mattilda stepped quietly in bearing a silver tray resplendent with flowers and linen and some exquisite dainties prepared by the heartbroken cook. Every member of that large household felt as she did. Gone was the merry spirit of the great old house; gone was the young bird whose trilling voice could be heard from the music room in the mornings; gone was the loving, gracious spirit that had lightened all their troubles. Mattilda set down the tray upon its stand and murmured, as she always did, "Any change, my lady?"

"No change," replied the Countess, as usual. For some weeks she had added "But there shall be soon, I am quite sure of it" with a bright smile of hope.

But no trace of hope remained in her bosom. Indeed, even Dr. Falmouth's hearty assurances had ceased to cheer her. And now even he had given up his usual refrain: "These young girls have a quantity of feeling, my dear Countess, but they have even a greater will to live. She shall be right as rain when the fever passes, you shall see."

But the fever had passed off some time before, leaving only a small fragment of the blooming life that had been there previously. Now Dr. Falmouth came, as often as ever, but he clucked over the poor child's pale face and, after the examination, passed out of the house with scarce a word. Poor Lady Harrington—to have been deprived of the one great love in her life, aside from her husband; to have been so cruelly robbed of the one bright, hopeful flower in her aging garden! The lines of sorrow were now etched into her once smooth brow, and her lips, which had been acclaimed as the most beautiful in England in her youth, were grown thin and drooping at the corners.

Again she sighed, and laying down her needlework, she took up the silver spoon upon the tray and commenced the unhappy process of trying to coax some nourishment into her daughter's mouth.,

But what of Lord Harrington, during all of this? How did that fondest of papas react to the effect his plot had had upon the creature who was dearer to his heart than anything on earth? Poor foolish Lord Harrington! He too was so saddened that he seemed to have aged a decade overnight. He tiptoed about the house as if it were a morgue and would not raise his voice above a whisper if he were on the third floor where Charlotte's chamber was. He hardly went out of doors at all unless it was to pace broodingly about the City, watching his old haunts through sorrowful eyes as if he were looking into a bright and cheerful room from the bitterness of a winter night.

To be sure, for a week he had kept up the same strain of optimism which he had first exhibited. When the fever struck he had grown frightened, as all men do when their womenfolk are taken ill. But, when the fever had passed off and the doctor's predictions were seen to be futile, he had panicked and now was so engrossed in his own misery and guilt that he could scarcely bring himself to speak, even to his wife.

One should perhaps say, especially to his wife; for her kind, sad eyes cried out to him like the direst knell of the hangman's bell. Hardly could he bring himself to meet her melancholy gaze at the table, and as soon as the meal was done, he fled from the dining hall into his own sanctum where he might be assured of no company but his own. And what sad company he kept there! What had begun as a complacent feeling of righteousness, the sensation that he had brought to pass single-handedly what would bring his daughter the greatest joy, had finally turned into a deep mortification and sense of leaden guilt. How could he bear to see his own reflection each morning in his glass? Well may we ask: but the hearts and minds of men are so perverse that we are often capable of hiding from ourselves the worst of our acts and, as if the sight might instantly kill us, pass our lives in a round of evasions and rationalizations too comical for the greatest idiot to believe. Nevertheless, Lord Harrington, who was not in all things so inane as he had been in this, who was, in truth, no more foolish than most people and a great deal more clever than some, had begun to see what dire consequences his actions had had. Indeed, were he not aware of it, he could hardly have behaved in so guilty a fashion until even his wife, so absorbed in their daughter's condition that she saw hardly anything else, began to wonder what had come over him. Several times she had put the question to him, and Lord Harrington, who had resolved a hundred times to bare his heart to her, commenced everytime to speak; but on each occasion he thought better of it and found some excuse or other for postponing the confession until so much time had passed that to confess was almost impossible.

Such was his state on this August afternoon as he sat in his usual place behind his desk with his boots upon the table top and his handsome old face creased in worry. Several times he had thought of going out of doors, but though the day was very fine—much finer than it had been of late, for a hot June had given way to a predominantly cool and rainy summer—he could not find the heart to move. So he sat on in the dimly lit room from which one could see nothing but the high garden wall some yards away.

It was thus that Mattilda found his lordship when she came rushing in, her face greatly flushed and her words all but incoherent.

"My lord, my lord!" she cried, nearly falling over the door ledge in her hurry to get into the room, " 'Er ladyship says you mun' come at once! My Lady Charlotte is risen from the dead! Oh, your lordship—do 'urry!"

"What, what?" exclaimed the Earl, gazing in befuddlement at the maid.

"My Lady Charlotte, my lord—oh, do 'urry! She 'as been asking for your lordship ever so long, only we couldn't 'ardly hunderstand 'er!"

"What's this you say?" cried his lordship, getting up at once. "My daughter is asking for me? Glory in Heaven, girl, well, move! Dear me, dear me." And the Earl nearly fell up the stairs.

He found a sight to bring tears into those old eyes. The Countess was standing, her own eyes brimming, beside her daughter's bed, and on that bed his daughter was sitting

up and staring at him from a face, though nearly as white
as snow, animated by something like life.

"What is it? Charlotte, my angel!"

"Hush, Desmond, do not exite the child. Charlotte has
been asking for you these past few minutes," said the
Countess, nearly choking for joy. "She wishes to know
what passed between you and Mr. Kirkland when he came
to say good-bye."

Now there were certainly subjects which Lord Harrington would have preferred discussing at this moment; but
he saw from the look of his wife that he must be calm and
reassuring and do what he could to make Charlotte better.
He therefore walked to his daughter's bedside and, taking
her small cold hand in his own, said with brimful eyes,
"What is it you wish to know, my angel?"

"I wish you to tell me exactly what passed between you
on that day," replied the young lady in a voice not strong
but full of determination. "You must tell me exactly,
please, and do not leave anything out."

"Surely there are other things for you to think about my
dear?" inquired the anxious Earl. But he saw at once that
his daughter was not to be put off. "Very well, then. He
came to me in a very gentlemanlike manner and told me
that, as your papa, I should know that he had determined
that the intimacy which had arisen between the two of you
must come to an end. He gave me to believe—though he
did not say so—that he thought a marriage to him could
not but end in disaster. He implied that you would be happier if you were to make a wiser match."

"But he did not—he did not mention his own feelings in
the case?" Charlotte pressed him. "He did not say that
he—"

But here, evidently, her courage gave out, and she
stared with imploring eyes at her papa, who instantly replied, "No, no, nothing of that kind. It would not have
done, you know, to say anything of that nature, under the
circumstances. He only let me know that, feeling a great
respect and affection for you, he could not honourably request your hand in marriage, which evidently he had intended doing. And I must say, my dear, that at the time I
thought him very wise to do so, and very honourable too.
I do not believe he could have made you happy as his
wife."

But Charlotte evidently heard none of this, for she was murmuring to herself "Affection and respect!" several times over. She seemed to fall into a kind of trance, and her parents, watching her, grew fearful that she was about to sink into the same state of apathetic inertia which had overcome her all these weeks. They watched her closely and glanced at one another, but at last Charlotte, two un-natural spots of crimson appearing in her white cheeks, exclaimed, "Then he could not have loved me! How could I have been so foolish as to believe he did? It was only a temporary infatuation, and then he came to his senses! Oh, Mama, how ever shall I live again?"

The Countess, seeing some colour in her daughter's cheeks and hearing from those lips more words than had been spoken in a month, could hardly contain her joy. Here, at last, was a natural reaction, behaviour she could understand and with which she felt confident of dealing. Gathering her daughter's slender frame in her arms, she pressed her to her bosom murmuring words of comfort.

"Oh, my precious angel, you *shall* live, and live to be a happy woman yet. He was not worth a hair on your dear head, I assure you! No man is worth so much suffering! Be thankful you have discovered his true nature now and not when it was already too late!"

"Indeed, Charlotte," chimed in the Earl, relieved at finding some object of his wrath other than himself, "indeed, your mama is right! The fellow was not worth so much as a moment's thought. Fancy his treating you so ill! Had I but known what your feelings were, I should have boxed his ears and with some glee! My poor girl, you shall see that there are still some gentlemen in the world, though you may not believe it now."

Charlotte, weeping into her mother's bosom with all the pent-up energy of six weeks' enduring agony paused long enough to sob, "I shall not hear one word against him, Papa! He was not to blame. It was my own fo-foolish fault. *Oh*, how I loathe him!" And once again she sobbed.

Some time was passed in this fashion with the daughter sobbing, her mother cooing and her father pacing up and down the room threatening direst consequences to the man who had treated his daughter in so ignoble a fashion. Indeed, the Earl had managed to work himself into such a state of anger against the young man that had anyone hap-

pened to point out to him the error of his ways, he should
have stared at them in amazement. This happy state of
oblivion took such a hold on him that he succeeded in
convincing himself thoroughly of his own righteous innocence in the case.

Lady Harrington was so relieved that she minded neither her daughter's weeping nor her husband's mutterings
and sat, rocking Charlotte back and forth like a baby, for
close to an hour.

From this moment, Charlotte's recovery commenced.
That violent emotion which can wreak such havoc but in
some instances can do more good than any other had
taken hold of her: sheer anger—anger at herself, primar-
ily, for being so foolish as to ever have believed that Gerald loved her; anger against him who had (as she now
thought) deliberately led her to believe it so; and anger
against a world which, having never before dealt her the
tiniest blow of pain, had so nearly felled her with this one
great disaster. Who can say at precisely what moment the
dull throbbing which had been in her head for weeks and
which had alternated only rarely with an intense renewed
awareness of her misery had begun to give way to the idea
that she might not deserve to suffer so? Who can say what
miracle of Nature was worked, transforming a determination to die of grief into a will to live? That the miracle had occurred is all we can be certain of.

From that moment on she began to make a wonderful
recovery. On that very evening she desired to be allowed
to sup below stairs but, of course, was prevented with
many assurances that before long she should do so every
day. She was, however, carried to the little sofa before her
fireplace and there consumed the first substantial meal
which had passed her lips in six weeks. For some days she
was treated like an invalid, brought her meals and fussed
over by everyone. During that time her frail limbs began
to strengthen, and the once dainty features, grown thin
with pain and illness, began to regain their old bloom and
colour. To be sure, she was still pale and fragile. But that
state is not always unbecoming to a girl, and in Charlotte,
whose loveliness was nearly perfect, it only increased the
allure of her beauty. To her doting parents she certainly
appeared the very epitome of feminine perfection.

It was about a fortnight later, when Charlotte, almost

completely recovered, had begun to spend nearly all of her day downstairs employed in quiet activity, that she declared herself intent upon going out into the world again. Indeed, nothing could have made her parents happier, and though hesitant about pushing her recovery too fast, they, after some discussion, agreed that it might be allowed.

Now Charlotte's thoughts were not all that her parents believed. She appeared outwardly calm and had regained her old customary cheerfulness and, though a trifle quieter than she had been before her illness, made a great point of demonstrating her affection to everyone she saw. If a spot of colour appeared sometimes for no reason in her cheeks and if her eyes were sometimes animated by a sparkle that more clearly resembled a glint, no one seemed to notice it. In the privacy of her own chamber she once or twice succumbed to that same unhappiness which had first caused her illness, but she never allowed it to be seen by anyone else. Indeed, in her whole attitude and manner was a quiet determination which had not existed before. She seemed somehow more grown-up, more in command of herself, and sobered by this first painful brush with life. Her innermost feelings and thoughts, however, remained a mystery to all those about her.

Chapter 10

Georgiana, Duchess of Devonshire, was the accounted favourite of London's many brilliant hostesses, and when a ball was given at that noblewoman's spectacular town mansion, no one who considered themselves anyone would admit that they had not been invited. Fortunately, no such admission was required of Lord Harrington and his family who were always amongst the first of the capital's *ton* to receive their cards of invitation.

On the first Monday in September Her Grace had planned her usual gala entertainment before leaving the City for her hunting lodge in Scotland. The Duchess made a habit of departing well ahead of the Season's end, for she grew weary of her many social obligations in London and always liked to be the first to reconnoiter the hunting grounds, to refresh her horses' memory of the terrain, and to oversee the hounds. It was whispered by some that she also liked to precede the Duke by several weeks, as she had for some years entertained a special affection for her chief groom; but it was a rumour believed by few. In fact, Her Grace had original ideas about a number of things, not the least of which was whom to take to her bed. Although a woman of well above forty, she retained her famous looks, her prodigious energy, and the stubborn nature for which she was renowned. Not only was she the acknowledged queen of London's hostesses, not only did she count the Prince himself amongst her most intimate friends, but she was, perhaps, the single-most influential person in the political world of the day. In her salon, graciously entertained and beautifully fed, both Fox and Pitt had fallen victims of her charm and wit. Under her subtle auspices the Whigs had gainsayed the Tories, and without the least bit raising the shackles of the latter against herself. It amused her, as she said, to "have a hand" in what the government did, and her elegant gloved hand was nearly always present in the great decisions of the day.

Georgiana Devonshire liked also to "have a hand" in those few marriages which she considered sufficiently brilliant to fall within her notice. She had quietly engineered several on her own and delighted in being the secret witness of matches which astounded the general public. Georgiana's second cousin, the Marquis of Beresford, was a particular favourite of hers. She had single-handedly taken it upon herself to see that he was presented in the most splendid circumstances to the great world of London when he had reached eighteen. Her success, most certainly, had been helped along by the almost feline good looks of the young man, by his uncanny green eyes, his droll sarcasms and his very substantial fortune. Be that as it may, the young Marquis had soon become one of the most brilliant figures in the *ton*. He was approved by Brummel, that great maker and breaker of social careers, and positively adored by the mamas of the City. No less was he adored by their daughters, who became like a brood of fluttering hens on the instant of his entrance into any room. His most disinterested glance at any female was sufficient to set tongues wagging for several weeks, and any sign of admiration for a woman, however slight, was greeted by a joy similar to that of her having discovered she was admired by Prinny himself. It was, therefore, a source of no little consternation—even outrage—when his very obvious interest in Lady Charlotte Harrington, his cousin, had gone seemingly ignored by the young lady.

George Beresford, indeed, would hardly stoop so low as to deign to look twice at a lady who had snubbed him once. And yet he had done so for Lady Charlotte. Some people wondered what he saw in the Earl's daughter, who, though admittedly very lovely to look at, and possessing a certain refinement of elegance which was not usual, was hardly the handsomest or most brilliant lady in London. A great many mamas worried over the fact and tried to make their strapping Helenas and Clarissas behave as quietly as possible, dressing them up in all sorts of absurd feminine fripperies in an effort to make them appear delicate. But Beresford evidently had no eyes for anyone else, unless it was the Duchess, who was, after all, his patroness and cousin. Quite stubbornly he kept at Charlotte and was treated, in return, like a fond sort of puppy, an attention which could not have done much for his considerable vanity.

It was a question, therefore, of great interest to everyone in the *ton*, whether or not she would pay him any heed at the Duchess' ball, where, as it had been whispered, she would appear for the first time since her mysterious illness. Now Lady Charlotte was not, in herself, subject for so great a debate between the fashionable onlookers. In fact she was an acknowledged belle and a good many young men found her intoxicating (though for what reason, considering her extreme quietness, her modest manner and reserved address, it was not perfectly understood), but she was certainly not considered to be the greatest catch in Town. Lord Harrington was well known for his pennypinching ways, and though his daughter was known to be well-provided for, he was not at liberty to leave her the bulk of his fortune, which was not very large in any case. Having no son, his title and income were entailed away to a nephew, and what was left could not have amounted to more than thirty or forty thousand pounds. Indeed, even this was an exaggeration on the part of the gossips, for had they but known, Lord Harrington was much less niggardly than he was genuinely out of pocket, for his sad confession to Sir James Kirkland had not been entirely an invention. In truth, he desired very keenly to see his daughter married well, for it would relieve his mind of the burden of her well-being after he was gone.

The general populace (at least the general populace of tonnish London, which was not very large) agreed that Lady Charlotte would do much better to marry the Marquis than he would to marry her. Why then did she not jump at the chance? Why then had she taken so suddenly ill at the very moment Gerald Kirkland's quitting London for America? She was a very foolish girl, said some; but others held their breaths and waited, for they had an idea that Lady Charlotte was not quite so foolish after all. This notion was strengthened, moreover, by some hints from the Duchess herself, who, as everybody knew, was set upon having Beresford married to his cousin.

The night of the ball arrived, and no one who was not infirm or uninvited stayed away. Lady Charlotte, with her parents, arrived in due course, and soon afterwards the Marquis stepped into the great salon. As usual, he was dressed in the very peak of fashion, having strayed so far from Brummel's dictums as to adorn himself in shades other than black, and therefore, in his silk gartens and silver waistcoat, stood out amongst the herd of other gentlemen like some exotic bird amongst a flock of falcons. Lady Charlotte, more astonishingly considering the rumours which had been circulating about her strange and dreadful illness, looked as radiant as the dawn. Her cheeks, to be sure, were a trifle paler than usual, but then she had never been ruddy. Her lovely, graceful figure was draped in a magnificent gown of turquoise silk threaded through with gold, which was rumoured had been a gift from Georgiana Devonshire upon hearing of her recovery. Her heavy chestnut-coloured locks were drawn up in perfect simplicity away from her face, with only a gentle fringe of ringlets framing her dainty features. Moving about the immense gilded salon, her fan fluttering delicately, she seemed like some lovely moth. There was surely no sign in anything she did or said that she had been dreadfully close to the grave but a month before. Her manner, certainly—gracious and warm as ever—did not hint at any secret unhappiness. Those who knew her best might have said that she had lost that innocent playfulness which she had once possessed, that she seemed suddenly less of a kitten and more of a cat. But as Charlotte, who treated everyone with equal affection, had no particular intimates to whom she told her secrets, there was no observer to say, "Ah! Look how she is changed!"

The Marquis and she did not at once notice each other, or, if they did, made no show of it. When Beresford was announced, Lady Charlotte was standing in another corner of the room, conversing with her mother and the Duchess of Norfolk. Beresford went at once to his hostess, who drew him into the circle of guests with whom she was speaking. When, a little later, she drew him aside and murmured something in his ear, it was not noticed—perhaps because she led him into a small antechamber away from the crowd. She gave him some meaningful looks, which he returned, and then they rejoined the other guests. Some while later, the Marquis was observed addressing Lady Charlotte and the Earl, and his remarks appeared to please the young lady. Indeed, they danced three country dances together almost at once, and when she was not dancing, Lady Charlotte allowed the Marquis to fetch her a goblet of punch and to sit with her in the shadow of some palms out of the way of the general commotion.

In the last part of the evening, after the late supper had been served, they were again seen dancing a cotillion. Charlotte was by now quite flushed and plainly encouraging the young nobleman. She laughed merrily when he made some witticism and listened intently to all he said in that flattering way with which a woman listens to a man when she wishes him to know she admires him. Though none of their conversation was overheard, it was quite plain to everyone before the evening's end that Lady Charlotte had finally been caught.

Charlotte made her departure rather earlier than was customary, curtsying to the Duchess slightly before one o'clock. Her mama, hovering nearby, hastened to explain that her daughter was still frail and must be treated accordingly for some weeks yet.

"Oh, I understand, my dear, to be sure I do," the Duchess assured her, giving the young lady's hand a warm pressure and bestowing upon her a brilliant smile. "The Duke and I are so pleased that you were strong enough to come to us. And I must say that you look splendid—splendid! That gown becomes you admirably."

Charlotte smiled and made her thank-yous very prettily, curtsying again to the Duchess, who looked as if she might have been her elder sister. Her Grace was, in fact, more than in her usual looks tonight—her high handsome bosom daringly exposed by a bodice of rich ivory lace, her still voluptuous mouth and dark eyes expressing her great pleasure over the young lady's wonderful recovery. Charlotte smiled again and moved towards the door.

"You know that you are always welcome here, my dear," said the Duchess, detaining her a moment longer.

And then, with a sly sideways glance at the Countess, she added, "Though I hope soon to welcome you as a married woman."

The Countess simpered, as would any mother whose daughter had been so significantly addressed, and followed her daughter out of the room.

Lady Harrington was delighted and very much amazed at the seeming rapidity with which Charlotte had recovered her good spirits. She would have been content if her daughter had danced all night with a groom, so long as she saw her laugh and smile; but to have danced all night with Beresford, whom she had never before given any sign of liking! The Countess, like her husband, had always entertained a secret wish to see her daughter married to the Marquis. Unlike the Earl, however, she had never pressed the matter upon her. Now she was overjoyed and even wondered for an instant if it had not been a good thing that her daughter had been jilted, if only for its having brought her so soundly to her senses?

If Lady Harrington was pleased, no words could express the rapture of her husband. He could not contain himself for a minute in the carriage going home but was moved to exclaim over her daughter's good sense and Beresford's good fortune at least a hundred times.

"My dear child, you can have no idea of what pleasure you have given me tonight! To see you dancing with young Beresford time and again, the two of you hardly seeing another soul in all the room! I can only say what joy it would bring me if you were to dance off into eternity together! He is so very sound a match, you know; but then, nothing as compared to you! Indeed, I hardly know which of the two of you would be the luckier—though as I am your papa, I am bound to say I should consider *him* by far the more fortunate! Heh, heh, well—we shall see, we shall see! I shall say no more until you wish to speak of it, I assure you!"

His daughter said nothing in reply and only smiled into the darkness of the carriage, but the Countess gave her husband a nudge in the ribs and exclaimed, "Heavens, my dear! It is very early days to be talking of such things! Cannot you see that poor Charlotte is exhausted!"

"I shall say no more!" promised the Earl still grinning

widely, and then he kept his silence for a moment before he was off again.

Charlotte bade her parents good night as soon as they were in their own hallway and, having kissed them both and received their silent congratulations and their voluble wishes that she might sleep soundly, hastened up the stairs to her own chamber. There, having stood a moment or two undecided by the bell pull, she turned away and went to her little ormolu writing table. In the third drawer she found a packet of letters tied up with white ribbons, and these she drew forth. Taking the packet with her to the window, she selected one and began to read it in the light of a candle upon the sill. Her lips formed themselves into the words at first, but when her eyes filled up with tears, she ceased to mouth the phrases and read on in perfect stillness until the tears were running in profusion down her cheeks and her breast began to heave. With a silent sobbing, she pressed the whole packet to her breast and gazed out into the darkness that was London.

After a while the sobbing diminished, and with a deliberate step she approached the hearth. Here she stopped, and taking the letters one by one, she threw them into the fire and watched as each curled up in flames and then fell as a small black cinder to the grate. She went to bed, at last, with dry eyes. But it was a long while before she slept.

Georgiana Devonshire's ball went on into the small hours of the morning. Having consumed a prodigious supper of lobsters, roasted veal asparagus, partridge, grouse and pheasant, an entire pig cooked whole with an apple in its mouth, a brace of canvasbacks and innumerable small dainties, sweetmeats and pastries, her several hundred guests found themselves sufficiently revived to dance on until the breakfast was brought forth at two o'clock. Even after this, many stayed—no longer dancing very much, but playing at cards, imbibing quantities of the delicious champagne punch and sharpening their wits. It was no wonder, considering what they had eaten and drunk, that few noticed very much after one o'clock. Certainly the Duke, who had retired rather drunk some time before to a sofa in the library, failed to note the disappearance of his wife and one of his guests. Indeed, it had happened often enough before in some more obvious instances, and he had never noticed. It was not astonishing, therefore, that this evening the beautiful Georgiana moved with utter complacency up the stairs of the mansion's west wing to a secluded suite of rooms, followed by a no less complacent George Beresford. Even the servants were safely out of the way—every one of the staff of two hundred and thirty-six being occupied with the entertainment in the main part of the house.

Georgiana slipped without a word down the darkened hall and, with the aid of the candle she had taken from a sconce below, unfastened one of the doors. Here, astonishingly (for this wing was never used except during the largest house parties and was customarily kept under dust covers, the beds unmade, the carpets rolled up), was a chamber which might have been occupied that very morning. A large four-poster bed stood in the middle of the far wall, its satin coverlet turned down. Fresh linen covered the pillows, and by the marble washstand in an adjoining room were a pile of small damask towels and a jug of hot water. The fire was made up and burned brightly in the otherwise dimly lit room, as Georgiana, turning towards her guest, gave a throaty laugh.

"Ha ha!" she laughed, throwing back her head in an abandoned gesture, "I wonder what Devonshire would say if he could see this!"

"Nothing, I don't suppose," replied the Marquis, advancing slowly upon the Duchess as if he were a cat stalking a choice morsel. "He seems to notice very little." His voice was lazy and distant as he lifted one hand to the soft swell of the Duchess's left breast.

She gave a quick intake of breath and then, as his dark eyes held hers and she felt the strong fingers closing over her nipple, sighed deeply.

"I'm not so young as your little friend," she murmured in a husky voice. But her eyes were teasing as she took his other hand and placed it upon the other breast.

George Beresford's reply was careless. "Don't mention her, please! We shall not discuss anything distasteful for an hour."

"You shall have to do more than discuss her, my dear boy, if you marry her."

"I shall do as I please," returned Beresford irritably.
"Now be quiet!"

The Duchess, unused to being ordered about, seemed
delighted to comply.

"I shall do as I please", retorted Beresford irritably. "Now be quiet!"

The Duchess, unused to being spoken about, seeme...

Chapter 11

The journey upriver from Manhattan proved to be a great adventure.

Gerald, who had been a little reticent about accepting the Browns' kind invitation, if only for fear of foisting himself and Canterby too forcefully upon their generosity, soon forgot his hesitations. The Americans' cordial treatment of their English friends was so warm, so completely without reservations, that it was impossible to resist. Their companionship was a source of enormous pleasure to Gerald, who found their plainspoken ways, their unaffected enjoyment of each other and of life; to be as infectious as the river air was bracing. The steamship *Arcadia*, too, gave him a thrill the likes of which he could seldom remember experiencing. It was invigorating to step up the slender gangplank onto a vessel so utterly different from any he had ever seen before. Her lines were long, but she was surprisingly beamy, and the two steam funnels rising out of her deck gave the impression of some great, powerful beast. When her engines were started, and she began puffing out of the river harbour toward the main stream, he felt a strange inward exultation. Here, at last, was man independent of nature, unfettered by the fitful winds, the sudden calms, the unexpected changes in the current's flow. Here, in fact, was modernity at last!

Standing upon the deck watching the passing scene, Gerald thought time and time again that he had never seen anything so beautiful. The words of the French traveller, Chastellux, came back to him as he watched the rocky outline of Manhattan recede and the steep forested cliffs begin to rise out of the current:

You at length take advantage of a spot where the mountains are a bit less high to turn to the westward and approach the river, but still you cannot see it. Descending slowly at a turn of the road my eyes were suddenly struck with the most magnificant picture I have ever beheld. It was a view of the North [Hudson] River, running in a deep channel formed by the mountains, through which in former ages it had forced its passage.

The Marquis, however, had not the advantage of travelling by ship from which vantage point the sparkling clear water, laced with the rose-coloured fins of spawning salmon, rushed past the sheer walls of rock, rising like black marble out of the River, and ending in summits of wooded splendour at the top. Nor, thought Gerald, had Chastellux the added thrill of making his way over this glorious natural turbulence in a vessel which swiftly and steadily carried them upstream, unmindful of wind or current.

The day on which they left New York was brilliantly clear and somewhat cooler than it had been in the past few weeks. The refreshing river breeze further aided the party's comfort, and perhaps it was the exhilaration of that breeze, added to the sense of starting off upon a true adventure into new and unspoiled territory, that gave the young Englishman a feeling of such inner exultation. He felt free, indeed, for the first time in months, as if he had at last shaken off the last shackles of European life with all its rules and confinements. Greeting the Captain with a broad smile and hearty handshake—the Captain of the *Arcadia* being as much a friend as an employee of Mr. Brown—Harry smiled into that ruddy face, those twinkling eyes. Even Miss Brown, Gerald noticed, shook him by the hand with a warm smile and solicitations after his wife.

The party soon retired, however, to the foredeck, where the other passengers were assembled either standing at the railings or seated in small clusters of chairs. Some read, some conversed, some merely watched the passing scene—and with these Gerald instantly sympathized. A number of other passengers—there were fifty-four, *in toto*—were acquainted with the Browns, and they soon came forward to greet the young Americans. Gerald and Canterby, being Englishmen and therefore a little exotic, drew their attention, and they desired to be introduced. Though not aware of it then, Gerald made the acquaintance that morning of half the wealth of the Hudson River. Gouverneur Kemble, Philip Van Rensselaer, Chancellor Livingston and his lady and daughter—all these luminaries of New York society and politics were aboard. Of particular interest to Gerald was a gentleman of thirty-five or thirty-six called Washington Irving, who had travelled much in Europe and professed himself to be an author. Irving was a charming man—unpretentious, sympathetic to an Englishman's situation here and a brilliant conversationalist. He was engaged presently, as he told Gerald, in writing a book about the legends of the Hudson River and its inhabitants. Unfortunately, his journey ended at Tarrytown, where he was considering buying an old stone cottage of what he termed "immense possibilities, though practically no amenities." Gerald watched him walk down the gangplank on the afternoon of their first day with a strange sense that he had met the gentleman before, or would meet him again, somehow and someday.

He was soon distracted again, however, by his own immediate party, who wished to partake of refreshment. They had already taken their luncheon in the formidable dining saloon, where certain peculiar rules of etiquette were observed. One of these was that no gentleman could enter the saloon until every female wishing to dine had been comfortably seated. Having waited a great while for this to be accomplished—the ladies taking their time in organizing themselves—the men all rushed in a great swarm, practically falling over themselves in their eagerness to get a place at table. Fortunately, Miss Brown had taken the precaution of spreading their possessions about on three of the chairs at their table so they were not forced, like one poor fellow, to stand and watch the meal miserably from the sidelines!

All this Gerald found vastly amusing, even refreshing, and he said as much when Miss Brown now inquired if he felt he could face the same ordeal again for tea. "I believe I could face it forever," he replied with a laugh. "Well, perhaps not quite forever but for tea certainly."

"And then supper, and then breakfast!" Chastity warned him with a chuckle. "But perhaps you will have become accustomed by then."

Canterby made some grumbling noises about having to enter an obstacle race every time he wished to take nourishment but soon accompanied the rest. Gerald noticed that his friend had not moved from Miss Brown's side during the whole course of the voyage. When he smilingly pointed this out to Canterby, the latter merely grinned and wagged his finger.

"You must not, my boy, take rights of proprietorship over the lady simply because she has seen fit to honour you with a smile or two! The fair sex is very fickle, you know, and I intend to prove how shallow was her attraction to you."

Gerald only laughed and held up his hands in a gesture of resignation remarking, "Well, if you do that, old chap, you know she is as like to be shallow in her devotion to *you.*"

Miss Chastity Brown, however, looking perfectly splendid in a fawn-coloured travelling costume, her auburn locks tucked beneath a fetching bonnet, seemed to take no notice of her constant companion. It was as if Canterby had been her little terrier, whom she really loved and enjoyed petting but over whom she had never considered losing her heart. Instead, all the considerable charm of her looks and smiles were directed at Gerald, who, not unaware of her attentions, could not deny that they were very flattering and altogether rather enjoyable. In fact, he had never conversed so easily with a lady before; or not, at least, upon such equal terms. This was certainly due in part to Miss Brown's forthright manner, which, though managing to be flirtatious, was rather like the companionable fraternity of a younger brother. Never had Gerald felt so inclined to say so much, and so openly, to a woman, and when, having been cross-examined about his life in England, he caught himself upon the point of mentioning Lady Charlotte Harrington by name, he was much astounded with himself. Indeed, he would have to be far more careful in the future, for there were some subjects too painful still for mention even to so sympathetic an audience.

His decision, however, was taken from him by Canterby. On the evening of that first exhilarating day, when Gerald had retired to the gentlemen's common quarters (for there were no staterooms on the steamer) to dress for the evening, Canterby detained Miss Brown, who was about to go below herself.

"Ahem, Miss Brown—I thought I ought to tell you something, something about our friend Gerald."

"Yes, Mr. Canterby?" returned Chastity, turning round with that alluring half-smile, "What is it you wish to say?"

"I thought you should know that his affections are engaged. Or rather—not his affections"—Canterby felt quite uncomfortable, but rushed on nonetheless—"but he himself; he is engaged to be married. A most unfortunate circumstance, really."

"Engaged?" she repeated coldly. There was certainly no denying that the news had had a very stunning effect. "Do you mean affianced?"

"Exactly. It is not a thing one likes to mention, you know, about one's dear friend, but I thought you should be told, as he seems not to have done so himself."

"I can hardly credit what I hear, Mr. Canterby! Do you mean to tell me that Mr. Kirkland has failed to tell us of his engagement?"

Canterby looked quite appalled at the idea but managed to nod his head miserably. "I suppose, you know—the whole thing is so unfortunate; he ought not to have put himself in so awkward a position—that is why we have come, really. Poor fellow! He can scarcely bear to think about it. He tries to hide himself from the truth, but naturally in the end it shan't do any good—I dislike saying anymore."

"You may spare yourself the morbid details, Mr. Canterby," said Miss Brown, drawing herself up with dignity. "I understand that a gentleman may sometimes get himself enmeshed in distasteful situations. I do not wish to hear about it. But he ought to have let us know, don't you think?"

"Most certainly he ought," Canterby hastened to assure her. "Most certainly, indeed! It was most improper not to, of course. Still, one can't blame the fellow—though, of course, he was mistaken. One oughtn't to travel under false pretences. Still, I know I may count upon *you* to be discreet. I shouldn't like him to know I said anything, you know. And I most definitely thought you should be told."

Miss Brown drew herself up still more, an act requiring a certain athletic ability, for she had already stretched her small frame to its greatest limits. "You were right to do so, sir! Most definitely right! But, I shan't let him know you told me. Still, I ought to tell Harry—"

"Ah! Pray do not do so, my dear Miss Brown—not as yet. He may still come forth of his own volition, you know. Give him another day or two. It was a most unfortunate circumstance—he can scarcely bear to think of it!"

Miss Brown gave only a little snort upon hearing this. "I expect he shall have to do more than think about it! A gentleman may not be released so easily from his promise!"

"Quite right, Miss Brown—quite right. The poor creature! Not at all what he would like, I suppose, but still—how dependent she now is upon him!"

Miss Brown, though utterly disgusted by what she had heard, still found it within her power to inquire who the young lady was.

"Ah! I ought not to say, in faith, Miss Brown. But I know I may trust *your* discretion—her name is Charlotte Harrington, Lady Charlotte Harrington. Poor thing! Had she not so great a fortune, I suppose he would not have taken any interest in her at all. But, Gerald is—how shall I say it?—rather embarrassed, poor fellow."

Now Chastity was really outraged. To think that she had admired so rapscallionish a fellow! She had, however, no leisure in which to indulge her outrage now. Her eyes widened a good deal as she stared at the gentleman before her, in truth a most strange and Devilish-looking fellow. She had not thought much of *him*, indeed, before this moment, rather prefering the handsome and charming Mr. Kirkland. But now all that was changed, of course. She felt bewildered and rather embittered to have been so shoddily used. But, as she had no alternative but to trust the judgement of Mr. Canterby, she put herself in his power.

"Do you not think I ought to tell my brother? He will be quite appalled."

"Ah, Miss Brown—I pray you will not," said Canterby,

making an affecting spectacle of comradely loyalty. "I pray you will not, indeed. Hold off a little yet. And do try to understand my poor friend's plight."

Miss Brown gave him a doubtful glance, but seeing how sincere he was, she could hardly do otherwise than promise to keep the horrid secret for a day or two more. "But I shall certainly not deign to speak to him," said she.

Saying that he could hardly expect her to do so, Canterby escorted the young lady to the stairway. Having watched her descend, he turned toward the passing mountains with a gleeful smirk.

Chapter 12

Chastity Brown was as good as her word. She was certainly not about to mention what she had heard to Gerald Kirkland, whom she now regarded as a cad. To have pledged his troth to a lady and then to hide the fact before his new friends—nothing could be worse, unless it was (as had been abundantly hinted by Mr. Canterby) to do so under the worst pretences. His friend had made it clear, without saying as much, that Gerald Kirkland had fallen into one of those unpleasant entanglements which she had sometimes heard her brothers speak of. What was still worse, he appeared to have entered the entanglement only for money. To a young lady who had been oft warned of fortune hunters by her parents and who had once or twice received their unpleasant addresses, nothing could be worse.

As she extended her pretty arms that her maid might slip on her camisole and then perched herself on the one chair in the draughty cabin to have her hair arranged, she pondered the misapprehension she had been living under. How much she had admired Mr. Kirkland but an hour before! How she had liked his manner, his modest air, his gallant addresses—and how she had thought he admired her! Indeed, they had become quite intimate that afternoon upon the deck, for had not he recounted for her entertainment a great many incidents from his childhood in England and made her feel that she was specially priviledged to be told so much? And yet, she recollected now, had not he, even then, hidden something from her? She re-

called how in the midst of reciting some adventures he
had had in Scotland at his father's hunting lodge, he had
abruptly stopped and gazed off into the distance with a
pained look. She had enquired if anything was the matter,
but he had only mumbled that he thought he had seen a
fellow lose his balance on the deck. Of course, she had
turned round, but, seeing no one on the deck, had laughed
at him. Now a blush came to her cheeks—or rather, a hot
rush of blood—for she realized that she had been flirting
quite shamelessly with him! To imagine what his thoughts
of her must be—the kind of person he was—it was too
outrageous to contemplate.

Clinging to the bedpost to keep her balance against the
occasional rocking of the steamer, Chastity bit her lip.
That percentage of her blood that owed itself to Ireland
grew hot indeed, and her cheeks very pink. She, who had
been the belle of New York since her come-out, to be
treated thus! To be lied to, to be scorned (for in her mind,
Gerald's failure to mention his engagement represented
much more than an untruth), indeed, to be made a fool
of! If she told her brother, she knew it would be the last
they would see of their new English friend. The thought of
Harry knocking off his block did not displease her either.

And yet she held back. Something—she knew not what,
for certainly there was nothing to condone in his behaviour—made her pause. A brief vision of his face crossed
her mind's eye: that noble face! She had thought but last
evening how little it would take for her to love him—he
who seemed so gentle, so chivalrous and was so admiring
of them all! How he must be laughing to himself to see
how well he had deceived them, whilst all the while he
was fleeing from his own ignoble conduct in England!

No, it was too much. Chastity would not give him the
satisfaction of being punished by a man. She could do the
job a great deal more efficaciously. Oh, how she would
watch him squirm!

When he was finally admitted to the dining saloon, Gerald was rather amazed to see that Canterby, having gotten
in just ahead of him, had taken the place to the right of
Miss Brown and that she did not look up as he sat down.
In fact, she was pointedly cold when she at last deigned to
look at him, and Gerald was appropriately confused.
Harry, on the other hand, was his usual amiable self and

commenced talking at once about a new business relationship he had struck up with some furriers in Canada. Gerald, who knew little about business in general, asked him several questions and found himself more and more intrigued with the problems of foreign trade.

"You see, we don't have the market in this country as yet for large quantities of furs," explained Harry. "If we strike up the deal with these Canadian gentlemen, we must first be assured of securing a foreign market."

"Couldn't you sell to us?" Gerald asked. "I know there is a great desire for furs amongst the English ladies."

"Well, of course, we should like it very much, and to sell to the French as well. But the Russians have dashed near cancelled us out altogether. They have been at it so long, you see—for centuries there has been no other source of furs. And amongst our own people they are chiefly desirable for capes and cloaks and such. But the workmanship required is very skilled; only the really wealthy can afford them. That is true, for the most part, in England, too, but there are more wealthy people there."

"Couldn't you approach the British government and strike up some sort of bargain? I know you have done so already with corn and other grains. We are already importing thousands of barrels per annum of those—"

"That is certainly what we should like," remarked Harry Brown. "But to do so we need an agent in Britain, someone with connections in the government."

For an instant, Gerald thought he saw the American give him a quizzical glance, but then, as if with an inward shrug, Mr. Brown raised his eyebrows and smiled. "The problem is, you Britishers are apt to despise business if you are well connected, and to be without connections if you don't."

"Well, that is hardly fair," protested Gerald, "After all, we are not known as the merchant nation of Europe for nothing. I suppose that to build up the sorts of empires dominated by some of our nabobs and princes of trade, they must have had some influence in Parliament."

Harry Brown only smiled and changed the topic to a description of his home upon the Hudson, a subject which interested Gerald a good deal. He had, however, sensed that his new friend had been upon the point of making him a proposition and, far from feeling insulted by the idea, was rather pleased. He believed Mr. Brown, for all his protestations to the contrary, rather despised men of no ambition and that, to him, men of business were the most enterprising and admirable of the species.

It was a view altogether contrary to everything Gerald had been brought up to believe; for Harry Brown had not been far off the mark with his comment upon the British view of trade. For one of Gerald's upbringing, to muddy one's hands with commerce was unthinkable. He was, after all, the son of a baronet. He would himself be Sir Gerald before many years had passed. Like the Prince of Wales, though in a far lesser sense, his whole life had been spent fitting himself to the task of taking his father's place. That that place included not only a baronetcy but all the encumbrances of his father's and his grandfather's extravagant way of life made fitting into the place all the more difficult. He was expected to be Sir Gerald, but without any of the trappings which made a Sir Gerald's position secure. Like a penurious monarch, he would be expected to rule his modified estates with all the dignity befitting his station, but without any of the fortune.

It was not the first time Gerald had pondered these facts. Once or twice, out of vanity, he had imagined what it might be like to go home to England a rich man. Not the least of his fantasies had been envisioning Charlotte's expression when she heard the news that he had made his fortune in America (quickly, of course, and without a bit of trouble) and had returned to marry her. But then the fantasy changed once again, and this time Charlotte, now the Marchioness of Beresford, wept at the news, which had come too late. Yet even this view of things did not displease him overmuch. There was a side of him as vain and vengeful as any other man. Indeed, although he felt ashamed at once for having felt so, he had taken a good deal of pleasure from the notion.

The trouble, of course, was that even had he the desire to enter the world of trade—which he was not altogether sure he had—he was certainly not equipped with a head for business. Though intrigued by some aspects of business and certainly willing to listen to Harry Brown's descriptions of his work, he did not very much fancy the notion of haggling with traders or mistreating employees. He knew from his slender experience of nabobs that upon such unpleasantness was their wealth founded. He had seen what sort of abject poverty the inhabitants of Liverpool and Manchester suffered and had once walked down into a coal mine and seen the poor filthy sods who toiled twelve hours a day in a living Hell. He found it sufficiently difficult to stomach the sight of misery without being a party to it.

On the other hand, he liked everything about Harry Brown, who seemed as open and honest and fair a man as he had ever met. He could scarcely conceive that this enterprising and charming young man could stomach it any more than he. He wondered, even as he listened to his friend's rather rhapsodic depiction of his family's home, what sort of destitution their fortune was built upon. But then a chance remark made him smile at his own fanciful thoughts.

"You shall tell me, Kirkland," Mr. Brown had been saying, "if you have ever beheld a prospect more magnificent than that which may be seen from our drawing room windows. The Hudson is at its most peaceful near Garrison. The water is like glass and in it are mirrored the Catskill mountains, the sweeping eagles overhead and the drifting clouds. My great-grandfather chose the site for its view, despite the difficulty of building a road up the cliff, which is very steep. In the old days the sailors had to transport their cargo of molasses from the West Indies up that cliff to a distillery in the mountains. That was in the days when the slave trade was on, and the molasses was exchanged for Africans. I don't know if you have heard much about it—what a horrible trade it is! And it is still conducted in some places and even by some people we know. To think one could build one's fortune out of so disgraceful a business!

"You may have heard that one of the first Browns made his fortune by it. It may or it may not be so, but the inheritance of the legend left my father so repelled at the idea of being associated with the slave trade that he long ago freed our slaves. He was the first man to do so in the Hudson Valley and received much criticism for it. A great part of the wealth in these parts is built upon the labour of Negro slaves. But my father has enlightened views and has put them all to work for good wages and in conditions which I believe may fairly stand against the best of any workers in the civilized world. I hope you shall go with me sometime to our warehouses so that you may see if I speak truly."

"I should be delighted to," said Gerald. "And I couldn't more heartily agree with what you have said about the trade in slaves. There has always been a great debate going forward in the House of Commons, whether or not it shall be outlawed. Most of us agree that it is an outrage, but as so many of the powerful figures in our government have had their pockets padded regularly by the Creoles, it is more than a question of the general view."

"And so it is here," agreed Brown. "There have been several times movements afoot to ban the importation of slaves, but they are inevitably put down before they have gone far. You will no doubt hear it said that it is chiefly the fault of the great plantation owners in the southern states, but I am convinced they are no more at fault than our northern mills."

Gerald, having heard this much, was elated to find that Harry Brown took as dim a view of human suffering as he. He was astounded, however, at hearing that the same Mr. Philipse he had met at the Van Cortlandt's dinner party was one of the great participants in the continuing slave trade. Mr. Brown assured him it was so and that of all the repugnant dealings of which he had heard, none were fouler than some which had been made by that gentleman.

"He has ingratiated himself with some of our governors," Brown told him, "and now, having descended from a family which was sent fleeing out of America for its rampant royalism, he has returned to make a fortune out of the worst commerce imaginable."

Gerald, astonished, said something of the kind had been hinted at by Madame Van Cortlandt the other evening, but that he had put down her obvious dislike of the man to a general bias against Tories.

"It is perfectly true," smiled Harry Brown. "The Van Cortlandts are surely among the greatest Patriot families in America. Their disaffection for anything which smacks of royalism verges on an obsession."

"But," remarked Gerald, surprised, "they were so very cordial to me—and was not Madame's uncle a royalist?"

"*You* are hardly a royalist—merely British, and of another generation, besides, from that which they hated. And so far as her uncle is concerned, I make no doubt but that his near relation to them—being as they were, amongst the first great families to declare their loyalty to the new government—has embarrassed them considerably. What is worse, he—the uncle, I mean—was not so very dislikeable a fellow from all I have heard. I believe their nationalist sympathies are in dispute with their personal affections. They make up for it by hating every other royalist the more. But in so far as Philipse is concerned, he needn't have been descended from a royalist to make anyone hate him. He is an odious fellow, worse, in my view, than the most despicable murderer. His avarice had taken hold of him so firmly that he has given up all claim to a moral sense. Indeed, there is hardly anything I would put past him."

These words were certainly very hard, and spoken, moreover, with a real intensity of feeling by the American gentleman. Gerald was amazed and would have begged to know more had not they been interrupted at that moment by a question from Miss Brown.

"Is it not so, Mr. Kirkland?" she was enquiring, her eyes full of a strange bright fire, directed at, but hardly into, the gaze of that young man.

"I beg your pardon, Miss Brown? I am afraid your brother was telling me something of great interest, and I did not hear you."

"Evidently," returned she in a voice full of sarcasm. "I do not wonder that *my brother* is full of interest to you. But I enquired if you did not agree with my view of the argument Mr. Canterby and I were just having. I say a lady will always open herself to reproach by her very eagerness to please, whilst a man will hardly ever do so. Mr. Canterby takes the opposite view."

Gerald glanced smilingly at his friend, who seemed intent upon an examination of the tablecloth. It was evident from the question that the two had been conversing in rather an intimate manner, and apparent, moreover, that something had been said to make Miss Brown think ill of himself. He hardly knew what it might have been, but knowing his friend and knowing Canterby's admiration of Miss Brown, did not doubt but that he had taken the opportunity to supplant him in her affections. His reply, therefore, was as ambiguous as possible. It was not, after all, a reply which seemed desired.

"As a man myself, Miss Brown, and I hope a gentleman, I must, of course, agree with Canterby. A gentleman will always allow himself to be reproved, if there is reproving to be done. A lady—if she be one—would hardly put herself in so vulnerable a position."

"Ah!" cried Miss Brown now, "but with that view I must take exception, for you are assuming that the lady would do so out of a lack of gentility, but I believe she would do so from an overabundance of generosity. If a lady admires a man, she will always give him the benefit of the doubt, thereby sacrificing her dignity to the whims of the gentleman. If she has chosen carefully for whom she does this great service, she will nearly always be rewarded by his greater regard. However, there are certainly those instances when the unhappy creature will be rebuked by his ungallantry and thereby learn to keep her counsel more closely in the future."

Her statement was pronounced with a certain defiant stress which Gerald could not help seeing was directed against him. He could not imagine what could have been said by Canterby to bring out this stream of venom from the lady—for it was hardly less. Her intense coldness reminded him of the words of Congreve concerning women who are scorned and Heaven's rages. But for what cause was Miss Brown's scorn directed against him? It seemed a little comical—this young woman, whom he liked and admired, behaving as if she hated him all of a sudden, and Canterby, that scheming devil, staring at his spoon for all the world as if it were the most amazing thing he had ever beheld.

Gerald could do little but smile and raise an eyebrow, which he did. Harry Brown gaped at his sister and looked curiously at Canterby, and then, as if the ways of women were too obscure for him to fathom, he remarked, "Well, I'm dashed if I know what you are talking of, the two of you; but I should like my port and cigar in quiet, if you don't mind. Kirkland, will you join me? Perhaps we should leave these two curious creatures to confound each other a little more."

Gerald bowed and smiled at Miss Brown. He merely cocked an eyebrow at Canterby who had the goodness to colour slightly. The two gentlemen retreated from the dining hall where smoking was forbidden and made their way to the gentlemen's saloon.

"He might have had the courtesy to blush!" cried Chastity, much vexed, upon seeing the last of their backs. "As if he did not comprehend me perfectly!"

"Ah, well—Gerald is the very Devil," sighed Canterby, leaning back with satisfaction. "He supposes you don't know what he has done, after all."

"Well, I shall make him know! I cannot bear the idea that he may go about pretending he is not a cad. You ought to have fought him!"

"I?" said Canterby blinking, "Why on earth should I fight him? He is a perfectly pleasant fellow. I don't know a more amiable travelling companion. Of course, I did not expect him to keep his condition a secret—especially considering that he was becoming intimate with another lady. Of that, I can assure you, I had no idea!"

"Of course, you did not! How could you? How could anyone expect such abominable behaviour? I have no idea what he can have done to this poor lady—this Lady Charlotte—and I do not wish to know! But to desert her, to rush off to America pretending himself a free man—"

Now Canterby was all very pleased to see the effect his little confidence had had upon the young and charming Miss Brown, for it had appeared to increase him in her estimation as clearly as it had lowered Gerald; but he did not wish it to go too far—certainly not to the point of her accusing him outright. For that would surely reverse the good effects of his actions and plunge him lower than ever in her regard if she found out the truth. Moreover, he did not relish the idea of Gerald calling him out, which was not unconceivable considering the antiquated thinking of his friend. Was it not all in good fun, after all? Was it not all for the sake of pleasure? And all was fair in love and war—still, he did not wish it to go too far. He endeavored, therefore, to assuage her anger a little.

"But you mustn't think too ill of him, Miss Brown."

"Too ill of him!" cried Chastity, growing crimson. "What is too ill to think of a man who has behaved as he has done?"

"Oh, but perhaps you do not understand. After all, he

was enmeshed in her web as surely as she was in his. It is not all his doing."

"Does not he desire her money?" demanded Chastity bluntly. "That is what you led me to believe."

"Well—yes; but then, she desires a husband. It is not so bad an arrangement, surely? In England it is done quite frequently, and no one is the worse. So long as they do not hurt anyone else—no innocent third party."

Chastity's cheeks grew really crimson upon hearing this. Drawing herself up coldly, she remarked, "You will find, Mr. Canterby, that in America we do things differently. And you will also find, I think, that I am no mere third party to be made a fool of. I am not without some friends, you know! Nor am I utterly without resources of my own!"

The sight of her so straight and hot, her eyes fairly sparkling with fire and her bosom heaving, was very pleasurable to Fitzwilliam Canterby. He had no doubt but that she had plenty of resources of her own, but "I make no doubt of it, Miss Brown" was all he said in quite a proper tone. "Indeed, I make no doubt of it at all."

Chapter 13

As can easily be imagined, Gerald was eager to discover what had caused Miss Brown's sudden disaffection. He questioned Canterby at the first moment of their being alone, which was not, however, at once. The steamer accommodated all the men together in one great bunkroom, and all of the ladies in another, only slightly more commodious. That night Gerald could find no opportunity to get Canterby aside, and so he told himself he would question the other on the morrow.

At dawn, as they had been told, the steamer docked at Garrison, which was hardly more than a village with some docks jutting out into the great stream and a small yard to attend the vessels. Along the banks of the Hudson, as they had neared the town, Gerald had seen several great villas on high promontories above the water, and one of these, barely visible from the river, Mr. Brown had pointed out as belonging to his family.

The party was met by a coach and four driven by a large black coachman who embraced Mr. Brown warmly and took the hand of each of them. Gerald was amazed—he had never seen a servant treated in so familiar a fashion before—but he was to see the same sort of greeting by nearly every one of the Browns' many servants who appeared to feel themselves a sort of great extended family of the master. They were all, Harry Brown told them later, freed slaves who had chosen of their own free will to serve for wages the same family for whom they had toiled without pay for so many years.

The trek up the mountain to the Manor House was in itself an adventure. Seldom had Gerald traversed a road more narrow or more rocky. The steep track wound up the mountainside with, on one hand, a sheer drop of five hundred feet, and on the other, a rocky ledge strewn with boulders, some of which had already dropped onto the road. Indeed, they were several times, at the steepest places, forced to descend from the coach to allow the coachman to lead his team over boulders and great holes. It was hardly the best choice of vehicle for such a journey, but as Mr. Brown told them with a smile, the coachman, Jenkins, refused to meet any new visitors to the Manor House in any less grand a style.

For all the difficulty of the drive, it became immediately apparent when they had crested the last rise that the difficulty was well merited. The view which burst upon them at the moment of coming over that final steep stretch of road was sufficient to take the breath away. On one side beyond a long and stately avenue of chestnuts lay the Manor House, a large and handsome edifice built in the Georgian style of brick and rubble stone. On the other, beyond a rich green lawn and rocky ledge from which grew pine and rhododendron, stretched the real vista. Floating far below them in the crystalline light, the majestic Hudson waved and turned like a river of blue glass. Upon its gleaming surface floated several pleasure boats, yachts with their sails bloated by the gentle breeze, and like stern beasts beside them, the *Arcadia* and another steamer churned the waters in opposite directions. Far beyond the distant bank rose up a steep cliff of granite to form the range of mountains called the Catskills. In the still and gleaming air, the distant mourning of curlews sounded like ghostly human cries, whilst overhead, a single bald eagle swept and circled.

It was a sight to be recorded forever in Gerald's mind, this noble panorama of Nature. The slight evidences of man far beneath them seemed to Gerald like a gentle reminder of his and all his kind's infinitesimal part in all this wild beauty. Though wild, it was soft; and though savage, peaceful like some sleeping beast. He turned to Harry Brown with a slight smile—all he could do to show his emotion. The American, however, seemed to understand and grinned back nodding.

"Quite a view, is it not, Kirkland?"

"I should say!"

"You shall grow accustomed to it in time. At first it tends to overcome one."

"Rather like growing accustomed to God," replied Gerald softly.

Canterby, who had shown less astonishment at the sight began to be restless. "But what about the house, eh, Brown? Shall we not have a go at that? I am awfully anxious to see it."

"All in good time, Mr. Canterby," remarked Miss Brown who had been watching the reactions of the two Englishmen with some interest. "But you can hardly compare our humble domestic comforts with this scene."

"Oh! To be sure, it is very grand," responded that gentleman, anxious to please. "I only meant that perhaps we shall have as good a view of it from the drawing room—for that is what you said the site was selected for, was it not?"

"Aye. My great-grandfather came up here, so the tale goes, with some of the rumrunners and was so taken by it that he set down his walking stick at a certain spot and declared it should be the situation of his favourite armchair. The house was built around that spot, and though it has been enlarged at various times, the original drawing room with his chair remains intact."

They were soon to see that chair, a solid old Hepplewhite of enduring comfort and virtue, together with the room which housed it. The original manor, they learned, had consisted of a main house and two adjacent buildings which housed the kitchens and laundries, and the stables. Since then the secondary buildings had been enclosed by an enlargement of the main house, and now what had been the stables was a most delightful modern wing containing below a sunny morning room and library, and above, several guest rooms. It was in this wing that Gerald and Canterby were to be put up and here that some hours later, having met the lady of the house and two of Harry Brown's younger brothers, Gerald managed at last to interrogate his friend.

"Canterby," he said when they had been left alone to dress for dinner, "what the devil have you said to Miss Brown to make her so cold to me? She has not spoken five words since last evening at dinner. The two of you have been as thick as thieves since then."

Canterby looked offended "What in heaven d'you mean, old man?"

"I mean that from having been most cordial she has suddenly taken to looking at me as if I was murderer. Come on, now, I know you have said something to get up her dander."

Fiddling with his snuffbox, Canterby suggested that his friend was imagining things. "Perhaps she has simply decided she likes me better," said he.

Gerald saw that he was not to get much satisfaction. Watching Canterby's back, which was turned towards him as he stood by the window taking snuff, he began to grow irritable. It was not, as he told himself, that Miss Brown had any special significance to him, save that she was a charming and appealing young woman. But he should like to know what had made her former good regard so obviously take a turn for the worse. As he continued to watch the back of Canterby's head, he started to feel a real resentment of the fellow, who, heretofore, had been an amusing companion on their journeys.

"Don't lie to me, Canterby, for Heaven's sake! I know you are hiding something."

To his great surprise, Canterby whirled round, his small puckish features grown perfectly red and wearing an expression of malicious disdain. "Oh, for God's sake, Kirkland, you are a fool! D'you suppose Miss Brown cares only for your drivelling love of views and your tiresome, Godlier-than-thou manner? Perhaps she likes a little more wit from time to time—yes, by Jove!—perhaps she actually thinks me more amusing than you!"

Gerald, grown rather red himself, gave an indifferent shrug. "I didn't know she meant so much to you, old thing. But, of course, if she does—if your intentions are honourable—I shall gladly leave the field to you."

"Oh, you *are* a boor! Honourable intentions, indeed! She simply likes a little diversion from time to time. She is not a complete simpleton, you know. Not like your pathetic little Charlotte Harrington."

Gerald's face turned suddenly white. It was the first time that name had been mentioned between them since

that fateful day in London two months before. It had been
an unspoken agreement—or so Gerald had thought—a
gentlemen's agreement, whose purpose need not even be
expressed. The name came like a knife into his heart. He
had hardly realized how great the wound had been till this
moment of feeling its lingering pain. He turned abruptly
towards the door to his own chamber without looking
back.

"Do not dare to mention her name again, Canterby.
The very sound of it from your lips sickens me."

Canterby stared after him, his mouth slightly open.
Having so little moral finesse himself, he found it astonishing in anyone else. After a moment, however, he snorted
softly and turned back to his snuff. What a bore the fellow
was, really! As if he thought it amusing to go parading
about the countryside, giving forth upon his own virtue
and actually supposing it were up to him to judge others
as well! Still Canterby had not realized what an effect
Lady Charlotte's apparent desertion had had upon his
travelling companion. To all intents and purposes he had
seemed cheerful enough. His behaviour had done much,
certainly, to reduce whatever faint traces of guilt had ever
been felt by Canterby for having carried out the little plot
put forward by Sir James.

And now that hundred pounds was nearly gone. The
cost of travelling was always great; and a hundred pounds
was always less than it seemed. He should obviously have
to do something to raise a little cash, though he knew not
what. His father was not about to send him any of the
ready, for so he had declared in no uncertain terms. Canterby turned thoughtfully to the window, the recent scene
between Kirkland and himself already replaced in his
mind by ideas of greater magnitude. After a little, a
thought suddenly struck him, and he gave a quick intake
of breath and moved to the writing table which stood
against one wall of the chamber. Taking pen and paper,
which he found readily at hand, he quickly inscribed a letter. After a moment's thought he took a fresh sheet of sta-
tionery and scribbled another note. These, having been
sealed, he now addressed respectively to Miss Joanna Van
Cortlandt at Cortlandt Manor and to Mr. Henry Philipse
of Philipseburgh Manor, Harlem.

Alone in this own room, Gerald stood staring out of the window at the superb view of the River it afforded.

He had scarcely realized how little it, or anything else, could mean to him without the hope of someday showing it to Charlotte. It was as if only half of him stood there, as if only part of him had moved through the last weeks, observing, enjoying, being astonished and exclaiming over all the novelties he had seen. In truth, how unsuccessful had been the deceit he had tried to work upon himself: that he was capable of seeing, hearing, feeling anything in all the world with his whole mind and heart, so long as *she* was not a part of it! His mild flirtation with Miss Brown: a moment's diversion from the real pain he suffered! For, compared to Charlotte, who was the very sun above him, the earth below, whose laughter had been his joy, and whose silences, his very soul, that quick, clever girl could be nothing but a dim candle. To be sure she was charming, and to be honest, his vanity had been not a little soothed by her evident interest in him. And that attention, being all he could hope for now, had been most welcome. But now he saw, with the clarity of intense pain which sometimes illuminates our deepest motives as clearly as it obscures the passing moment, that he had endeavored to trick himself into believing his suffering less than it was.

At first he had felt only the wound to his pride, he having been robbed of the act of sacrifice by Charlotte's eagerness to marry another. That punctured pride had been soothed by Miss Brown's flattering attentions, and now that they were removed, he saw how superficial his first pain had actually been. Pride and vanity—what were they to the soft inner core of him? That self hardly ever noticed unless it was jabbed with knives as he felt it to be now. His heart! How strange a word it was—was it not rather his whole being, mind and legs, stomach, shoulders, arms, every drop of blood in him, his whole life which now cried out for the comfort which only that one small, fragile being could provide? An image passed across his mind, one as eternal to him as a painting, the image of Charlotte sitting lost in thought in the little dell in Hyde Park. Had it been at that very moment, when he in his vanity thought she was dreaming of him, that she had made up her mind to marry Beresford? And now the image of that man, closed out of his imaginings till now by hatred and envy, came clearly back to him. That she should forevermore be his, a piece of property as surely in his possession as his infernal cape or his Yorkshire estates—the thought was repellent. In his disgust Gerald turned from the window and commenced pacing back and forth across the carpet.

There are some moments of suffering almost too horrible to be endured. If the pain be physical, we writhe and grown and sometimes clutch at the bedsheets or any object which is at hand. If the pain is mental or—how much worse—spiritual, we have hardly any recourse but to clutch and moan and writhe about inside ourselves, endeavoring most desperately to discover some little patch of oblivion within our minds. Thus did Gerald struggle, pacing as if the pacing would help him to find peace, but in his anguish and rage at his own impotence, he was unable to find even the smallest thought to give it to him.

Charlotte had sought peace in oblivion, gazing unseeing at the ceiling of her room for all those weeks and wishing more to die than to live if life was to be thus. Gerald—perhaps because he was a man or perhaps because his strength was a little greater (though Charlotte's strength must not be supposed slight only because her love was so great)—found his oblivion in sheer rage. The anger was directed first at himself for having failed to find some means to keep his darling despite the world. It was next directed against the world at large for having arranged things so despicably as to make it possible for a man to lose the one thing in all of it he desired—nay, needed—most. And last, he raged against the particular world into which he had been born, whose rules and expectations were both petty and unreasonable, presuming, as they did, that human beings could find happiness within the bounds of fashionable conduct and only within those bounds.

Here, on a rocky promontory above the great Hudson River in a land which had been built upon the breaking of those rules, Gerald wondered if things might have been different had he and Charlotte been Americans. Might they not have resolved their difficulties in a country where to stand against the tide of complacency was an act to be admired? In America, could he not have chosen from a range of possibilities of honest work which could support their physical needs and still preserve his dignity? Would it have been necessary for Charlotte to marry a marquis, here?

Something in Gerald rose up to that unspoken challenge and made him for the first time in his life desire to prove himself without the aid of family or connections. Charlotte was gone; there was no remedy for that. But must he live forever under the yoke of his own helplessness? Could he not at least prove to himself that he was capable of changing his situation?

He thought of Harry Brown and the proposition which Gerald was sure had been nearly made. He thought of why it should be that Brown had not made it and rebelled inwardly that it should have been so. And as he paced, unaware that the instrument of his torture and of Charlotte's was sitting in the next room oblivious to all but his own scribblings, he determined to reopen the subject with Harry Brown himself. For if he was destined to lose Charlotte, was it also destined that he should lose himself?

Chapter 14

How little do we know ourselves and our own strength until some accident of fate forces us to look inward as the last recourse for our salvation!

Such was the case with Gerald, who, having once made up his mind that his destiny lay within his own grasp, moved with new purpose in the days and weeks ahead. Such also was the case with Charlotte, five thousand miles across the Atlantic Ocean.

Whatever miracle of Nature or of will had made her first rise from her bed—that bed which might so easily have been her death bed!—had given her equal strength to endure the still more difficult time which lay ahead. No one, seeing her, could have imagined from her quiet, cheerful manner that the spirit within that delicate frame was every moment waging war against itself. Certainly her parents, watching with joy as every day gave back a little of her colour and filled out that poor ghostly figure, did not realize that their fragile-looking daughter was in fact the most gallant of soldiers. How could they suspect, when the play was acted by such an unlikely trouper, that the whole charade was for their benefit?

For Charlotte, once determined that she would live, but having no reason of her own to do so, had chosen to do it for her parents' sakes. How well she knew their dependence upon her, those two older and apparently stronger beings, whose whole life had been devoted to spoiling her! The uncanny wisdom which had allowed her, even as a small child, to divine the motives of her elders enabled her to see how much of their strength had been derived from her weakness. And in the infinite cycle which is Nature, she had begun to see that it was now her duty to spoil them. The sight of her once beautiful mother, now grown stout and her brow creased with worry, wrung her heart. And her father, who had once set her ahead of him upon his hunter, holding her gently between his great strong hands, whilst with two fingers he controlled his horse, now with his flesh hanging about his bones and his still sharp eyes peering sadly out from beneath his bushy brows— what grief did not that cause her? And when she saw what suffering she had laid at their door, she was ashamed that she had ever loved a man who could hurt not only her but them!

She set about the business of restoring their cheerfulness, therefore, by seeming to regain it herself. With a will she bent to the task of building up her strength, eating heartily, taking exercise as much as she was permitted, and moreover, seeming to regain her old joy in life. She was rewarded soon enough by seeing them both shed the burden of the past months. Her mother regained her old animated manner, and though two or three new creases had been added to those already on her brow and at the corners of her eyes, she was nearly as she had been before her daughter's illness. The Earl, even more so than his wife, seemed to undergo a metamorphosis. The stoop he had acquired during Charlotte's illness disappeared, he put on weight and seemed to have shed the burden of ages from his look and walk. Indeed, he was more merry than she ever could recall seeing him, and were it not for his continual jubilation at the match he thought was coming off, his manner might have pleased her altogether.

In fact, Charlotte might well have been supposed to be falling in love with the Marquis of Beresford and he with her. Having made a concerted effort to rejoin the living, Charlotte had not stinted in the enjoyment of living society. After having once ventured to the Duchess of Devonshire's soirée, she began increasingly to go about. As it was drawing towards the end of the London Season, there were a good many entertainments given, and she appeared at nearly all of them. And all of those she chose to attend were frequented by George Beresford.

Had people not known better, they might actually have

accused him of pursuing the Earl's daughter, for it had
been noted that he deigned not to attend those amuse-
ments where she did not appear. And yet it was well
known that the Marquis pursued no one, but was pursued
by everybody. Lady Charlotte, of course, did not pursue
him and never had, and some said this was the secret of
her great coup. The idea would have made her laugh, im-
plying as it did a long period of scheming for the attentions of a man she had never much cared for. Indeed,
Charlotte had been used to laugh whenever Gerald teased
her about the nobleman and how her papa wished fer-
vently that she would marry him. She had known him, after all, when he was a gawky youth in breeches, and at
about the same time that she had fallen in love with Gerald, she had determined that her cousin Beresford was, at
fifteen, a "silly goose."

But, of course, that had been long ago before that part
of her life in which she had known joy had ended. The
"silly goose," who used to walk with his knees knocking
together and had pursed his lips at the sight of a cow, had
metamorphosed into a handsome man and brilliant match.
That he paid her as much court as he did—positively an
avalanche, for Beresford—could not help but flatter her
vanity now that any deeper emotion was closed to her.
And so she let him flatter her and dance with her and generally monopolize her at three or four balls and dinners,
after which it was said universally that she was a scheming
creature and had somehow caught him in her net. It was
even rumoured that her flirtation with Gerald Kirkland
had been nothing greater than a contrivance to get the
Marquis's attention.

Naturally Lord and Lady Harrington were not loath to
believe the rumours they heard—at least the ones about
Beresford being set upon marrying Charlotte. They believed from what their own eyes saw that she did not dislike him and they managed to convince themselves that
she was actually falling in love.

When a girl who has been very ill, that illness making
her pale and thin, gives away to good health, she naturally
regains her colour and her curves. It was easy enough for
the Earl and his lady to believe that good health had no
more part in the increasing brilliance of their daughter
than the age-old glimmer of love which is known to ani-

mate the palest flesh and dullest eye. As they saw Charlotte beginning to bloom again before them, and saw, moreover, that she was accepting the attentions of so desirable a bachelor, they naturally believed her to be in love. At first only Lord Harrington remarked upon it, which as we have seen, he did very freely. But, at last, even her ladyship, who was somewhat more contained a personality, was inclined to mention it.

"My dear," said she coming into her daughter's room one evening after a ball at Almack's, "may I speak to you?"

Charlotte, who had been taking down her hair with the help of her maid, bid her mother sit down by the fire and sent the girl away. "Why, of course, Mama. What do you wish to tell me?"

"It is rather what I would wish you to tell me, my angel. A mother knows more about her daughter in some ways than anyone—but I now find myself rather at a disadvantage."

Having finished brushing out her hair, Charlotte joined her mother by the fire. She was wearing a brocaded dressing gown of palest green, embroidered all over with dragons. Her rich chestnut tresses, falling heavily about her slender shoulders, were lit into a thousand glimmering colours by the firelight. Watching her sit down before her, the Countess thought she had never seen her look so lovely.

"You know you may say anything to me, Mama."

"Yes, my dear, I know." Her mother paused and, feeling strangely ill at ease, smiled nervously. "I do not like to ask you to tell me what you had rather not. I suppose I had always believed you told me everything until I realized how deeply you were attached to Gerald Kirkland, which, of course, I hadn't the slightest knowledge of—"

Charlotte coloured, despite herself, and looked fixedly into the fire. "I had rather not speak of that, Mama. Anything else—"

"Yes, my dear, of course." the Countess hastily rushed on, "But I did not mean to touch upon that painful subject. It was rather a more cheerful one I had in mind; tell me, my dear, if you feel you can, do you think George Beresford could make you happy?"

Her ladyship peered furtively at the young woman opposite her, a woman who had suddenly ceased to be a girl. Charlotte was still staring into the fire, but with a sudden smile she looked into her mother's eyes. "Why, I do not know, Mama! The subject has never come up between us."

"But, if it should, my love?" her mother pressed on.

"If it should, then I shall have to decide. But I cannot learn to regard him as anything other than a friend until it—if it—does. And really, I don't imagine it will."

"Oh, but I think you are wrong, my dear. In fact, if I may believe my own instincts, which I generally may, I think the subject will come up sooner than you think it will."

"But I do *not* think it will, Mama!" laughed Charlotte, leaning forward and patting her mother's folded hands. "I have learned a good deal about that, you know, in these past weeks. I was once punished for thinking too much before it was time, and I shall never do so again."

The Countess regarded her daughter, who, having leaned back once more in the small armchair in which she sat, had suddenly ceased laughing. There was a look of bitter irony in her eye which she seemed trying to hide with smiles. This one glimpse of her daughter's true state of mind did much, however, to sober her ladyship. She found herself of a sudden in the awkward position of one who suspects much suffering in a loved one, but who is prevented from showing her suspicions.

"I think," she said at last, gently, "that you may find your cousin is a good deal better behaved than some other gentlemen." But a warning look from her daughter prevented her going on. She rose, sighing, and went to the door. But with her hand upon the knob, she turned back.

"For what it may mean to you, my dear, I believe you know how fond your papa is of the idea of your one day marrying the Marquis. I, too, should be made very happy, if it would ensure *your* happiness."

Charlotte watched the door close upon her mother's back and was at once overcome with a sense of shame for having given away even a hint of her lingering pain. She had started up, even before the door had closed, longing to rush into her mother's arms but at once sat down again. As she stared fixedly into the licking flames of the fire, her lips drew more firmly together, and her eyes grew brighter.

What use was she if all she did was cause her parents unhappiness? Foolish creature that she was! Could not she bring herself to do so simple a thing knowing it would be all the world to them who loved her most? Did not she owe them this one simple act?

She had but to make one sign to George Beresford and she knew he would propose, knew it with the same uncomplicated certainty which told her that he would never love her. How she knew so much since he had done nearly all within the power of a man to show his admiration of her is a question which cannot easily be answered. She knew it, that was all, from the tips of her fingers to the soles of her feet. And she was, if anything, still more certain that she could never love him. Honour him—yes; and respect him; and even perhaps, with time, enjoy his company. To be sure she would not revel in it, as she had done with Gerald. There was only one living presence capable of making her whole being come alive and that was now deprived her forever. But still, might there not be some comfort in sharing her life? Might she not with time grow numb to those needs which still cried out within her? A sudden picture crossed her mind, and she flinched slightly. It was an image of George Beresford kissing her, and she drove it at once from her mind, though not from any prudish motive. She had enjoyed—nay, adored—the feel of Gerald's lips upon her own, had longed for his touch and dreamt of his caresses. It worried her that her unreasonable loathing of intimate contact with Beresford should overcome all her rational motives.

Having driven the picture of Beresford from her mind, she commenced walking up and down, much as Gerald, in a room overlooking the Hudson River, had walked up and down on that same day, but so many miles distant! Her thoughts, like his, were of her own power, of how easy it might be for her to take her life into her own hands. Was it not possible that she could shake off this devastation of her heart, this obsession which seemed to hold her in its clutches, preventing her from breathing freely and from walking in a path of her own choosing? That an emotion which had once animated her whole life, had thrilled and intoxicated her, should have dwindled into so horrible a parasite! She walked, more and more quickly, as if her haste might shake it off, and suddenly at the moment of her deepest despair felt that it had begun to slip. It was but a flicker of light seen through a curtain, yet it gave her hope. She stopped abruptly in her pacing and, with a strange brightness in her eye, turned round.

In future years, when she had ceased to wonder at the strength which had suddenly come over her, she would wonder if, had the strength come sooner, she might not have averted all that had occurred and was still to occur. She would ask herself if, had she but shown the same courage to Gerald before he had gone away to America, he would ever have left her? For was it not partly her own weakness which had driven him away, thinking, as he must have done, that she was too fragile to endure any hardship which their lives might bring to them? Had it not surely been for her that he had gone away? For she had long since given up the dread that he had never loved her or had fallen in love with some other woman. She realized now that he had been afraid—afraid for her—but also for himself, and though she could forgive the latter, she could not forgive the former.

But all that philosophizing was to lie in the future. At that moment, with her cold, hard eye fixed upon some object by the fire—the brass poker perhaps, or the ash can—she made up her mind to marry George Beresford.

Chapter 15

He took the hint at once.

In fact, he had expected it a good deal earlier and had begun to grow restless thinking perhaps Georgiana had been mistaken in her assurances to him. But no, she had told him in her last letter from Scotland, "There is sure to be a sign. Take my word, my darling, for I was once a girl myself, though this you may find hard to believe. But I shan't apologize to *you*, who makes me feel that I am once again in that first flush of youth . . ."

Skipping over this part of the epistle—a dreary, but inevitable addition to all of Georgiana's letters, wholly unlike the woman as she behaved in the flesh—Beresford's eye had shifted to the bottom of the page: "A girl always gives a sign when she is ready to be caught, just as the fox, before he is driven to the ground, turns round for one last glimpse of the hunter. Take care you see it, however. It may be as fleeting as a look or gesture. And then, my own dear George, do the thing at once. The sooner you are man and wife, the sooner we shall be free of public disapproval if you choose to come to me here or even in Devon. No one minds what married men and women do, so long as they are discreet. Devonshire will never suspect a newly married man, and surely that sweet little creature who shall be your bride won't notice. And remember what I have always told you—an expedient marriage can only do you good. As for me, I shall never mind whom you marry, so long as she does not rob me of you."

This last bit, which might normally have caused him a

certain irritation (for Beresford disliked being lectured to
as intensely as he disliked Georgiana's occasional drifts
into the maudlin), only made him thoughtful now. During
all of his affair with her, the Duchess had never once al-
luded to the future. She had urged him to marry, and
marry well, but always for his own sake, and they had
agreed—each for his own reasons—that Lady Charlotte
Harrington was an excellent choice. But this time Georgiana had gone a shade too far, for she had dared to intimate—though in the lightest possible way—that he was
her property and might continue to be so.

Beresford had been attracted to the Duchess for many
reasons other than her passionate sensuality. Of these, the
chief was her independent spirit which had always served
to assure him that he would never be throttled by her. On
the contrary, she had once or twice let him know that she
would not be expected to remain celibate simply because
he was not about. The idea had shocked, and then titil-
lated him. He sometimes lay in her great bed imagining
her making love to a series of other lovers. He desired her
only the more thereafter and delighted in the constant attention needed to keep Her Grace intellectually amused
and physically sated. But certainly, should she commence
to exhibit those little cloying signs of possessiveness which
had successfully extinguished his passion for a number of
other ladies, he would find it difficult to continue to pay
her court. The idea occurred to him now for the first time
and made him wonder all the more what reason he had to
get married.

The answer, of course, was perfectly simple. His uncle,
the Duke, had let him know that his nephew's way of life
was not pleasing to him. His Grace had a sentimental
streak about him, due, no doubt, to the fact that he had
sired five daughters and no sons. He was addictively domestic, fond of his dear old drafty abbey and relentlessly
abused the scandalous ways of nearly all his friends. He
would not himself leave the country or stay in town. But
he possessed a prodigious string of spies or else an astonishing clairvoyance, for he seemed to know nearly as soon
as Beresford did, what his nephew was about. It had come
to his attention some months before that the Marquis, his
heir, had been keeping a lady of dubious reputation in
high style with his uncle's allowance to him. That al-

lowance was very large and supplied the needed padding to Beresford's own income from his private estates. Almost at once the Duke had summoned him and given him in no uncertain terms his views upon such conduct.

"You ought to marry, George," said the elder man, who had risen from his bed for the occasion (for he did not wish his heir to know just how near the young man was to having the full run of the estate). "In fact, you ought to marry at once. If you do so and if I approve your choice, I shall be most liberal in my allowance to you. You may count upon my generosity, you may be sure."

"And if I do not, Uncle?" inquired the Marquis, who was capable of looking most bashful when it suited him.

"If you do not, then I shall feel myself forced to reduce your present allowance. I believe you now get ten thousand a year from me—which is very ample when added to your own income. It makes the difference, I believe, between your present comfortable circumstances and a certain—shall we say reduction?—of your style of life. Obviously, it strikes you as sufficient to support all sorts of undesirable creatures as well as yourself."

Beresford flushed slightly but saw that he was cornered. "And whom do you suggest would make an appropriate wife for me, Your Grace? I presume you have some views upon the subject."

The Duke most certainly had his views, but he did not like sarcasm from his dependents and said so. "Don't be cocky, George. I am an old man, but not too old to give you a poke in the eye—or in the pocket, where it shall certainly pain you more. But, however, I do have my private wishes in the matter if you desire to know them. I have long cherished the idea that you might one day marry one of your cousins. Don't scowl so. I know that Priscilla's children are not very comely—which is due to her husband's blood, of course—but Charlotte is my idea of a perfect rose."

"The perfect rose" had thus made her debut into the heart of George Beresford who, after many hours of agitation, had resigned himself to the facts. His uncle might yet live another ten or fifteen years. Was he to make do upon the six thousand pounds he had from his Yorkshire estates for a whole decade? Impossible! He had already developed a thoroughly tonnish style of life in London, which required him to keep two carriages and a good many other expensive appurtenances aside from the infamous mistress. He could hardly be expected to continue his success with Georgiana Devonshire on limited means. The idea of marriage, therefore, seemed a distasteful necessity. "The perfect rose," for some other reasons, had struck him as a not entirely unhappy suggestion.

Lady Charlotte was all the things which he absolutely required in a wife: beautiful, well connected, impeccably well-bred and, better still, demure. In an age when females were beginning to have a great many ideas about their own importance and particularly their own importance in their husband's affairs, Charlotte made a refreshing change. He could not imagine her bullying him, as he had seen some of his friends' wives do, nor interrogating him whenever he chose to go abroad, nor arguing with his taste in clothes. So long as he presented a discreet facade to her, he was perfectly sure that she would not interfere with him over much. She would be a gracious hostess and would no doubt redecorate his house and reconstruct his staff, all of which would cost him something—but no more than a pittance beside what he might lose if he did not marry!

Charlotte, therefore, became his object, and to woo her became his most consuming occupation. He was amazed to find that one admiring look in her direction did not send her fainting to the ground, and her distance, her apparent ignorance of being courted by the most desirable bachelor in London, piqued his interest. He was amazed to discover that she seemed more infatuated by that young Kirkland fellow than by himself, which got his dander not a little and made him determined to pursue her more hotly. Surely a hot pursuit by George Beresford was a thing impossible to ignore by any woman.

Gerald Kirkland suddenly quit London and was rumoured to have gone to America, and then Lady Charlotte herself disappeared for some weeks. It was said that she was ill with influenza, but some knowing ladies raised their eyebrows when they said it. By the time she rose from her bed and went back into society, it was pretty well understood that her heart had been broken by Gerald

Kirkland. Nearly discouraged in his efforts, Beresford had all but given up and said so to his uncle.

"Oh, but you haven't tried, dear boy! Go to it! They are a dafty lot, these women. Give her a poke or two!"

It was an interesting proposition, certainly, but one which Beresford could not fathom how to implement. But Georgiana, who had by then become his mistress, assured him that it was the best possible moment to propose.

"Women are all vulnerable when they have recently been ill-treated by a man. If you but treat her kindly and make her feel that she is still beautiful and desirable, she will be yours in a flash."

The Duchess, evidently, had been correct. Beresford had done what he was bidden, and for the first time, Charlotte had really seemed to warm to him. But still her behaviour was more friendly than infatuated, and it was during this period of their intercourse that he had begun to really admire her.

Admiration would perhaps not be the correct word. Let us say, rather, covet. He was a man who had been spoiled since birth; nothing had ever been denied him. He had expected an instantaneous and most favourable reaction from this young lady, and instead he had had a long period of coolness, followed by a short period of cordiality. She allowed him to court her, which she had not done before—but it was so very passive a thing! He knew enough of women to be capable of reading those small signs of their physiognomy which tell if they are cold-blooded or hot-blooded, witty or tender. Charlotte, because she was unreadable, intrigued him. On the one hand he saw that her lips were very full and sensually curved, and on the other that her cheek was pale and chaste. The soft swell of her bosom and the open manner in which she looked at him contrasted with a certain reservation in her manner and frequent impenetrable silences. As he grew accustomed to Georgiana Devonshire's abandoned embraces, he began to wonder what secret rivers of heat ran through those slender limbs of Charlotte's.

And so when the hint came, he took it. There was, moreover, never any question that he should miss it.

They were seated on a marble banquette near the end of the formal gardens at Gore House when it came. They had wandered off a little from the crowd near the house, which was watching a game of croquet between the Frenchman, the Duc d'Amboise, who had introduced the sport to London and Lady Blessington, their hostess. The game had raised a good deal of curiosity, and the hilarity which had ensued upon its demonstration had become quite raucous. It was one of those ripe afternoons in early autumn when the summer still seems to hang about the air touching the leaves with gold and the grass with silvery light, and Beresford himself had suggested they walk in the famous grounds. They had circled the rose gardens, and then, as if by implicit understanding, had moved farther away from the house and the noisy laughter of the guests. They had come finally to this spot, and Charlotte had declared herself desirous of sitting down.

"Are you fatigued?" he inquired, as solicitous as ever.

"Hardly at all. I simply wish to sit in quiet for a little. It is such a lovely day!"

"You ought not to tire yourself unduly so soon after your illness."

"Oh! I am perfectly well now. It has been weeks since I was ill."

"Still, a convalescence from so severe a bout of influenza ought not to be rushed." The Marquis was amazed to see a sudden smile animate Charlotte's lips. "Have I said something amusing?"

"It is only that you are so delicate. You needn't pretend to believe that I had influenza, my lord. I know it is not believed by half of London. You needn't protect me from the truth."

Much taken aback, Beresford feigned astonishment. "The truth? What do you mean, cousin?"

"What you already know: the truth. That I no more suffered from influenza than you do now. That I succumbed to the age-old malady which besets young women when they are badly treated by a man. That I was heartbroken." Charlotte was looking at her hands which lay folded in her lap. She spoke without apology; her voice was clear and rational and perfectly distinct.

"And," inquired Beresford, taking his place beside her on the bench, "is it true? Are you heartbroken?"

"I used the past tense, my lord," said she with a smiling

sideways glance. "But would it make any difference if I were?"

Beresford paused a moment, thinking. "No. Why should it?"

"It is not generally thought very flattering for a man to be told he is not the first love a woman has had."

"You flatter me, Cousin!"

"No, Cousin; you flatter me."

They were now looking each other directly in the eye. Beresford was astounded by what he had heard, but much more by what he saw. It was as candid a glance as had ever been granted him by any man, much less any woman. He was the first to glance down, against his will.

"Indeed, Lady Charlotte—I had not believed I had reason to hope so much—"

"It is not very much!" she said with a short, high laugh, and then suddenly, in humbler tones, "I give you leave, if you require it."

He said, looking her again straight in the eye and with more feeling than he had exhibited in some months, "I do require it, indeed. You amaze me utterly, dear Charlotte!"

There followed a silence, uncomfortable for both. Beresford knew neither what to say, nor what to do. He had been prepared for some sort of scene at such a moment—a falling down upon his knees, a spouting of poetic thoughts, and a proportionate sentimentality from the lady. But here he had been spared the task so much dreaded—and he was not sure if it made him glad or not. He thought he would like to kiss her, but her face, expressionless and closed, admitted nothing of the kind. He glanced at the grass and grimaced.

"I am not very experienced in such things. Do you like being proposed to from the ground?"

"I do not know! It has not been done to me before."

He glanced up again and smiled. She had resumed her former self and was once more vulnerable.

"I assure you it is very pleasant if it be properly done—or so I hear."

"Then perhaps you will show me, sometime."

"I am perfectly prepared to show you now, my lady!"

"No—I had rather not. I wish you to consider it more carefully, for I do not wish to be one of those women who discovers, too late, that she has taken advantage of a gentleman's weak moment."

"But," protested Beresford, who was really astounded by the girl's manner, "I assure you, I have given it a great deal of thought already."

"And so have I," smiled Charlotte, "so have I. Still, I think it would be kind of you to speak to my father first."

"But I have already done so, Charlotte, I assure you! Why—did not you know?"

"No," said Charlotte, genuinely surprised, "I did not. When was that?"

"Why, in June—very early in June. But you were so cold to me then and evidently in love with another—"

Charlotte held up her hand, and again she smiled, as if apologising. "If we are to be man and wife, my lord, I wish you would do me one favour. Never speak to me about that—subject."

Beresford nodded his understanding but was too pleased with his evident success to notice anything strange in her expression. "It is all arranged then?" he enquired, rather anxiously.

"It is all arranged, my lord."

Then, to his astonishment, she stood up and waited expectantly for him to do the same. Really, it was too odd for words! Certainly nothing like what he had imagined. He was still as they walked back toward the house, Charlotte talking of the weather, of the beautiful gardens and the lovely park, as if she desired to avoid any further mention of the subject so much in his own mind, he being unsure of what had transpired. Were they engaged or not engaged? Had she accepted him? Had he even proposed? "It was arranged" she had said as if he had agreed to buy a filly from her. And just when he had been upon the point of kissing her, which he thought would be the proper gesture, she had stood up, and now she would hardly look at him! Too odd for words, really! He wished of a sudden for the sound counsel of Georgiana Devonshire, who might have some insight into this strange young woman's behaviour.

But, if he was puzzled by the manner of her acceptance, he had no doubt as to her meaning. Whether or not the formal words had been spoken and replied to, they were sooner or later to be consummated. Thus encouraged and given, moreover, a new view of this woman who was to be his wife—a view which tantalized as much as puzzled him—he went jubilantly to her side, fairly bursting to get back to town where he could write to Georgiana and his uncle of his success.

Chapter 16

"What do you mean, my dear?" said Lady Harrington when she had been told the news. "You say you are to be married, but that he has not proposed? I do not understand you, I am afraid! Though, of course, I am very happy! Very happy, indeed! But still—"

Charlotte smiled at her mother's confusion. She saw that the first joy her announcement had caused was marred a little by this detail.

"I told him to wait, Mama, until he was perfectly certain."

"But he said that he *was* certain, did he not? So then, did he not declare himself?"

"What is a declaration exactly, Mama?" enquired the young lady, putting her arm through her mother's. "I have never been quite sure of its form. Are there certain words which ought to be used. Does it not count if the words are different?"

"Why! I hardly know what to say to you, my dear. I only know that your father made his intentions quite clear and that I must have accepted him as clearly. But there were certain words—Love, Honour—of course, they are old-fashioned, I know—"

"*I* do not think so, Mama!" exclaimed Charlotte still smiling. "I think them perfectly lovely."

"Then, of course, it is all right? Oh, my dear, I am thrilled, perfectly thrilled! I hardly know how to tell you sufficiently. Your papa shall be overjoyed, and the Duke as well. Oh, my angel, what a bright future you shall have!

A duchess, only think! I never shall forget how frightened you made your papa and me all those weeks. I thought you would not live, and then I was afraid you would live forever unhappy and bitter, but now you are well, and your future is so bright! I cannot think what could make me happier at this moment!"

Charlotte did not suggest that perhaps if those old-fashioned words, Love and Honour had been mentioned but once by her future husband, it might have increased her own joy not a little. She did not, however, dampen her mother's pleasure, nor her father's, when he heard.

"What! What is this!" he cried, jumping up from his chair. "What did I tell you, Daphne, eh? Heh, heh! And I was right about it all along, after all! By Jove, I cannot stand about thus. Come here, my dear, and give your old father a kiss. There, my pet; well, what a pretty bride you shall make, to be sure!"

"The prettiest bride that ever lived," murmured her ladyship with eyes growing peculiarly shiny. "It shall be a great occasion, and you shall be the happiest woman in the world!"

"Tut!" exclaimed the Earl, good-humouredly, "and what are you, my dear? Well, well!"

Charlotte was made much of in those next hours and days, and the Marquis, when he came to call, was treated as if he were one of the family already. If there had been some question that he ought to make a formal proposal, "on his knees," as he had put it, it was now taken as done, at least by Lord and Lady Harrington. Charlotte, if she had desired such an event, made no mention of it, and in the general jubilance which overtook the house in Mount Street, her reticence was not noticed. Beresford, indeed, found her less ardent than he had expected; but then, he had dreaded what he thought she would be like. Now on the contrary, he found himself fairly dandling after her. Once or twice he was brought up by the thought that she was actually trying to evade him, for in that first week of their engagement he was not once alone with her, save for the interludes of five minutes or so when they awaited a carriage together at some ball or were left consciously by her parents in the music room. But Charlotte, whose inner state of mind was quite the opposite of what a girl's generally is when she has just agreed to be a duchess, contrived whenever possible to have a third party in the room with them.

Her reluctance—which she never allowed her parents to see—sprang from more than one source. First, she did not believe, had never believed, that Beresford loved her. Canny as she was, she could not guess why he should wish to marry her above a dozen or so other young women whose characters would have more perfectly suited him. She guessed, however, that he had a motive and that his motive was not love. Was not his conduct that afternoon at Gore House ample proof? Where any other lover would have professed himself amazed and overjoyed—falling down upon his knees or over himself with happiness at her blunt acceptance—he had merely enquired if she would like him to do so. More than that, any *real* lover would have sensed her own indifference and would have behaved accordingly. But Beresford—Beresford had merely accepted her offer as if she had enquired if he would like a leg of mutton for his supper. To be sure he had seemed pleased, but his pleasure was so cold, so empty of any real human feeling! The thought of his words and of his looks that afternoon haunted her for many nights.

But was it fair for her to demand love from him for whom she herself could feel no warmth? As little as the thought of being a duchess moved her, it moved her more than the thought of being his wife. Had she devoted a year's meditation to the task, she could not have thought of what could be less pleasurable, less easy, less satisfactory, from any human point of view than to walk through life by his side. Where she craved warmth and softness, there was ice and stone; where she desired a mutuality of interests, there was none; where she would have prayed for a mate in whom she could confide everything, whom she could succor and support, there was a man whose inner being was a mystery and to whom she could not fathom confiding a single thought. He did not need her help or her support, for he was like an island, entire unto himself. She thought of these things late into the night and tried to give them less importance in her mind; but she could not.

To be sure, there were worse things than marrying him. There was, for instance, the thought of her parents should she grow into an old maid. To her it did not matter—what mattered anything so long as the one being she had ever loved had fled? She supposed in time she would learn to take satisfaction in small things—in the running of a household, in raising the children which she prayed would come—but never, never in her own heart's fullness! She supposed she would grow older and that with age would come a certain philosophy of mind, and with this hope, she learned to live.

The whole of London seemed to know of the engagement, though it had not formally been announced. Lady Harrington was planning a great ball at which her daughter's expectations would be trumpeted aloud, but she might have spared herself the trouble. Everyone in the City seemed to have heard: servants learned the news from the Earl's domestic staff, and their masters imbibed it from the very air. Nowhere was Lady Charlotte not greeted by a round of admiring titters; nowhere was her hand not held an instant longer than any other lady's. Secret smiles followed her wherever she went; she even received the supreme flattery of all: to be scowled at by the dowager circle at Almack's, for she had cheated them of their daughters' hopes.

All this Charlotte vaguely knew. She passed through it and over it as if she were in a dream, smiling and laughing, appearing to be vastly pleased, and all the while some part of her was weeping. She clung to a pitiful hope that Gerald might return even now, that he might yet claim her for his own. Hardly did she dare admit it even to herself; and as day followed day and the engagement party drew closer, her hope began to dwindle into nothing.

But then one day, something occurred to scatter into pieces the frail tranquillity she had attained.

She was following her mother about the pantry making an inventory of the larder and the wine cellar. Lady Harrington was all a-twitter, for she had finally set the day for the engagement party and was making up a menu for the hundred guests she had invited to sup and dance. The whole kitchen staff buzzed with her—even the old butler, generally above such jollity—was practically hopping from one foot to the other as they discussed plans for the party.

"What have we got for claret, Baldwin?" the Countess

demanded of him. "I cannot recollect if we have any of the '87 left."

"That was all drunk at the ball last May, your ladyship, but we have a great deal of the '89 still in the cellar, and, of course, there is the La Tour '93, a very fine wine, my lady. His lordship would know."

"Yes, but his lordship is away this morning. Have you got the wine list here?"

"No, my lady. His lordship keeps it in his desk."

The Countess turned to Charlotte. "My love, will you run up to your papa's study and bring it me? Which drawer is it in, Baldwin?"

"I think it is the second or third on the right, my lady. I am not quite certain, but I do recall his lordship always puts it away with his right hand."

"Well, see if you can find it, my dear. Here is a key if you need it."

Charlotte ran up the stairs, glad to be useful and glad to keep busy on this glorious autumn day. There was a smell of dry leaves in the sunshine coming in beneath the doors and windows; she could just believe, so long as she was occupied and in the cheerful presence of the Countess, that she was perfectly happy. She paused at the door to her father's sanctorum and sniffed the lingering scent of a cigar. A thin stream of pale-lemon sunlight fell across the rich Turkish carpet and the marqueterie desk. All seemed peaceful, warm, and as it should be. How long it had been since she had felt this sense of rightness in the world!

She moved across the rug, took out the little silver key her mother had given her, and fitted it into the first lock. Her eye fell upon a stack of tradesmen's bills and correspondence. The wine list, which she knew to be contained in a morocco binder, was not there. The second drawer was not locked. She saw the binder with its neat golden letters and drew it out. As she did so an envelope fluttered to the floor. Stooping, she picked it up. As she began to slip it back into the drawer, her eye caught something which made her stop and suddenly draw in her breath. She pulled it forth again and saw the words written in that dear, familiar hand:

For Lady Charlotte Harrington
Kindness of Lord Harrington

The seal was still in place!

Forgetting everything—the wine list in her hand, the open drawer, the sunlight and the sense of peace which had so quickly been shattered—she dropped into her father's chair and stared at the words, as if, by staring long and hard enough, she might succeed in making its contents come into her mind without reading them. In those seconds—no more than three or four—it was as if the last weeks and months had all fallen away, as if she had never heard of Gerald's sudden flight, never been ill, never recovered—and never accepted Lord Beresford. She was once again the girl who had sat waiting that fateful afternoon in June on the bench in Hyde Park, hoping that she might soon be, not a lofty duchess, but plain Mrs. Kirkland. Her heart beat so fast that she pressed her hand against her breast to make it stop.

Only after some time did she open the letter, draw out the folded paper, and read:

> Sunday evening, 14th day of June
> Dover Street

My dearest Lady Charlotte,

I have this day spoken to your father and have informed him of my intention of setting sail to America tomorrow at dawn. I go with a tumult of thoughts and no little sadness. But my heart is not heavy, as I have been assured that your intended engagement to your cousin, the Marquis of Beresford, is the result of your own free choice and dearest wish. My only regret is that I did not understand sooner your desires, for then I should have absented myself a long while before this and not imposed my presence upon you, which must have been a great burden to your ladyship and caused you no little distress; for I know that you are, of all females, the most softhearted and that you must have dreaded telling me the news yourself. For this kindness I am deeply grateful.

Your father has told me that while you have every intention of accepting the Marquis's offer, you have not done so yet. May I take the liberty of urging you to do so at the earliest possible moment? If you will accept the advice of a very true friend and humble admirer, you will see that there is no longer cause for hesitation. Indeed, it has long been my belief that the life which Lord Beresford is capable of offering you is far better than anything I, in my present difficulties, could ever proffer. Nothing is dearer to me than the thought that you shall ever be the happiest of women, and with this marriage, I know that you shall be.

I take my leave of you with every wish for that same happiness and the promise that I shall remain,

Your obedient servant,
G. Kirkland.

For some minutes Charlotte stared at these lines, uncomprehending. The tone was so unlike his! So stiff—so formal—she could not at first be sure that it was the Gerald Kirkland she had known and loved. But other truths began to come home to her, so many at once, and so difficult to understand that at first she was tempted to think it all a terrible joke. She read the letter through again and yet again, and only then did she begin to see how it had come about.

When Charlotte did not return, her mother sent a maid to see what was the matter. The servant girl came back some moments later with a frightened look. "She's gone off again, my lady!" cried the girl running down the pantry steps. "Right as rain, she's gone off again! She's fainted dead away, my lady!"

It took but an instant for her ladyship, hearing this, to reach her daughter's side. With a face drained of colour, she beheld Charlotte's slight form draped across the Earl's desk, a letter in her hand. Sending for salts and the doctor, she set to the business of reviving the young woman, of rubbing her wrists and temple and getting her onto a sofa. Charlotte's eyes began to flutter as her mother picked up the letter which had evidently caused her daughter's collapse.

"Read it through, Mama," she murmured softly. "Read it quite through, and tell me—was ever a girl so deceived by her own father?"

Lady Harrington did as she was bid. She read the letter

through and then read it again. At length, she looked up, still confused.

"What does it mean, my dear? I do not understand."

"Don't you see?" said her daughter. "Papa told him I was about to accept Lord Beresford. He let him think that it was what I wished! Oh, Mama, that is why he went away!"

The Countess was dumbfounded. Certainly she understood the cause of her daughter's distress, and she began to understand the Earl's deception. But, even now, she could not see—perhaps because she did not wish to—how the letter had undone the work of all those weeks. Her greatest desire, even now, was to restore her daughter's recent good humour.

"Oh, my love! How distressing! But you must not let this piece of news destroy your happiness! You have come through your illness and now are to be very shortly a marchioness. You shall be happier than you could ever have been with Gerald Kirkland, I am quite sure of it."

But Charlote was not listening. A sort of wild look had come into her eyes, and she sat up. "How shall I ever look at him again, Mama? How shall I ever know him again?"

The Countess was bewildered. "Know whom, my love?"

"Why, Papa, of course! He always wanted me to marry my cousin, and so when he saw I would not do so of my own free will, he took the choice away from me. He devised a scheme that would make me hate Gerald, whom I loved more than life and force me to look kindly upon Lord Beresford, though if there had been no other man upon earth, I should not have been induced to marry him, before—before—"

Her ladyship, thinking of the invitations which had been sent out, of the wine which had been ordered, the masses of edibles and flowers from the greenhouse which had been cut, began to panic.

"My dearest girl, think what you are saying! You must not speak so of your father. He only did what he thought was best for you. It was not right; most assuredly, it was not right of him. But still, he did it only out of love. You must not hate him for it! And after all—has it not come out in the end? For you do love George Beresford now, do you not? Perhaps you did not at first, but now that is all changed, surely?"

"Has it, Mama?" enquired Charlotte with a smile. Her face was so pale, her voice so strange and her eyes so wild that Lady Harrington could hardly suppress a shudder. "Has it changed? I shall tell you: nothing has changed. I still love Gerald, more if possible, and I still hate Lord Beresford. Yes; I hate him! He has not a feeling bone in all his body, he could not understand what it is to love if his life depended upon it! I do not understand how you and Papa can be so gratified that I have given up the one man in all the world who could ever make me happy and consented to marry a man who *must* make me miserable!"

"Hush, child! You don't know what you are say—"

"I know perfectly what I am saying! I agreed to marry him for one—for only one reason! To make you and Papa happy! And, in return, what have I received? Deception and cruelty, that is all!"

"You mustn't talk like that—"

But Lady Harrington, staring into her daughter's fevered eyes, suddenly forgot all about the invitations, the gossip, the flowers and wine. The deception she had worked upon herself in the past weeks—making herself believe that Charlotte was perfectly happy, that all was right with her family—began to fall away. She had been too blind and too unwilling to see the signs which only a mother is able to read, signs which should have told her that Charlotte was pretending to be happy, to wish what her parents wished. She remembered those innumerable small looks and glances which ought to have told her at once that this engagement was wrong and that Charlotte could never be happy as George Beresford's bride. And now—with what consternation—she began to understand the extent of her husband's well-meaning cruelty, and her own anger was born.

"How shall you ever forgive us?" she mumbled, humbly sinking onto the sofa at Charlotte's feet.

"You did not know, did you, Mama?"

The Countess shook her head. "But I should have seen—I should have seen!"

"I must go to America, mother. You must arrange it with Papa. Perhaps Aunt Gertrude will accompany me. I must go to find him! If it is too late . . . perhaps he has fallen in love with another woman—perhaps he is already married. But it does not matter; I must go to him. So long as there is any chance, I must go to him."

In vain did her mother endeavor to persuade Charlotte against so foolhardy a step; in vain did she set forth the complications of a young woman travelling by herself, even with a chaperone, and of the difficulties which must be overcome in order to actually find one man in all of that vast Continent. But Charlotte was adamant; she saw only one course open to her and that one must she follow. If the country was vast, than she would trace his steps until she found him; if it was difficult for a young lady to travel alone, then she could surmount the difficulties. Of one thing, and one thing only, was she certain: Gerald should know, as soon as she could tell him, that she loved him, that she had never deserted him for another. She knew she had some money of her own. If her father forbade her going, she would be obliged to defy him. The journey would be paid for by herself, she alone would undertake the search, she alone would take the financial risk.

"But what of George Beresford?" enquired her mother at last. Was he to be told anything? Or only made to await her return in case she might still marry him?

Charlotte did not blink at her mother's ironic tones.

"You will be breaking your engagement, you know, my dear. If you were a man, you might be liable to Breach of Promise. It is not, even in a woman, a very slight offence."

"But I shall be breaking no engagement, Mama," replied Charlotte with a smile.

Her mother regarded her in astonishment. So vast a change had come over her daughter in the last minutes, she felt she scarcely knew her. "Do you mean you will marry him after all?"

"I shall not marry him. But I never said I would!"

Now her mother stared and begged her to be more lucid.

"I told you, Mama, that he never actually asked me to be his wife. He made no declaration, and I accepted none. Let him try, if he likes, to accuse me of breaking my promise, for I never promised anything!"

The Countess could only stare, dumbfounded by what she heard.

Chapter 17

Having made up his mind to be the oracle of his own fate, Gerald Kirkland set about the task of changing his life with a vengeance.

To those who had not known him before, his behaviour was not much different. Only a new light in his eye, a greater animation in his manner and something like an obsession with seeing and learning everything about him hinted that some great inner battle had been fought and won. Even the one person who had known him since childhood—Fitzwilliam Canterby—was not aware of the revolution his old acquaintance had endured. Had Canterby been less absorbed in his own thoughts and desires, he might have guessed something; but as it was, he seemed himself transported by some new idea.

Of those about him, Chastity Brown was the only being who remarked the change in Gerald, and she was disinclined to like anything she saw in him. Try as she might, she had been unable to elicit any word or sign from him which betrayed his dishonourable conduct. At the most pointed taunt, he merely shrugged and smiled as if to say "I do not understand you, miss, but if you are determined to hate me, then I cannot change your mind!" Nothing could have irked her more than this indifference made more loathesome by his friendly manner, for it betrayed not only an insensibility to the wrong he had done his friends, but a hardness of heart she had not suspected in him before. She was more than ever determined to confide her knowledge of his conduct to her brother's ear and was only prevented from one day to the next by Mr. Canterby's pleas.

"Pray say nothing about it just yet," he urged her while they were walking one crisp autumn day by the mountain brook which ran behind the Manor House.

"Each day that passes without his confessing anything makes his conduct more repulsive," returned Miss Brown. "I really do not think I can endure it any longer. I *must* tell Harry!"

"And yet—I pray you won't, my dearest lady"—for Mr. Canterby had so ingratiated himself with that young woman that he was allowed greater and greater freedom of address—"I pray you won't! It can only anger your family against us both, for *his* lack of honour will surely be interpreted by them as including my own."

"But I shall explain it to them!" protested Chastity, who had not thought of this. "I shall make them see it was only your loyalty to your friend which kept you from revealing the truth yourself. In any case, you have revealed it to *me*—why not, then, to the others?"

Here Canterby paused in his walking and, turning around, assumed one of those expressions of deep thought and inner resolve which had deluded half a dozen unfortunate females at home. "Ah! But you were the only one he might really have injured had you not known the truth," he remarked.

Chastity looked much affected. After a moment, she said, "How right you are! To think how I admired him before you unblinded me! I might, had I not known better, have gone to all sorts of lengths for him! To think of it makes me shudder, Mr. Canterby. Let us talk of something more pleasant."

This Canterby was glad enough to do. He was much better at making agreeable conversation than at playing the righteous and honourable young man, which in truth, he was perfectly willing to do, if by no other manner could he accomplish his ends.

After some poetic remarks about the dew-lit grass, the sparkling stream and crystal air, which Chastity just barely managed to stomach (for Canterby was much less an aficionado of the poets than he cared to reveal), he turned to the subject uppermost on his mind. "I suppose you have heard that your brother and Kirkland intend going up the River tomorrow?"

"Do they?" inquired an indifferent Chastity. She was not much concerned about the comings and goings of the latter gentleman any longer.

"Why, I was sure your brother would have told you. He is taking Gerald on a tour of the warehouses at Albany. They expect to be away for two or three weeks."

"Then I shall have two or three weeks' tranquillity, Mr. Canterby. It makes no difference to me, only I do pity poor Harry."

"As well you might," mumbled Canterby quite audibly, pretending to stare across the stream into a wooded copse at the other side. "How gorgeous are the autumn leaves in this place!"

"They are accounted the most beautiful in New York," replied Miss Brown. "People come from miles away to look at them. They are nothing yet—but you shall see in a month how brilliant the colours are."

"Alas! If only I could be here," murmured Canterby.

"What! Are you not staying? Do you go with Harry and—the other gentleman, then?"

"No! Oh, no, Gerald would certainly not want me about, I am positive of that. He would regard me as interfering with his plans, you know. But I have received a most gracious invitation from Madame Van Cortlandt to stay at Cortlandville. I cannot decline her without excessive rudeness, I think, especially as she knows I have already stayed out my welcome here."

Chastity made some polite noise to the contrary, but, less concerned with Mr. Canterby's assurance of welcome than with another remark he had made, she demanded, "Plans? What plans can Mr. Kirkland have that you could interfere with?"

Now Canterby contrived to look as if he had said something he did not intend. "Why, did I say anything of the kind? I do not know what plans, I assure you, my dear Miss Brown!"

He was instantly gratified for Miss Brown stopped dead in the path and, taking his arm, looked him very keenly in the eye. "Do not attempt to protect your friend, Mr. Canterby, I beg of you! Already you have protected him far more than he deserves. If you know something that ought to be said, pray say it!"

Canterby made a slight moan and turned his head away. "How keen you are, Miss Brown! I could wish a hundred injuries inflicted on me rather than being forced to tell you what I know!"

If there had been intensity in Chastity's gaze before, it was nothing to the expression of piercing distaste which she now wore. All of the anger she had felt against Gerald Kirkland for what she considered his mistreatment of her before was now multiplied a hundredfold. "I do not know what you are speaking of, sir, but I am bound I shall! Do not spare my feelings—only tell me!"

Canterby, his head turned away, gently unfastened Chastity's gloved hand from his elbow and slumped against a convenient oak tree, his palm shielding his eyes from the slanting rays of the sun. "By God, I wish I did not believe it! I should give anything—anything—to be spared my susicions!"

"Pray go on, Mr. Canterby! Spare me not!"

"Would that I could, Miss Brown! I believe—well, in all frankness, I must say that I am convinced—that Kirkland has laid an evil scheme against your brother."

All the blood drained out of Chastity's blooming cheek and, as quickly, rushed back again. "Evil! What evil can he intend for Harry! What can he do to him?"

"Hush, my dear lady, I beg of you! I shall explain it all, if only you hear me out. It is not exactly that he intends to injure your brother, but I fear, in his avarice, such might be the consequence of whatever he intends. Believe me, even Gerald is not capable of outright evil; but what evil may result from his schemes, I do not think he minds. You see—oh, that I did not suspect it!—he has long hoped to make his fortune in America. He confided as much to me time and again on the voyage across the ocean and has several times hinted since we have come to Garrison that he has layed a plan to achieve his goal. I believe, from countless chance words that have slipped unintentionally from his lips, that he now hopes to go into business with your brother. Rather, he shall get your brother to agree to such an arrangement in order that he may cheat him of a great amount of money."

Words cannot express the consternation with which

these words were greeted. Had Chastity been the sort of
female who is given to fainting, surely now she would
have lain draped across the knotted roots of that venerable
old tree against which Canterby was leaning. Not being so
weakly made, she stood rigidly in the same spot, her boots
rooted to the earth, her fists clenched and her white lips
drawn tight together. Not even the scarlet hue of her walking cloak could match the brilliance of the two spots in either cheek. Her lips parted at last, as if she was about to
speak, but then they were again pressed firmly together. At
length one gloved hand was lifted to her breast, and her
eyes grew round.

"Then we must stop them!" she cried, whirling about
and beginning to run pell-mell down the path towards the
garden gate.

"Stop!" cried Canterby, at length catching her up and
grasping her arm with less gentleness than firmness, forc-
ing her to obey him. "Stop, I beg you!"

"You shall not beg me anymore, Mr. Canterby!" returned a panting Chastity with flashing eyes. "Your loyalty
to your friend has gone too far. Now it is time for me to
show my sisterly loyalty! I must warn Harry before they
go to Albany tomorrow. There is no telling what may pass
between them if they are left alone together for so long.
Harry is so susceptible. You have seen yourself how devoted he has grown to your friend! Indeed, we must stop
them at once."

Now Canterby nodded sagely. "I begin to see that you
are right, Miss Brown. Only, perhaps it would be wise if
we decided beforehand what ought to be done rather than
rushing in pell-mell without an idea. They may all think us
crazed if we act too rashly."

In the interests of further developing their own arguments against Harry's consorting any longer with Gerald
Kirkland, Chastity was persuaded to see reason.

"I think I ought to warn Gerald to leave of his own ac-
cord," remarked Canterby. "It would be the most chari-
table thing to do. If I could persuade him to go to
Cortlandville with me—or at least to appear to—for I
think he may not be much more welcome there than
here—at least he will have the chance of preserving appearances."

"I don't give a fig for his appearance!" cried Chastity.

"I would be delighted to see him tarred and feathered as they used to do in the old days to good-for-nothings!"

"Still, you know—it is not quite calculated to delight your mother if she discovers she has been sheltering a rapscallion. Do you not agree it would be kinder to her to let her remain in ignorance awhile longer? Then, after we are gone—"

"Well, I *shall* tell Harry, however!"

"Very well," sighed Canterby, affecting a most resigned manner. "Very well, then—if you must."

Chastity declared that she certainly must and set off at a brisk clip for the Manor House, which lay some quarter of a mile beyond. Marching beside her, Canterby prayed that his calculations as to the hour had been correct.

It appeared they had, for, upon reaching the mansion and bursting in through a side entrance, Chastity demanded of the nearest footman where her brother could be found.

"Why, Miss Brown," replied the servant, "your brother went off an hour ago with Mr. Kirkland to catch the steamer. They were looking for you everywhere to say their good-byes, but you were nowhere about. Mr. Brown left a letter for you though. I believe your mama has it."

"Gone!" cried Chastity, growing pale. "But they were not to leave till tomorrow!"

The servant, an elderly Negro whose wife had nursed the present Mrs. Brown, smiled. "They was all in a rush; said they wouldn't wait. Something to do with the *Clermont*'s last voyage."

"The *Clermont!*" cried Chastity. "Of course! She was to make her last trip up the Hudson today! Oh, my Lord—where is Mama? Mr. Canterby, you had better come with me."

Canterby, whose idea it had been for Harry and Gerald to take advantage of that historic vessel's last voyage in their journey to Albany, looked as appalled as anyone. Muttering admonitions to her to be restrained, he followed Chastity to the sunny little room where Mrs. Brown was accustomed to passing the morning hours. That lady, as softspoken and soft mannered as her daughter was passionate, was ensconced at a large table over which was spread her sewing. A damask cloth was folded on one side ready to be hemmed, and in her hand she held an elaborate lace collar. From this she looked up when her daughter burst into the room.

"Why, good morning, my dear! Good morning, Mr. Canterby. Have you been walking? Your brother was looking for you everywhere. He and Mr. Kirkland determined to take the *Clermont*'s last sailing up the River. Harry left you this letter, dear."

Chastity ignored the proffered envelope and stared straight into her mother's mild brown eyes. "Mama! We must stop them!"

Mrs. Brown smiled. She was well accustomed to her daughter's sudden bursts of emotion. "Whatever for, dear? They shall be back in a fortnight or thereabouts. Harry wishes to show Mr. Kirkland your papa's business. They are only going up to see the warehouses."

"But that is why we must stop them! There is no telling what may happen in a fortnight!"

Now Mrs. Brown began to see the extent of her daughter's distress and, bidding her sit down, wished her to tell calmly what was amiss. With great consternation did she listen to the ensuing tale and, with a look of deep sorrow, asked Mr. Canterby to confirm it.

"It is only what I suspect, madam—but I thought it sufficient to warrant my warning you. Kirkland is—well—he left England in some straights."

"Do you mean that he requires money?" demanded Mrs. Brown very much distressed. "Poor man!"

"Oh, tosh, Mama!" cried Chastity. "You would take pity on a murderer if you liked him. But I shall tell you *why* he requires money: he left a poor lady behind him to whom he had pledged himself against his will! I suppose he wishes to make a fortune that he may break the engagement, do not you, Mr. Canterby?"

Canterby sighed. "I suppose that may be his motive, ma'am. In truth, I don't know any more what I think of him! He was not always like this, I promise you. Indeed, I had great hopes that this journey might work some miracle upon him. I should not have allowed ourselves to be forced upon you had I the slightest suspicion—"

"Of course, you would not, Mr. Canterby," Mrs. Brown assured him. "Of course, you would not. Still, I don't know what I can do until your papa returns, my dear. Certainly it would not do to have Mr. Kirkland come back to us—and yet I cannot think how to avoid it! So long as your father is in Boston, I am afraid we shall simply have to wait."

"Could not you send a message to Harry, Mama? Or better still, one of the other boys?"

Mrs. Brown looked grave. "I do not like to accuse anyone on paper, my dear, before there is proof of a wrong doing. Your father would surely be most angry with us if we were to take things into our own hands and act without his knowledge. Really, my dear, I think we shall have to wait for them to return. Then your father will be home again, and he may ask Mr. Kirkland to leave himself. There is surely not much that can happen in only two or three weeks."

Thus was the matter settled, and Chastity was forced to see that no other solution could serve. She knew her father would be irate to learn of their guest's ingratitude; but he would be quite as irate to discover that his wife and daughter had taken it upon themselves to punish him. Indeed, Mrs. Brown's distressed look spoke more clearly than words what her misgivings were about accusing a man of something which had not been done, even if his intentions were the most deplorable. However, she was not averse to expressing her heartfelt gratitude to Mr. Canterby, and this she did with real feeling.

"Be assured, sir, that your actions will be looked upon by my husband as favourably as those of your friend will be condemned. I am inclined to believe he may make his thanks to you with some little reward for warning us."

Looking gratified, Canterby protested any such idea, saying, "No reward could be greater than to avert any possible harm to you or your family, madam. You have showed me the greatest hospitality: let that be my thanks."

"What a surprise that young man has been, my dear," said Mrs. Brown to her daughter when they were alone a little later. "To be honest, I never liked him much before. I always preferred Mr. Kirkland, thinking him the more gentlemanly of the two. And now look how deceived I have been!"

"You are not the only one," admitted Chastity, sitting down beside her mother and taking up a piece of embroidery. "Before Mr. Canterby told me of his friend's engagement, I was on the point of falling in love with him!"

Mrs. Brown, who was mild mannered and gentle but not devoid of humour, smiled at the vivacious girl at her side. "I should be more impressed, my dear, if you had not said that a half dozen times before about half a dozen gentlemen!"

Chastity pretended to pout. "Well, I cannot help it, Mama, if my heart is like a bell—"

"which tolls at every passing face," her mother finished for her.

"Oh, Mama, what a funny thing you are! I am not so bad as all that, though I wish heartily I had showed more circumspection with Mr. Kirkland. *How* I hate him!"

Mrs. Brown paused in her sewing and regarded her daughter thoughtfully for a moment. "Well, my dear, are you in love with Mr. Canterby now?"

"Of course not!" Oh, he is pleasant enough—but he *does* rather look like a weasel, don't you think?"

"Yes, my dear—very like! And I am glad you are not going to run away with him after all, although he has warned us against his friend."

"Run away with him! What an idea!"

But her mother only smiled and bent once more over her sewing.

Chapter 18

He who looked like a weasel but was blissfully unaware of the fact had other fish to catch beside the Browns. Saying his good-byes with every sign of regret and, indeed, with a very real distress at leaving behind the slim-waisted and tantalizing Miss Chastity Brown, he departed the next day for the lower reaches of the Hudson. As he was driven off in the gig to catch the next steamer going downstream, he contemplated what he was going towards and, in his mind, set it against what he left behind.

To be sure Miss Joanna Van Cortlandt was nothing like Miss Chastity Brown—neither so tempting to touch, nor so quick of eye and brain—but then, was not that partly why he had settled on Joanna? And then, of course, her family home was quite a lot closer to that of Mr. Philipse, whom he was most desirous of meeting again. Regretful as he was, therefore, he could hardly feel himself deprived of all amusement in the next weeks, for having satisfactorily spoiled Gerald's porridge, he was about to sweeten his own by a good deal. And if, in the coming months, he should find himself in close proximity again to Miss Brown, how could he swear he should not at last taste the honey of those tantalizing lips, those lips which had so irritatingly been turned away from his own whenever he had tried to get close to them? No indeed, there was no swearing anything in this land of bounty, where riches were the reward of any man clever enough and quick enough to turn a trick or two! Whistling very happily, he reached the pier at which the steamer *Titania* was berthed, and ignoring the

155

large black hand held out to him by the coachman (for there was no one about to condemn him for not taking it) he leapt aboard the vessel and commanded a porter to take his trunks below.

His friend, meanwhile—he whose porridge had been spoiled—was as yet blissfully unaware of the treachery from which he had suffered. Having made a glorious journey up the remainder of the Hudson on the majestic old steamer *Clermont*—the first of those great animals to plough the river waters without aid of wind—he and Harry Brown had docked at Albany and there begun one of finest periods in Gerald's life. The upper reaches of the Hudson were, if anything, even more grand than the lower. The River's mighty current was here a greater rush, a more savage roar than at Garrison. Calm as she appeared upon the surface, the powerful currents beneath were visible by means of the salmon's golden fins which tore the placid surface. Albany, too, was a great town, almost a city. Countless mansions lined the wide avenues, and stately churches, halls, and libraries surrounded the several lovely squares. The autumn was here farther advanced than at Garrison—the great oaks and elms were already a splendour of crimson and russet, and the air bit one's ears with a playful foretaste of the harsh winter.

The cold air was not unwelcome to Gerald who found it as exhilarating as everything he saw. After a fortnight of leisure at the Brown's Manor House, he was eager for new sights and new experiences. How eagerly had he accepted Harry's invitation to accompany him on a tour of the warehouses and how much closer he felt they had become on this solitary excursion. Indeed, he had hardly ever known companionship as satisfactory as that of Harry Brown. On the river steamer they had sat up a good part of the night staring over the dark and silvered waters rushing past the vessel's sides, talking as he did not remember talking to any being in all his life. His only other taste of real intimacy had been with Charlotte, for he had neither brothers or sisters. His father and he had never been accustomed to any kind of intimacy differing as they did on nearly every point—from the fundamental traits of their characters to their ideas of enjoyment—Sir James and he had shared little enough. He had hardly deemed it worthwhile to call upon his father before he left England and had been amazed when Sir James had actually come to say good-bye himself.

"Well, my boy, I hear you're off to America," he had said in his careless way, taking a chair before it was offered him.

"Yes, Father. How did you know?"

"Eh? Oh, I heard it about the Club yesterday. You could do worse, you know. They say there are fortunes to be made out there."

Gerald had let that slide and, taking a chair himself, poured them both a glass of sherry. "I spoke again to Mr. Bantree, sir, in case you are worried about that. He has sworn to do his best to settle these obligations of yours. There shan't be much left over afterward. However—"

Sir James, miraculously, waved his hand in an airy way. He who had come nearly upon his knees, begging to Gerald to "see it all right with old Bantree," seemed to have lost his anguish over the question of his debts, or, rather, his shortness of cash.

"Never mind, never mind, my boy. I shall see him tomorrow or the day after. Mind you look out for some pretty bit of native interest. Wouldn't hurt at all if you was to marry a millionaire's daughter."

Gerald had grimaced into the empty hearth. "I shall do my best, sir."

"Heh, heh—well, mind you do, my boy! Mind you do!"

Gerald recalled the conversation now, reclining in the plain armchair by the fire of Harry Brown's Albany digs. His friend had not come down from dressing yet. They were to dine on this, their first evening in the City, at the home of a business acquaintance. The memory of his father's manner on that afternoon in early summer still had the effect of giving him gooseflesh. For years he had put off admitting to himself his own parent's foolishness and lack of conscience. Now, removed from the physical and mental surroundings, which had kept him in chain to a set of traditions which no longer seemed either pertinent or reasonable, these traits of his father's took on a new harshness. Between them, Sir James and Gerald's grandfather had frittered away a huge fortune on drinking and gambling and a variety of other merrymakings. And yet their style of life, though it robbed their heirs forevermore of the luxury they had taken for granted, was condoned by everyone. Why should not a baronet keep five houses at full staff in case he should decide to visit one? Why should he not—if he could afford it—gamble away half a year's income in one evening at White's or keep a mistress in a style which might have put to shame a duchess? Ah, but there was the rub—if he could afford it! But, was it not a rather shabby way of going for one who might eventually fall on the mercy of his own son to make up his debts? For Gerald had some while since consigned to his father's use the modest inheritance left him by his mother, and now that, too, was gone. For the first time in his life he allowed himself a small shudder of revulsion at his father's conduct and swore that he should never be the cause of any of his own children's penury.

Children! Ah—the thought gave him a stab. The one woman he had ever desired to bear him heirs was gone, by now no doubt halfway to being a duchess. He thought of Charlotte, thought of her slight, upright form, the mobile neck and graceful set of her lovely head, of her wide hazel eyes regarding him as shy and candid as a doe. He thought of the soft touch of her palm and the softer touch of her lips and made himself stop just as a step was heard in the hall.

"Ready?" demanded Harry Brown. "I'm glad to see you've helped yourself to sherry—we do things very rough up here."

"I like it," said Gerald simply, gazing about the unadorned square room with its plain furniture and crackling hearth. They were in what passed as parlour for the suite of rooms.

"I'm glad," said Harry, just as simply helping himself from a decanter of sherry on the sideboard. He turned back to Gerald with a grin.

"I shall admit to you now, I thought you might stick your nose up at it."

"Eh? Why on earth?"

"Oh, the humble aspects—not ornamented or particularly couth. Neither satin nor French, if you take my meaning."

Gerald bowed his head. "I'm not so fond as all that of French or satin. In fact, I've grown quite sick of both lately."

"Is that why you came over here?" enquired Harry,

sinking into the opposite armchair and stretching out his evening-slippered feet. "I never could fathom it exactly."

"Partly," admitted Gerald with a smile.

"And what's the other part? Or do you mind saying? Curiosity, perhaps?"

Gerald smiled again and again inclined his head. He did not mind saying, in fact he would have told Harry Brown before anyone—but the painful remnants of his recent thought of Charlotte lingered on. He did not know why, but it prevented his confessing.

"Well, shall we go?" inquired Harry, standing up. He seemed to have read his companion's disinclination to speak further and tactfully prevented it.

As they walked down the cobbled street to the river-front along which their host for the evening dwelled, Harry explained his reason for wishing to dine there.

"Old Caldwell has a connection in Canada with the fur trappers. It was he, in fact, who got them organized sometime after the Revolutionary War. Before that, they all conducted their business on their own, each selling his pelts at the auctions in Quebec to the highest bidder, who, in turn, would bring them down the river to Albany and sell them to the shipping merchants for ten times what he had paid. It made for a great deal of ill feeling and led to one or two unpleasant incidents. But Caldwell had the inspiration to get them organized into a group that could command their own prices. The cost of furs has gone up markedly as a result, but the relations between trappers and merchants have improved accordingly, and, as the middlemen have been cut out, the trappers receive more of their fair share of the trade. As I am interested in taking up the shipping of furs, I had better get Caldwell on my side first."

Old Caldwell turned out to be a character of the first water. A great bear of a man with whiskers nearly covering his face, his huge hand enveloped that of Gerald, causing the latter to wince as his hand was wrung warmly and he was patted on the back. The old man—he must have been close to seventy years of age, though as agile as a man of his size could ever be—lived alone in a great square house fronting the River. From the look of its furnishings and embellishments, Gerald surmised the fur trade had done well by him. But the great man lumbered about the place as if he could not abide the delicacies with which fortune had showered him.

"Give your cloaks to Barney," he commanded them, gesturing towards another immense human, this one got up dubiously in the garb of a butler. "Bring us our wine, Barney."

Barney did as he was ordered, soon serving them with a remarkably fine vintage of claret in the ornate drawing room.

"Now then, young Brown, what can I do for you? I prefer to get business out of the way before we set to—always ruins my digestion if I try to think while eating."

Harry, with a diplomatic and yet plainspoken clarity which Gerald instantly admired, broached the subject on his mind.

"So you're interested in furs, are ye? I should think you might be, though what can possess your father to want to expand anymore, I can't hardly understand. He must have half the river trade by now, don't he?"

"Not quite that," demurred Harry Brown with a grin, "but we intend to get as much before the end of the decade. Now that Vanderbilt has moved into the passenger trade, we think it time to expand our business in cargo, and my father has an idea the fur trade is bound to do well."

"Always has, my boy! Your pa always was a clear thinker—couldn't of robbed so many of us blind, if he wasn't, eh?"

"Not robbed, Mr. Caldwell!" laughed Brown. "All legitimate trade, you know."

"Legitimate trade!" snorted old Caldwell with a twinkling sideways gleam at Gerald, "There's no such thing, I'll warrant. You listen here, Mr. Kirkland—don't go believing anything you may hear from some rackety merchant or other. Never was such a lot of thieves, I'll swear it!"

Gerald received the admonition with a laugh and continued to enjoy this original exchange of dialogue.

"Now then, Caldwell, don't you go and poison Kirkland here against us. I've every hope of persuading him to help us out, if it suits him."

"That so?" demanded Caldwell, regarding the Englishman with real interest for the first time. "Well, if you're to get into trade, young fellow, you could do worse than to do it with my friend Brown. Never was a more honest dealer on the Hudson River, and I've known plenty!"

Hearing of his possible connection with trade for the first time in the company of a third party, Gerald nearly coloured. He was more pleased than he let on, only saying, "I am certain there is none, sir."

"Hmph! That's correct. Well now, young Brown, what may I do to help you?"

With a succinctness which betrayed a good deal of mental preparation, Harry Brown put his desires before the older man. He wished first to have Caldwell's help in negotiating an agreement with the trappers and then to have a formal meeting set up between their leaders and his father and himself.

"And when d'you want it to be?"

"Yesterday, if possible. Father is presently in Boston, but he will be home in Garrison before two weeks are up. He charged me to get an arrangement worked out with you as soon as possible."

"Hmph! Not the most convenient time o' year, young fellow! The fur starts thickening about this time, and the animals must be caught before they go into hibernation for the winter. The trappers'll be out in the wild by now."

"Well, if they'd like to earn the prices for their pelts that we are willing to give them, they'd better elect one of their friends to represent them at a meeting. My father wants to begin trading before Christmas."

"Afore Christmas!" muttered the old man, shutting his eyes and puffing on a briar pipe. "Don't see how it can be done!"

Gerald glanced at Harry Brown who seemed undiscouraged and gave him a wink.

"Well, then, sir," he said rising, "perhaps we are wasting your time. Never mind, we shan't stay to sup—"

"Hold on, there, young fellow!" bellowed Old Caldwell from the depths of his armchair, "Just you sit down. Sly bit of baggage you are, ain't you? Just like your pa. Well, I reckon I can do something to oblige you, only it won't be free."

"Of course not," put in Harry with alacrity, regaining his seat. "I am permitted to offer you a generous commission on the year's shipments—say, six percent?"

"Twelve," snapped Caldwell, his eyes still closed.

"Nine—that is my limit, sir."

"Done!" cried Caldwell, springing up and grasping Mr. Brown's hand. "BARNEY! You can give us our supper, now!"

Much struck by the ease of the bargain and the singular manner in which it had been accomplished, Gerald followed their host into the imposing dining hall. As they passed through the double doors, Harry touched his arm and gave him another wink. Beginning to understand the purpose of the bargaining—not only for monetary reward but also for entertainment—Gerald grinned back.

After a meal as notable for the originality of the conversation as for the manner in which it was served, the two young men walked back through the starlit streets of Albany, pausing at the chief pier to watch a steamer, lit by a hundred twinkling lanterns, came into dock.

"I am beginning to understand your family's intoxication with this piece of water," said Gerald after a long silence.

"It is pretty gorgeous, isn't it?"

"Yes, perfectly. I wonder now how I ever believed myself aware of any natural beauty before I saw it."

"I can't imagine living anywhere else," replied Harry Brown simply. "Here we have got it all—the torrential fall of the Upper Hudson, Nature at her mightiest; the tranquillity of Garrison with her soaring mountains and swooping birds; the excitement of City life in New York. I don't think I could do without any one of them."

Gerald said nothing, staring out over the inky waters toward the few twinkling lights on the opposite shore. He was thinking of the places he had always called home, of London, the country seat in Devon and of that hunting lodge in the Scottish heath which had always been his favourite. Now it was gone, and Charlotte, too. He began to wonder if he would mind never going back.

"Did you mean what you said about wanting my help?" he inquired at last.

"Dashed right!" pronounced Harry turning towards him. "If—that is—if you have no scruples?"

"About actually earning an honest wage? None. But, I'm bound to say, I don't see what good I'd be to you."

The light from a street lantern fell halfway across

Harry's face as he replied, "You needn't understand that, so long as I do. But I'd better wait before I tell you what I have in mind; give you a chance to look round for yourself, you know?"

Feeling a small sinking in his heart—for he had hoped to learn at once what his friend's thoughts might be—Gerald agreed, and together they walked back to their rooms.

The next morning they commenced their rounds of the warehouses. These lay a mile or so away from the town on the banks of the Hudson and covered about four acres of land. Gerald was astonished at their size, their organization, and, most of all, at how handsome the structures were. They were made of rubble stone, Georgian in design, but with the Gothic influence currently fashionable in English country houses. About five hundred men were employed here, white and black, and all greeted Harry Brown with glad smiles. If Gerald had been hesitant about the idea of "slave driving," his reservations were at once dispelled. Every one of the workers looked well fed, well exercised and healthy. An old man hunched over a ledger sheet was the only being he saw above the age of fifty or under fifteen, and he was pointed out by Harry as being "an old faithful dog, our Peter—incapable of retirement from work."

"Have you child labour here?" inquired Gerald as they were looking around a huge empty vault that had just been finished.

"None here. There is a good deal at the mills. Just you glimpse what horrors go on at Massachusetts and Rhode Island! The mills make a mockery of what we have tried to do here. They employ anything, male or female, infant or crone, that has the use of its limbs. Father won't stand for anything of the kind. Everyone tells him he is losing his shirt for fear of muddying his hands, but he contends he gets more efficient and more cheerful labour from the able men he employs than he could from twice the number of children and nursing mothers. Besides, our work requires brawn as well as sheer movement. Just you look at that man over there."

Gerald looked and saw a huge brown man with a bundle the size of a dinghey upon his shoulders. He gasped.

"Can he carry that alone?"

"Alfred? He'll do!" laughed Harry, going towards the man, who put down his bundle and grinned at his employer. "Alfred, my friend Mr. Kirkland wants to know if that bundle is too heavy for you."

"Yaz, suh?" said Alfred, "Ah kin take three of *him*!"

Thinking "him" was himself, Gerald smiled nervously causing Alfred to roar with mirth.

"He means the bundle, Gerald," explained Harry. "It's full of cotton from the mills. Looks huge, but weighs less than coal. How're Minny and the baby Alfred?"

"Jez fine, suh. Minny made a batch o' buns for Miz Chastity. Said she looked mighty peaked last time she saw huh."

"Minny was Chastity's nurse," explained Harry as they moved away. "She has nine children of her own—God only knows how she manages them all—and they still keep coming!"

Gerald, confused, asked how old Minny was.

"Couldn't tell you—she was a young thing when she took on Chastity, but she must be eight or nine and forty by now."

"And still bearing children?"

Harry nodded. "Amazing isn't it? My own mother called a halt after six of us, and that was a good while back!"

The empty vault, Gerald learned, was meant to house mill-stuffs and, hopefully, furs.

"Do you think you can count upon old Caldwell to get you a contract?" he asked.

Harry raised his eyebrows and grinned. "The old fox! He'll do it for nine percent—robbery, I call it."

"Still, you were quick enough to let him have it!"

"Cheap at twice the price—for without him, there should be no furs to run. Old Caldwell has made his fortune scalping merchants like ourselves, but when he's gone, I don't know where we shall look—or the fur trappers, either."

They toured the last of twenty-two warehouses and then retired for lunch, taken at crude table in the foreman's shop. Never had brown bread, cold meat, and ale tasted so fine to Gerald. He leaned back replete and smiled at his friend.

"What next?"

"I'm off to go over the inventory with old Peter. Perhaps you'd like to walk?"

Gerald agreed and while he paced the rocky shores, looking back towards Albany at the small spot of civilization in this wilderness, his mind raced on. What could Harry want with his help? Well, he cared little enough! He should be glad to set sail that evening for the ends of the earth given the feeling in his soul just then.

The next week passed much the same, and the next, though now Gerald felt a familiarity with the place and its people and had begun to call some of them by name. Much of his time was spent idling about while Harry inventoried, checked books and consulted with various employees. Hardly ever had he been less idle, but never had he felt more so. He longed to be part of all this, to be greeted with wide grins like his friend, to be initiated into the mysteries of money-getting. In the evenings they supped—generally alone and talked late into the night, but never did Harry bring up the subject he had broached that night on the pier. One night, however, he did allude to something of great interest to Gerald.

"Your friend, Canterby," he said—looking uncomfortable—"tell me about him?"

"Not much to tell. He was a comrade of mine at Eton and again at Cambridge. His father is a great mover in the House of Lords—or rather a great immovable object, rather the same thing in that House!"

Harry laughed. "As bad as all that, eh? I had that impression a bit myself when I was over there. On, yes"—in answer to Gerald's inquiring look—"I was sent over after college. Like a good tourist, saw London and Edinburgh, and then the Continent. Very quick, though. I wish now I had spent more time though, *now*. Then I was impatient to get home away from the stuffiness and gadding about. I never *did* know what to say to a lady with scarcely any clothes on at a *soirée*!"

There followed a moment's silence, whilst each imbibed his champagne and his own thoughts. Then Harry turned to the subject, But this Canterby chap—somehow he doesn't seem at all your cup of tea. How did you come to be travelling together?"

Gerald sighed and wondered if it was to come out at last. Somehow, now that it was imminent, he felt it too far off to allude to. He said, after a moment's silence, "He was the most convenient thing when I left England. Not knowing him well made it the better. I was in a bit of a mess."

Harry looked sympathetic. "Pater?"

Gerald nodded. "Partly. Partly money and partly—a lady. I was in no mood to confide to anyone. Canterby was wit and froth but no penetration."

"Sorry, old man." A look of understanding passed between them, and no more was said on that particular head. But Harry still seemed inquisitive. "I ask, you know, only because Chastity was showing him so damn much attention before we left. Had you had words?"

"No! I'm as at a loss as you on that score. She was all smiles and charm one moment and ice the next. I suppose—"

"Well?"

"Canterby may have said something—I'm not sure. One doesn't like to jump to conclusions. He admires her a good deal and likes flirtation."

"So does Chastity." Harry looked slightly grim. "The girl will get herself into a mess one of these days. I was so pleased when she showed a shining to you—thought perhaps she'd turned out sensible after all."

"Sensible!" exclaimed Gerald. "That's not a compliment, I think!"

"In my book it is. You European light-o-loves may think differently."

Gerald would have protested had not any protestation demanded more truth than he cared to tell. Instead, he sipped his champagne with a secret smile and gazed into the firelight.

"Well, I'm off to bed, old man," remarked Harry after a little. "Seven o'clock too early for you? Good. I trust the thing smells all right, so far."

"As sweet as a rose," murmured Gerald. After his friend had gone he stayed up another hour counting the flickers of the log and the random hopes in his breast.

Chapter 19

His business at Cortlandville accomplished, Fitz Canterby took ship for Albany on the day following the departure of Gerald and Harry Brown from that city. The mission given him by Mr. Philipse was to visit one Thomas Caldwell, an agent for the fur trappers, and to complete one other piece of business.

His lodgings at Albany lay not fifty yards from the house where Mr. Brown kept rooms, and from there he walked, on his first evening, to the same large square house when his friends had been entertained not a fortnight before. His greeting there we shall not detail, as it differed but little from the one accorded Harry Brown and his English companion. Like them, he was ordered to give his hat and cloak to Barney, and like them, led into the ornate drawing room. Even from this point, his meeting with the estimable gentleman was not much different from that of his predecessors, with the exception that he compromised at eleven rather than that nine percent and was given four courses instead of six. It seemed Mr. Caldwell was less inclined to feed his employers, the more they offered him.

From the square house by the river, Canterby returned to his rooms and supplemented his dinner with a bottle of the best claret in the house. With this he offered himself a toast in the looking glass above his basin, grinning from ear to ear, and said, "Fitz, my boy, you are the very Devil! Fancy leaving England with a hundred pounds and coming out, barely three months later, a millionaire!"

Though the first part of this speech was undoubtedly
true, there was yet left some little business to accomplish
before the last was indisputably consummated. This last
was to be taken care of on the morrow, however.

Leaving his rooms just after dawn—for Canterby, in his
new enterprising role, was growing used to rising with the
sun—he walked a mile up the River, heedless of the mud
on his shining Hessians. Having reached an outcropping of
the rock which provided a clear view of the warehouses of
Brown & Sons, he kept a chilly vigil there for nigh on
twelve hours, watching the comings and goings of the employees. A little discouraged—for he saw not one man en-
feebled by work nor any sign of grave illness—he at last
settled upon an elderly person of perhaps seventy. This
gentleman—for though poorly got up, he possessed an extreme spryness of manner and walk which impressed Canterby—by happy fate quit the premises sometime after the
others. Clutching a portfolio beneath his arm, he was in
the process of hopping down the path leading to the main
road when Canterby accosted him.

Some words were spoken on either side: those of the
old man, with at first a suspicious look and then increasingly a happy one; those on Canterby's side were spoken
volubly, clearly, like those of a man who has got nothing
to hide and a great deal to offer. Some gold changed
hands; more, perhaps, than the old fellow had earned in a
year. And then Canterby vanished, leaving old Peter
Judkins to scratch his balding pate and murmur at all the
coins in his palm.

Once home again, Canterby sank down into his armchair before the fire and laughed outloud. His mirth sated,
and his thirst, he sat down at the writing table to pen a
note to Mr. Philipse. "All is accomplished," ran the cryptic
message, "just as you advised. Caldwell's in the pocket and
the other, too. I shall be arriving in New York no later
than the evening of Saturday, the twenty-second."

With much to look forward to in that City, Canterby
was not the least eager to see the effect his stratagem
might have had upon Gerald Kirkland. That fellow irked
him—he always had. From the first time he had seen the
clear-eyed boy in knickers walking ahead of him up the
chapel path at Eton, Canterby had despised him—despised

his air of openheartedness and honesty, despised his premature sense of honour which prevented his joining in the general pranks upon the masters, despised his quickness in the schoolroom. Though without realizing it, he had wished, even from that early age, to do the fellow harm. When the opportunity had been handed him by Sir James at the Solarium Club, he had taken it eagerly. But even after wrecking his love life, Canterby was to find the other man still had an edge on him. When they had arrived at New York, who had entranced Miss Brown and who the plain-faced Joanna Van Cortlandt? Who had ingratiated himself with Harry Brown, and who was the obvious favourite of all their acquaintances? Gerald Kirkland, the knave! But all that was to be put to a stop now—all that and more! Canterby envisioned Kirkland's return to Garrison with glee, imagined the somber faces of Mr. and Mrs. Brown, the consultations in the library, the summoning afterwards. But most of all, he imagined Gerald's face when he was told he was no longer welcome in their house. It was only a pity he could not be there to see it!

He had sufficient business of his own, however, to keep him busy without much thought of Gerald. His first mission was to the offices of Mr. Philipse on Wall Street, where, having signed his name to a document he scarcely bothered to read, which entitled him to a certain fixed fee at once and then to a share of the profits of a particular transaction, he was handed a draft for four thousand dollars. It was the equivalent of above a thousand pounds. He had not seen so much money at once in a decade. He then hied himself to the Park Hotel, quite a few notches in price and luxury above The Lion, and there commanded a suite of rooms. Gazing down upon Battery Park and the Hudson, he murmured to himself what a lovely river it was. For the first time since coming to America, he was truly moved by a thing of natural beauty.

Natural beauty—though not of the same grandeur—was the next order of the day, as well. Miss Van Cortlandt, whose affections he had made sure of in Cortlandville, had arranged to visit her friends, the Livingstons, at their townhouse, so as to see him once again. He was invited to dine there that evening, and feeling himself somewhat drab for the confrontation, he called for a barber to be sent to his room. His hair trimmed and pommaded, his whiskers shaved and curled, he sauntered forth to the best tailor in the City and ordered two new coats, four waistcoats, a dozen shirts of the finest cambric, and three pairs of trousers. Having capped off his purchases with a visit to a nearby haberdasher where he bought three pairs of kid gloves and one of riding pigskin, two new hats, and an ebony and ivory walking stick, he returned to his hotel to dress. By six o'clock he was standing in the entrance hall of Number 34 Beekman Place.

Mrs. Philip Livingston, his hostess, was a young woman of about four and thirty. She and the Van Cortlandt girls were very friendly, especially the elder ones, and they often came to stay with her in New York when their mother and father were not in residence. Mrs. Livingston was a handsome woman—tall, high coloured, and with a mass of reddish-black hair pulled away from her brow. She greeted him cordially, saying Miss Van Cortlandt and her sister would be down presently, and led him into the drawing room.

Here were already assembled three gentlemen whom Canterby recognized: a member of another prominent New York family; a well-known lawyer, Mr. Briggs; and a Dr. Shipley of Philadelphia. Their talk ceased abruptly when the newcomers entered the room and Briggs coughed, as if embarrassed.

"I wish you to meet a great friend of the Van Cortlandts, gentlemen," said Mrs. Livingston. "Mr. Canterby is visiting us from England."

"Very pleased, I'm sure," they all said in their various ways and then stood regarding him silently.

"Well! I should tell you, Mr. Canterby," resumed his hostess with one of those expressions of eagerness worn by people whose guests have nothing to say to each other, "that you will meet some compatriots of yours tonight. Perhaps you know them? A Miss Dunfey and her niece— they are just arrived on the *Penelope*."

A Miss Dunfey rang no bells for Canterby, and this he stated. "But, of course, I shall be happy to make their acquaintance," said he. "You do not know the niece's name?" He was hoping he should not be going to meet one of the wounded from his battles of love, nor yet a sister, cousin, or friend of such for these were often worse.

Mrs. Livingston's handsome brow creased. "Her name

was not mentioned in the letter," said she. "My sister, Mrs. Grantly, required me especially to welcome them, for Miss Dunfey was her hostess several times in England." This pleasant chitchat could not last forever, and soon Mrs. Livingston was required to look elsewhere for sustenance of the conversation. "My husband is in Philadelphia at present," she remarked for Canterby's benefit, "else he should be here this evening. He is in the Congress, you know—or perhaps you don't. But then, why should you?"

"Anyone who is not aware of Philip Livingston's reputation," said the gallant Dr. Shipley, an elderly man of strong but diminutive stature, "cannot be aware of much. He is one of our great men, Mr. Canterby."

Canterby bowed. "I have heard of him, indeed, ma'am. The Van Cortlandts were full of his triumphs in the House."

The member of the distinguished family coughed. "Very true, very true. Livingston is a fine fellow. He does us proud!"

"Indeed!" put in Mr. Briggs, a very tall man with shaggy brows and whiskers.

Again the conversation ceased, and Canterby looked round him with some nervousness. At the Van Cortlandt residence he had been taken in as one of the family at once and had done his best to stand their sentimental gossip. But here in this living room he began to see what life with Joanna Van Cortlandt would be like—tiresome evenings with tiresome old braggarts as stiff as icicles and about as witty. He was afraid to initiate any conversation himself for fear he might let slip some irreverence unfit for those long ears. He gazed earnestly into the fire, his own pointed acoustical appendages jerking.

"Well, I had better see that the card tables are properly set up," said Mrs. Livingston.

"May I help you in any way?" demanded all four gentlemen in unison, and Canterby made a mental note never to arrive at any American dinner party before at least half past the hour specified.

At length, however, Miss Van Cortlandt came downstairs with her sister, and her plain face above her sturdy shoulders for once looked to him like a gift from God. She blushed and hemmed and hawed, as was her wont, and having imbibed one glass of champagne, began to giggle. Canterby felt a great desire to move away until he thought of the three gentlemen comprising the rest of the group. He almost looked forward to the arrival of Miss Dunfey—improbable name!—and her charge.

His expectations were soon rewarded, for a footman came in to announce them a moment later. At the sound, Canterby's jaw dropped. "Miss Dunfey; Lady Charlotte Harrington," came his distinct articulation.

There must be some mistake! Canterby's first instinct was to dive beneath a chair, but he contrived to stay upright, somehow, and glanced swiftly over his shoulder. She stood poised in the archway, her small head on its long neck tilted slightly back as if she were about to walk onto a stage. Her slender figure looked more lithe than ever, and the pallor of her cheek contrasted brilliantly with the strange sparkle in her eye. There could be no mistaking her—it was the very one! How the devil—?

"My dear Miss Dunfey," Mrs. Livingston was saying, moving toward the elder person who wore the lace cap of a spinster.

Joanna Van Cortland breathed heavily and murmured, "Isn't she a beauty?" glancing at him sharply. Canterby winced.

But when the introductions were made, Charlotte smiled evenly at him. "Mr. Canterby? Yes, I believe we have met before. At Almacks, perhaps?"

"Most probably," mumbled he and then remembered, in great relief, that she could hardly know anything of the part he had played in the scheme. But why on earth was she in America?

They were not seated together, Mrs. Livingston having fondly placed him next to Miss Van Cortlandt. Another time, indeed, he would have not thought it so kind, but though he was anxious to learn why Lady Charlotte was in New York, he was not a bit anxious to sit next to her, despite her very apparent charms.

Canterby, who had watched her from a distance in England, noting her beauty as the seasoned breeder of horseflesh notices the hooves and mouths of every passing mount, was now allowed a close look at her with the beneficial distance of ten feet of mahogany between them. She seemed demure, indeed, as she had always been; but there was a difference. As her swanlike neck pivoted back and forth between Dr. Shipley and the prominent American, smiling and frowning as was called for, her eye wandered about the room, as if too restless to stay in one place. Even Canterby, who was not renowned for his sensibility toward women's feelings, noticed the change. There was something—ah, yes!—something indisputably determined about her.

"Now," thought he, gazing absently into his sherbet, "what can the Earl's daughter be doing in America and looking determined, above all?"

The answer came quicker than he would perhaps have wished. In one of the infrequent lulls in Joanna's chatter, he overheard the fragment of a question and its reply:

". . . not by any chance met a great friend of my family's who is travelling here? A Mr. Gerald Kirkland?"

The icy stare which greeted this inquiry answered a question which had been uppermost in Canterby's mind for some time.

"The young man who was travelling with Mr. Canterby?" said the prominent American, glancing secretively across the table.

Lady Charlotte coloured and glanced also, but he was too quick for her. He had already begun to laugh heartily at some particularly drab jest of Joanna Van Cortlandt's. He timed his laughter, however, so that he might overhear the rest:

"No, I have not—er—had the pleasure of meeting him, your ladyship, though I have heard his name mentioned."

"Oh! Then is he in New York? I did not know he was travelling with Mr. Canterby—"

"I don't know, I don't know!" the gentleman hastened on. "Perhaps—indeed, it is most likely they have gone their separate ways, you know? You ought to ask *him*." He nodded at Canterby.

Canterby noted the coolness of the man's tone and his evident eagerness to have done with the subject. So he had heard already of Gerald's "treachery"! And if he—then how many others? He failed not, as well, to notice the gentleman's astonishment at finding an Earl's daughter was acquainted with him. Canterby smiled inwardly at the man's evident confusion as to whether he ought to continue speaking to the young lady.

Between Joanna's tiresome patter and the ensuing four

courses, Canterby was given time to consider what his position ought now to be. Obviously, the sooner he disengaged himself from any association with Gerald Kirkland, the better. But as to Lady Charlotte, what ought he to do? Her only possible motive in coming to America must have been to find Gerald. Had she somehow discovered the scheme to separate them and come here to make it up? But such conduct from that demure lady was almost too amazing to credit. A more likely solution was that she had come here, much like Gerald, on one of those long journeys so often prescribed for young ladies suffering from broken hearts. But why to America if she knew *he* was here? And why inquire the moment she set foot in the country as to his whereabouts? But then Canterby recollected the blush which had suffused her cheek when she mentioned his name and with what difficulty she seemed to have pronounced it. No doubt she wished to know where he was so that she might be sure of avoiding him! In either case, whether she wished to meet him or not, it must be Canterby's task to see that she did not. He saw that these Americans who professed themselves so abhorrent of titles were nonetheless impressed by one when it actually shook them by the hand. He had seen the favourable impression Lady Charlotte had created and did not wish to undermine his work by having her now claim a friendship between Gerald and her family. And suddenly an idea dawned upon Canterby, an idea so simple that it had very nearly eluded him and yet which might accomplish both his aims at once.

As soon as dinner was over and the ladies had retired, he took his opportunity. The four gentlemen moved toward the end of the long table, and the port and the cigars were brought in.

"Charming lady, what?" said Dr. Shipley smiling affably at him.

"Lady Charlotte?" Oh, yes! A delightful young woman. It was—well—it was rather tragic."

Nothing could have been more keyed to raise the eyebrows and the interests of these three old sticks.

"Tragic, did you say? Dear me, what happened?"

It was just the opening Canterby had looked for, and now he took it in both hands, playing his cards, at first with some discretion, but gradually with growing confidence, allowing himself to be thoroughly pumped. "I don't know that I ought to—it involves the lady's honour, don't you know? Scoundrel!"

"Honour?" cried Dr. Shipley overcome with kindly concern. "Don't tell me that young creature has been abused?"

Three pairs of accusing eyes were focussed upon Canterby, and he sighed heavily, focussing his eyes on the crimson liquid in his glass.

"Ah, if only it had been that simple. Indeed, had I but known what the fellow's intentions were, I should never have agreed to travel with him."

Three sets of ears visibly perked up.

"Ahem!" coughed the lawyer, Mr. Briggs. "I don't suppose you are referring to that—er—Kirkland person, are you?"

Canterby looked up in evident amazement. "Then you know? Good God, don't tell me he has already been boasting of it?"

Confused looks were exchanged, and three pairs of eyebrows raised. A silent agreement seeming to have been made, the prominent American spoke up, "It has come to my—er—our attention that that gentleman you speak of—er—Mr. Kirkland—has behaved in a most treacherous fashion to a family which showed him nothing but kindness."

"Quite!" added Mr. Briggs, nodding vigorously. "One might say scoundrelish, in fact. As lawyer for the family in question, it is my unhappy duty to prosecute the fellow. I—er—we supposed he was your friend. We had no idea you had parted on less than amicable terms?"

"Amicable!" exclaimed Canterby, wondering at his good fortune in having the opportunity to chat thus with the legal counselor of the Browns'—for he surmised at once the family spoken of was that one. "We parted after a quarrel. Indeed, as soon as I discovered what his real motives were in coming to America, I had no choice but to leave his company. There was no other honourable alternative."

"Then, perhaps—" ventured the lawyer carefully, "you already know what he has done?"

"Done! Don't tell me he has already *done* something? I only knew he had an idea of making his fortune in America and then, when he became so friendly with young Mr.

Harry Brown, it occurred to me, he might—but I ought not to say what I suspected. Still, you say he has done something?"

Another silent conference seemed to go on between the three Americans, after which, Mr. Briggs having been apparently elected as their spokesman, the lawyer cleared his throat. "It appears the—uh—person in question accepted the hospitality of my clients with every intention of abusing their friendship. Apparently my client's son was about to offer him a position—a most favourable position representing their interests in England—when they discovered the fellow had already taken advantage of them. By happy chance, this painful knowledge reached their ears before the position was offered."

Canterby looked all aghast. "You are not—I hope you are not—speaking of the Browns? Good God! It is what I feared! What did he do?"

The lawyer hesitated. He was not sure whether he should reveal every aspect of the case to this young man, however sympathetic he seemed.

Canterby groaned slightly and struck his forehead. "I warned them, I did indeed! I thought it my duty. But, I ought to have done more. I ought to have followed him to Albany when he went with Mr. Brown. I suppose it happened there?"

Mr. Briggs nodded gravely, relieved that it was not up to him to recount every detail of the horrid story.

"At Albany, I am informed, he was given an elaborate tour of the warehouses and acquainted with the most intimate details of the business. While Harry Brown was occupied, he took advantage of his friend by bribing the chief clerk, an elderly gentleman, who was thought immune to any treachery of the kind."

"Bribing the clerk! By Jove, it is almost past believing."

"So it was thought by my clients," agreed Mr. Briggs. "But the old fellow has vanished without a trace, and his accounts are in disarray. There was, moreover, a letter found with Kirkland's signature upon it giving particulars of their transaction—a most astonishing slip, if I may say so, on the part of your—er—of the gentleman. Moreover, an agent with whom the Browns had dealings has suddenly gone back upon an agreement made with them during a meeting at which Kirkland was present."

"What I don't understand," said Dr. Shipley, who had been listening to all this with great avidity, "is what the fellow hoped to gain. You told me no money was lost, and apart from hurting the Browns, how was Kirkland to come out any better?"

"That is indeed the question," remarked Briggs gravely. "And we shall find out presently, I dare say. Apparently Kirkland confided sufficiently in young Harry Brown to let him know that he was not in monies."

"That is so," put in Canterby with a nod. "His father, Sir James, has run through nearly all his fortune. It is why he became engaged to Lady Charlotte in the first place."

"Engaged to Lady Charlotte!" The cry was made in unison, and three pairs of eyes were again directed at the Englishman.

Canterby contrived to look as if he had said something amiss, but he needn't have troubled himself. His audience was so thoroughly hooked, he could not have made a wrong move had he tried. He heaved a heavy sigh. "It is an appalling tale," said he.

"Well, do go on!"

"I'm afraid now I must. You see, Gerald Kirkland, when he first discovered his penury, immediately made a proposal of marriage to Lady Charlotte, whom he had known since childhood and who still retained a sort of childish adoration of him. She has a fortune, and he knew her affections were secured. After a month or so, I suppose he began to grow bored with her. He always lived very high in London—far beyond his means, I should say, which were modest—and he was used to his independence, especially with females. It was about this time that he proposed to me the idea of coming to America for a few months. Naturally, I thought it rather odd that he would wish to leave his fiancée during their engagement, but having always been eager to visit this country, I accepted. I did not know him well—we were at school together and then at Cambridge but moved in rather difficult circles afterwards—" A little emphasis on this aside led Canterby's audience to believe that Canterby's circle had a greater degree of morality.

"Anyhow, we set off, and during the voyage over he began to confide in me little bits and pieces. At first he let me know he was feeling trapped by his engagement, but this I chalked up to a young man's restless nature upon being first engaged. Gradually, however, I began to get the impression that he would break it off if there was any way to do so. And as he kept harping upon the subject of trying to make his fortune in America, it dawned upon me that this might be his idea of a solution. If he could get money from any other source, apparently it would relieve his need of Lady Charlotte. Naturally, I did not like to think so and succeeded quite well in deluding myself as to his real intentions until we reached New York." Canterby paused and sipped his wine.

Several impatient glances were given to the glass, and the lawyer cleared his throat. "Do go on, sir. What happened then to make you think otherwise?"

"Well, he met Miss Brown—Harry Brown's sister—and commenced what I considered a rather wild flirtation with her."

"Flirtation! Dear me!" said kindly Dr. Shipley, looking appalled. "And an engaged man!"

"Exactly—only he did not tell her so."

"Failed to tell her of his engagement!" said the prominent American. "Good Lord!"

"I urged him repeatedly to do so, but he laughed me off. 'Canterby, old thing,' he said to me, 'Miss Brown doesn't care if I am engaged or not. Besides, what harm am I doing?' Naturally, I began to be concerned for Miss Brown's honour. I mean, in England, at least, it is frowned upon for a young lady to entertain any sort of—er—intimate acquaintance with a gentleman who is promised elsewhere."

"Well, naturally!" grunted the lawyer, his shaggy eyebrows bobbing.

"Well, my concern on that head, anyway, was relieved presently, for Miss Brown appeared to grow tired of him. Perhaps his flippant manner annoyed her."

"Sensible girl, always was!" declared Dr. Shipley.

"Do be quiet!" muttered the prominent American.

"She appeared to converse with him less, which I may tell you relieved my mind considerably, especially as he had compared her once or twice to his fiancée, and the latter had not come out altogether favourably. I had begun to think he might be trying for Miss Brown's hand, instead!"

"Cad!" cried Mr. Briggs, forgetting for a moment his legal demeanor.

"Infamous scoundrel. Well, what then?"

Canterby paused briefly, glancing round the table. "He said something which utterly amazed me. One evening, as he was dressing for dinner, he came into my room at the Manor House in Garrison and said, 'What do you think of this, old boy? Harry Brown asked me to go to Albany with him and have a look 'round the warehouses. D'you suppose I might get something out of him?' 'What on earth do you mean?' said I. 'Come on, Canterby, don't be a dunce. He's rich as Croesus. Has more money than he can know what to do with. If I can't get his sister to share her portion with me, I don't see why he would mind if I took a little of his. He'll never miss it, you know! And I am in the devil of a bind monetarily.'

"I could scarcely believe my ears. Naturally we quarrelled, and I said I should have nothing to do with him from that day forward. I warned him if he attempted any thing foolish, I should see him squared, but he only laughed and went out. The next day he left for Albany, and I came back here. Only first I hinted to Mrs. Brown and her daughter that he might be up to no good. I didn't like to give him away if he was only talking through his hat, but I could hardly leave the lambs to the slaughter."

"I should say not."

"Well done, young man, well done!"

"Pity it did so little good, however," said the lawyer, always practical. He furrowed his considerable eyebrows ominously and glared at Canterby.

"But you never told us what Lady Charlotte is doing here, did you?"

"Poor creature!" breathed Dr. Shipley.

"Poor, indeed!" exclaimed Canterby. "I have an idea she may have come looking for her fiancée. She is desperately in love, I believe. But I think it would behoove us all to protect her from him if we can."

All agreed. It would be monstrous to throw that dainty little thing into the jaws of so mean a beast! To be sure, she would have been well rid of him had he broken the engagement.

A thought struck Mr. Briggs. "Do you suppose he will

want to marry her after all, now that his other expectations have been dashed?"

Canterby nodded. "That is why it is essential we keep them apart. Someone ought to tell her he is a cad."

All three nodded and looked at each other.

"You are the obvious one, young man," said Dr. Shipley.

"Oh, I think not," said Canterby, adding, "She is bound to credit the story more if it comes from one of you—an older gentleman with greater distinction. Perhaps you, Mr. Briggs—you would be in a position to tell her quite authoritatively, as you are acting for the Brown family."

Mr. Briggs, having had his vanity thus oiled, agreed with some reluctance. "Well, I shall undertake the task, if I must. There must be an opening made. Perhaps I should confide in our hostess? She will know what's best for a young woman. But there is still another matter. Kirkland was sent off from Garrison with his tail between his legs, all right. He was advised that if he did not quit America at once, he would be prosecuted. I have sent a man down to the wharfs to make sure he embarks on a vessel, but so far he has not appeared. His whereabouts, I am afraid, are a mystery."

"Well, if *you* can't find him, then I doubt she can," remarked the Doctor sensibly. "So at least we may be easy on that score."

"Still," said Canterby, who did not like to leave anything to chance and who was more eager than any of them to be sure of Gerald's leaving the country, "there is no guarantee that she may not meet him accidentally upon the street or something."

"Perhaps we ought to arrange to have her invited to the country?" suggested the prominent American, who had been mostly silent during all of this.

"Capital idea, Morris. Perhaps Mrs. Livingston will arrange it. We must speak to her."

Having lingered rather longer than was usual over their port, the gentlemen prepared to join the ladies, rising with important looks and clapping each other upon the back. Canterby's earlier cold reception had indeed undergone a radical change, for they now conversed with him as freely as with each other. Reviewing the conversation as he followed Mr. Briggs into the drawing room, he congratulated himself on his lastest coup. Indeed, it was beginning to look that there was little he could not accomplish once he had put his mind to it. What ever could have possessed his father to call him, on those several occasions, a "useless rotter"?

Chapter 20

Miss Marianna Dunfey peered into her trunk and looked doubtful. There seemed an abundance of lace and not much else, save for grey taffeta and her one black satin gown. "My dear," said she, sitting up, "I do not know whatever I shall do. I had no idea they were so modish here!"

"Why don't you get something new?" suggested Charlotte, who was sitting by the window watching a doleful rain come down. "Mrs. Livingston told me last night there was a very good little seamstress in Pearl Street, wherever that is. But I'm sure it shan't be hard to find. Shall we go?"

Miss Dunfey looked shocked. "Go out, my dear? In this weather! You should get your boots all muddied and catch your death."

Miss Dunfey, the elderly personage finally selected by Lord and Lady Harrington to accompany their child to America on her strange mission, was much averse to mud and wet weather, especially when it affected the feet. Her own were very small and dainty—her one great vanity. She always decked them out in brilliant slippers covered with bows and jewels, which went very oddly with the rest of her drab attire. She was also excessively careful, and especially so now, as she had been given this charge with the most severe warnings to watch Lady Charlotte like a hawk. Her cousin, the Earl (for she was not a real auntie, but the sort of distant maiden relation always called so by even the most remote of her relatives), had admonished her that his daughter had taken an absurd notion into her head of finding the young man she thought she wanted to marry, or who wanted to marry her, but who had chucked her to come to America, or vice versa. At any rate, it was all most perplexing and bizarre. Fancy a young unmarried lady flying off to a strange continent in search of a young man! They had not behaved thusly in *her* day, she was sure! And fancy it being Charlotte—demure, sensible little Charlotte—whom she had always regarded as the most feminine and proper of her young female cousins! She breathed a little sigh, embodying all of her reservations about this journey and its outcome. Surely the voyage over had been quite bad enough with that dreadful storm and the two of them clutching their plates at table so as not to get their suppers all over their laps! Thank Heaven they neither of them had been seasick, however. But now Charlotte was insisting upon staying in the hotel, though they had been offered a place by Mrs. Livingston, that kind woman, which she was sure would be infinitely preferable to any hotel.

The sound of the raindrops pattering upon the copper roof above their heads was dismally regular. Outside, the Hudson was black and churning, the cobblestones black and shiny. One or two people walked quickly by, holding packages over their heads to protect their hats. Really, it was a very dismal country!

"Perhaps I should go alone," murmured Miss Dunfey looking doubtfully out of the window. "I could get them to call me a carriage and take Jenny with me—that is, my dear, if you don't mind?"

"Oh, no! But oughtn't you to wait a bit? The rain may let up pretty soon."

"I doubt it, my dear," said Miss Dunfey peering ever more dubiously into the street. "This sort of storm usually lasts a great while."

"What a pity!" murmured Charlotte and was silent again.

"Still," went on Miss Dunfey, "you do need those new ribbons for your frock. I could get those on my way. Pearl Street, did you say?" And Miss Dunfey consulted her small map. "I don't see it—oh, yes—here it is. Quite a small affair, I must say. But not very far off by the look of

it. Well, my dear, I shall just be off, then, if you are quite
sure you don't mind?"

"I'm quite sure, Auntie," responded Charlotte almost irritably.

Miss Dunfey peered at her. Tut tut! The child was
grown quite strange of late! It was as if she was possessed
by some sort of demon!

The elderly lady sighed a small sigh and went to fetch
her walking boots. Charlotte stared after her, frowning
and already feeling a pang of guilt. It was really awfully
plucky of the dear old thing to have come along with her!
She knew a number of much younger women who would
have shied at the idea. She promised herself to make it up
to her, one way or the other.

But then her head turned back towards the wet outside
world, and her frown deepened. Last evening, their first in
New York, had promised such hope, and then it had all
been dashed! When she had learnt that that fellow, Mr.
Canterby, was travelling with Gerald, her heart had leapt.
She had determined to interrogate him as soon as the men
came in from their port. But then he had behaved so
strangely! As soon as she had walked up to him, he had
ducked his head and looked afraid of her, and then, when
she had enquired if he was in fact travelling with Gerald,
he had shaken his head vigorously and said no.

"But you were?" she had pressed him.

"Well, yes," he had admitted, as if reluctantly. "We
were at first. But I have been on my own these last three
weeks."

"Where did you part?"

The question was quite simple, it seemed to her, and
considering the eagerness with which it was asked, he
might have behaved more gallantly.

"Er—that is to say—a town on the Hudson. You will
not have heard of it."

"Mr. Canterby," she had said with great urgency but
carefully keeping her voice low for she saw they were already attracting some attention from the others, "I beg of
you to tell me where he is! I must speak to him. It is a
matter of the greatest urgency!"

Whereupon he had looked at her very sharply and muttered, "You had better not, your ladyship. No one knows
where he is!" And then he had walked off!

From that moment the evening had been ruined. None of the solicitations of the American ladies, none of their kindness nor consideration could help her. It was as if, after walking for a great while in the desert, she had seen a clear stream and, running up to it, had found it vanished into nothing! For so she felt—as if she had been walking and walking for years in a vast infertile wasteland with only the hope of seeing Gerald again to keep her alive. Her feverish state had carried her through the arguments with her father, the weeping of her mother, even the stony silence of Lord Beresford. It had carried her onto the ship and through the tedium of Miss Dunfey's monotonous chatter. But all at once, about a week before, the fever had left her, and it its place had come a sense of supreme hopelessness. How, indeed, was she to find Gerald in this vast country? What hope had she of even hearing of him, much less seeing him? And if she did—what then? At first her almost insane determination had answered that question with "I shall know when I see him!" But now—the thought of actually seeing him almost frightened her! It would end her doubts, her longings, and her fears—but with what result? Then last night, when she had seemed to be so near to finding him, all her old resolution had come back, only to be smashed but an hour later!

Charlotte stared out at the dismal rain, the dismal street, the great, turgid river, and wondered what could have possessed her to come to America? She heard Miss Dunfey call, "Well, I'm off, my dear! It's getting less wet, after all!"

"Good-bye, Auntie! Take care you don't catch cold!"

The door to the hallway closed, and Charlotte was alone. It was a relief, in fact, not having to call up her last reserves to be cheerful to Aunt Marianna. She slumped a little on the windowseat in which she was ensconced and stared about her. It was a pleasant enough room—so far as hotel sitting rooms go—cozy and warm, despite the damp. But she was not looking at the furnishings, nor at the wainscoating and moldings. Her eyes saw something else entirely: it was as if she had ranged about her, in her mind's eye, all of the people who were dear to her. On the small settle by the hearth, she saw her mother—dear, dear Lady Harrington! Without her, life would be unbearable, would it not? No, not unbearable. Much sadder, certainly—she would miss her dreadfully when she passed on. And then, with his booted leg propped upon the footstool, his elbow on his knee and his chin in his hand, was the Earl, her father. Papa! But then a cold sort of shiver passed down her spine. How dear he was, but how little she could now bear to think of him! She had always been his pet, and he had nearly petted her death at last.

Next, on the divan, were ranged all her cousins, aunts, and uncles—a great number of them! They were a jolly, laughing set, and with some of them she had shared many happy hours. Her grandfather, the Duke, sat very erect in a straight chair and glared at her. He had always been very fond of her! She thought him a dear and knew his heart would be broken when he heard she was not to marry—George Beresford—who slouched, booted and spurred, in a large armchair, his long legs crossed negligently before him. How she could ever have thought of spending her life with him, she did not know! And yet she could not help feeling a certain pity for him. So arrogant and stiff despite his cultivated slouch! Had he ever known one really happy moment in all his life?

And then, at last, she saw Gerald sitting a good way from the others, half turned away from her, as if, staring into the air, he could see something she could not. How sad he looked! As sad as that day in the Park. Her heart was wrung. To think of him sad, cold, alone, lost—she could not bear it! There was something, to her, more dreadful in the thought of that strength and virile certainty of his brought low by misery than in anything else she could imagine! It was like the thought of a wounded lion gazing up pathetically at his tormentor, unused to being weak and therefore the more anguished at his impotence. Oh, where was he?

And all at once she knew, knew with a certainty she had never felt before, that there was but one being on earth without whom she could not bear to live. She would find him—find him if it took the last drop of her strength, if it took to the end of her life. So—it was not to be an easy task? Very well, she could face it, so long as it was over at last!

She rose from the windowseat with a new brightness and went into her bedchamber where she commenced to change her frock. But just as she had reached up to pull the pins out of her hair, a maidservant knocked and entered the suite of rooms. "Lady Charlotte Harrington, mum?"

"Yes, what is it?"

"There's a gentleman to see you, mum. Here's his card."

Charlotte picked up the small square of paper, her heart stopping for a moment. But she saw at once the name was not his. "Be so good as to show Mr. Briggs into the sitting room, then. I shall join him in a moment."

"Yes, mum."

What could that old gentleman want? Puzzled, she finished her dressing with all haste and, peering into the glass, arranged a shawl about her shoulders.

Mr. Briggs was standing before the fire when she came in. His great frame turned round, and his shaggy eyebrows gathered together as he made his bow.

"How good of you to see me, Lady Charlotte."

"The pleasure is mine, sir. Shall I ring for sherry, or perhaps some tea?"

"Thank you ma'am, I am not thirsty."

"Very well, then. Shall we sit down?" She motioned him to a chair before the fire and, as she sank onto the settle, wondered at the stiffness of his manner. But then an idea struck her—perhaps he might be of some help! She coloured slightly and fought down the eagerness of her voice. "It was a very pleasant dinner last evening, was it not? Miss Dunfey and I are both astounded at the hospitality we are being shown."

"Ah, yes—very pleasant, your ladyship. Mrs. Livingston is a fine woman, and her husband is a very fine man." Mr. Briggs, however, had evidently not come to talk of dinner parties. He seemed to hurry through these niceties until he reached a point where he could safely come down to what he had to say. "A—hem, Lady Charlotte, I am afraid I have not come altogether on pleasant business."

Charlotte grew white—could it be—? But he rushed on, and what she soon heard was much worse, even, than what she had feared.

"I have it from your acquaintance, Mr. Canterby, that you have—er—entered into an engagement with his friend, Gerald Kirkland?"

The name brought her up short, but she managed a smile. "No—that is, I am afraid you are mistaken. Mr.

Kirkland and I are very old friends, but we are not engaged. I have, however, a great interest in seeing him. Can you tell me where he is staying?"

"Not engaged?" said Mr. Briggs, puzzled. "I am quite certain he said you were engaged! Are you quite sure?"

Charlotte smiled despite herself. "Quite sure, Mr. Briggs. A lady generally remembers to whom she is engaged, you know!"

"What, eh? Quite, quite! Dear me—well, perhaps I should not have bothered you about it, then."

"Have you some news of him, sir? I beg you, if you have, to tell me at once, for I have come a great distance to see him, and though we are not engaged as yet, I hope we shall be, very soon!" All this came rushing out of Charlotte's lips almost before she knew what she was saying, for in the panic of seeing Mr. Briggs rise, she desired to say anything that might make him stop. She bit her lip and fell silent as the gentleman gave her a puzzled look.

"Well, this is all very strange, ma'am. However, if you have such an interest in the gentleman, perhaps I had better tell you all. I suspect, however, that when you have heard me out, you will change your mind about wishing to marry him."

Charlotte's candid gaze that seemed to say "I challenge you to tell me any such thing!" must have disconcerted him slightly, for he walked to the fire as if to arrange his thoughts. "I am very sorry to have to tell you, your ladyship, that this gentleman—er—Mr. Kirkland—has behaved himself very badly while he has been in this country. So badly, in fact, that I have been directed by my clients to bring a suit against him if he does not at once quit America." Briggs let this sink in for a moment before turning round. When he did, he saw a pair of very bright eyes burning into his.

"I will believe no such thing of Mr. Kirkland, sir! I beg you to explain yourself!"

The lawyer heaved a sigh and took his seat again. "Very well, young lady, if you must know everything, I shall tell you. Believe me, I have no desire to bring this action, and I would give much to be able to say that I have told you an untruth. But the facts of the matter are indisputable, and I shall lay them before you, that you yourself may judge."

Mr. Briggs proceeded to do so, recounting everything he had learned from Mr. Brown and much that he had heard from Mr. Canterby. He desired suddenly to do whatever lay in his power to prevent this pretty young woman from making a fool of herself over a cad, and therefore he spared her nothing; not the flirtation with Miss Brown at which she winced; not the camaraderie with Mr. Harry Brown, which did not affect her; nor the lurid details of his visit to Albany and subsequent dismissal from the Manor House at Garrison.

At these last words, her mouth fell slightly open, and she looked almost inclined to laugh. When he had finished, she sighed deeply and said, "Well, I am afraid there must be some mistake! Surely you are speaking of someone else, for Gerald Kirkland is incapable of any such kind of thing!"

Mr. Briggs looked into his lap and frowned. "My dear Lady Charlotte, I am not mistaken. I can well understand your disinclination to believe any wrongdoing on the part of your—er—your friend. However, I am quite sure it is the same person. Let me ask you, is his father not a baronet, Sir James Kirkland?"

Charlotte was very pale. "Yes."

"And, is that same baronet, Sir James, not practically penniless?"

"Yes." It was a very faint sound.

"Is not his son equally poor and, as might be understood of anyone in his position, eager to improve his—er—his financial status?"

Charlotte, pale though she was and trembling, managed to look fierce. "Not at the cost of his honour, Mr. Briggs, nor of the law!"

Mr. Briggs looked pitying. "My dear young woman," he said gently, "I am an old man and have been in the law for nigh on forty years. I have seen a great many fine young men turn callous when their pockets are empty."

"But not this young man!" exclaimed Charlotte, rising from the settle. "Not this young man, sir! Good day, Mr. Briggs. I trust when we meet again that you shall apologize for your mistaken accusations!"

Mr. Briggs looked resigned. Clearly there was nothing he could do but leave. He moved towards the door. "Ah,

Lady Charlotte—" he began, turning round with his hand upon the knob.

"Yes?" Her face and voice were like cold stone.

Poor thing—Mr. Briggs could not but pity her—to be in love with such a one! "If you doubt my word, perhaps you will not doubt that of my client, Mr. Robert Brown. He is a respected man in this country."

"Thank you," said Charlotte icily. "I shall think about it."

But when Mr. Briggs had left, she was not capable of thought. She fell down, limp, upon the settle, not in a faint, but in a state of utter collapse—emotional, physical, and mental. Could there be anyone who had borne as much as she in these last months? To be told that her lover was deserting her, then that he was a blackguard! To have been through so many ups and downs, so many revolutions of sorrow and of pain? For a time she gave way to self-pity and wept her heart out.

But Charlotte's grief did not last above an hour. Before that time was up, she was upon her feet again, pacing back and forth across the little room, as defiant as she had seemed to Mr. Briggs.

"How dare they!" she cried out loud. "How dare they accuse Gerald of treachery—Gerald! I will not—nay—I *cannot* believe it! Never was there a kinder, better man! Did he not leave England for my sake, and for my sake alone?" If a shadow crossed her mind at that moment, the merest suggestion that what Mr. Briggs had said was true, she swept it away at once. "No!" she exclaimed, as if in defiance of her very thoughts, "No!"

And then another sob escaped her lips, but this one was not from pity for herself but from anger at the injustice of the world. Some little while did she pace, thinking frantic and outraged thoughts. But by the time Miss Dunfey came in from her shopping—much bedraggled and very muddied—Charlotte was as calm as the eye of a hurricane.

"Auntie," she declared before the poor woman had had time to shake out her cloak or take off her muddy boots, "we are going up the Hudson tomorrow."

"Up the Hudson?" demanded the elderly woman, dumbfounded. "Why, my dear, we have only just got here!"

"Yes, yes, I know it. But nevertheless, we are going up the Hudson tomorrow. I have some business with a family called Brown, and they live in Garrison. It is not much of a journey—you shall see—only a day and half, I think, by steamer."

Miss Dunfey trembled in her wet boots.

"Steamer, did you say, dear? Oh, my! I don't think I shall like that at all! Must we, dear?"

"We must," said Charlotte firmly, and then, with an anxious look at her chaperone, she enquired, "Is it too much for you, dear? I can go alone, if it is."

"Alone? My Lord, no! Whatever should your father say to me? Very well, Charlotte—I shall go pack my trunk."

"That is very good of you, Auntie," said Charlotte humbly. "I wouldn't ask you, you know, if it wasn't absolutely required."

"Yes, yes, my dear" and Aunt Marianna twittered off. Really, these modern young girls were altogether a puzzlement!

Charlotte looked after her receding back with a grim smile. Well, if it was true, she would have it from the horse's mouth. And, if it wasn't—well, she would not cross that bridge till it was burned behind her!

Chapter 21

The excitement of the treachery having died down some days before, Miss Chastity Brown was somewhat at a loss as to what to do with herself.

It had been a time of great fervour and passion—things Chastity adored and without which she could not live. Indeed, so fervid and so passionate had everyone become that she had hardly known them. Even her normally gentle mother had succumbed to the general hubbub, and one evening Chastity had actually heard her mother and her father exchange one or two angry words—an event unprecedented in that house. Harry had been disbelieving from the start and was so angry with her that he would not speak. Really, it was a shame, when she had single-handedly saved them from a blackguard! Or very nearly single-handedly—there had been that funny little man, Mr. Canterby, but he had fled after dropping his tidings. But whoever had averted the disaster, or created it, the result was the same—Gerald Kirkland had gone off, not even endeavoring to defend himself, and now Chastity's life was very quiet and dull. Whether or not he was a scoundrel after all, he had been very good looking, and her quarrel with him had added liveliness to her existence. But now life was getting back to normal at the Manor House, and she was restless. She was not the least disappointed, therefore, when, upon coming in from a dull walk one mild afternoon in late October, she was greeted with the news that two visitors had come to call.

"Visitors?" she inquired of the butler. "Who on earth?

Not Mr. Bunk, I hope?" Mr. Bunk was her eternal suitor—a most pathetic specimen of the opposite sex.

"No, Miss Chastity. They are two ladies—English ladies, I believe. They are upstairs with your mother."

Chastity promptly went up and, opening the door, was amazed to see a very old, and mousy-looking but bright-eyed female and a perfectly lovely young one.

"Oh, my dear," said Mrs. Brown, "we have some visitors."

"Yes, Mama, I have eyes," said the young woman.

"Don't be impertinent, my dear. I should like you to say how-d'you-do to Miss Dunfey and Lady Charlotte Harrington—they have come all the way from England."

"Lady Charlotte Harrington!" echoed Chastity, staring in amazement at the younger of the two. Lady Charlotte! Was not that the name of the lady Mr. Kirkland had so ill used? Chastity stared in fascination. Was this her rival then? For they *had* been rivals, after all, for a few days before Mr. Kirkland was disgraced, had they not?

"This is my daughter Chastity," Mrs. Brown was going on. "Perhaps she can be of more help than I."

"How d'you do?" said Chastity, sitting down. "What help, Mama?"

Mrs. Brown looked uncomfortable. "Lady Charlotte is concerned about a friend of hers—Mr. Kirkland, my dear. She says she heard from Mr. Briggs in New York that we had a disagreement with him."

"That's right," said Chastity, looking with much interest at the pretty young lady. "And it was high time, too!"

"Now, my dear—" said Mrs. Brown.

"Well, after all, he *did* desert you, didn't he?" said Chastity to Lady Charlotte, who turned white and looked away.

"My dear Lady Charlotte," said Mrs. Brown very rapidly with a vexed look at her daughter, "you mustn't mind Chastity. She is much too candid—"

"This is hardly the time to mince words, Mama!" said the candid young lady. Moving into a chair closer to Lady Charlotte's, she patted her hand. "You're well out of it, I assure you, your ladyship! He was nothing but vile, perfectly vile! Imagine, he never even told us you were engaged to be married! Mr. Canterby told me all about it, you see, and—"

Charlotte's graceful head on its long neck swung round and her eyes sparkled. "But there was nothing to tell, you see! We were *not* engaged! He never asked me to marry him because he thought himself too poor! Miss Brown, I tell you that someone has been deceiving you, and Mr. Briggs as well! Why does everyone think he was trying to break our engagement when he came to America?"

Chastity did not know what to say. At last she settled for: "Are you *quite* sure you are Lady Charlotte Harrington? I am positive it was the name Mr. Canterby told me. And you have a great fortune and—"

Charlotte could do nothing at this moment but smile. "I only wish what you say were true, Miss Brown! I am indeed Charlotte Harrington, and my father is an Earl, but I have no great fortune. I am sure that you are much richer than I."

Mrs. Brown felt the afternoon was not a success. In bewilderment she looked from one of her guests to the other and was at least relieved to see that Miss Dunfey looked quite as puzzled as she.

"Do you understand what they are saying?" inquired the elderly lady. "I do not even know what we have come about! Indeed, had I known what a confusing country this was, I should never have agreed to visit it! First the storm on the ship, and then the great puffing barge, and all the rain, and ruining my boots, and— Well! I don't know that I shall be able to bear any more!"

"Hush, dear," said Lady Charlotte, patting her relative's hand. "It shan't last much longer, I hope."

"I should say so!" cried Chastity, jumping up. "My lady, would you mind dreadfully coming into my sitting room for a few moments? I think we have a great deal to say to one another."

"Gladly," said Lady Charlotte, rising. "Auntie, will you be all right?"

"Oh! I shall take care of your aunt, my dear!" twittered Mrs. Brown, giving the elderly lady now wearing a scowl a reassuring glance.

"They are too fast for words," muttered Miss Dunfey watching them out the door. "Not at all what young ladies were like in *my* day!"

"I dare say so," ventured Mrs. Brown in what she hoped was a tranquillizing voice. "Girls are very lively nowadays."

"Hmph!" grunted the chaperone, whose really very generous spirit seemed to have been taxed to the limit.

In Miss Brown's sitting room things were still more lively. Having taken the chair offered her, Charlotte was listening in amazement to the tale recounted by the young American lady. It was a slightly abbreviated version of the one told to her by Mr. Canterby.

"But—why on earth should he tell you such a thing?" gasped Charlotte when she had heard the whole. "Unless —unless, of course, it was to discredit Gerald!"

"Then you never *were* engaged, after all?" demanded Chastity, fixing upon her companion the full force of her bright dark eyes. "And he never ran off?"

"He "ran off" as you put it, Miss Brown, only because he thought I wished to marry my cousin who is very rich. But, you see, it was only a trick of my father's who thought I shouldn't mind. Only, of course, I did—I nearly died of a broken heart. And all the while I thought Gerald had discovered he did not love me. So, you see, we have all been deluded. Only now that I have found out the truth, I am determined to find Gerald, if only to tell him that *I* never wished to desert *him*."

"Well!" declared Miss Brown, her eyes snapping, "What a pretty kettle of fish this is, to be sure! Fancy how wrong I have been, believing that dreadful Canterby person. I suppose he was jealous of Ger—of Mr. Kirkland, don't you?"

"Quite possibly," murmured Charlotte, thinking of the small weaselish person she had spoken to at Mrs. Livingston's. "Was he—were they—flirting with you?"

Chastity opened her mouth, then closed it again.

"No," she said, very positively, "not they. Mr. Canterby threw himself at my ankles and barked, like a funny little dog, only I did not let him nip me. Ger—Mr. Kirkland was excessively nice. I mean, we had some very pleasant conversations and all that, until I learned he was hiding his engagement. Naturally, I thought it was because he was dishonourable, so I did not speak to him after that. But how wrong I was, Lady Charlotte, how very wrong!" The young woman's face looked exceedingly earnest, and she bent forward as she spoke. "I blame myself now for what happened afterward. Perhaps if I had been more civil, he would not have tried to rob—er—to deceive my brother. D'you suppose it might have prevented it if I had?"

Lady Charlotte had risen abruptly from her chair and now moved toward the window. "I do not believe," she said very quietly and with great intensity, "that Gerald is capable of any such thing. I never knew a man who was better, nor more honourable. I never knew a man who felt more deeply!"

Impressed by the manner of her companion, Miss Brown sat silent for a moment. "You're right," she said, "quite right! It does seem strange that a man who would give up his lover out of gallantry would be inclined to cheat his friend! Harry still won't believe it, you know. He has hardly spoken to me since that day."

"Do you think *I* could speak to your brother?" demanded Charlotte suddenly, spinning around.

"Harry? Why yes—I suppose so! I shall send for him." Miss Brown went to the bell, and a maid came in. "Go and fetch Mr. Harry, will you, Bertha?"

"Mr. Harry is gone ridin', Miss Chastity."

"Oh, what a bother! Well—ask him to come up here straight away when he comes in, will you?" The maid ducked and went out.

"He shan't be long, my dear Lady Charlotte," said Miss Brown, who had begun to adopt a quite proprietary tone in her conversations with the former. Whatever envy she had felt on first seeing this breathtaking creature had now given way to admiration and affection. Already her heart was given to the lovely pale creature in the sky-blue travelling costume, whose quiet manner masked so much passion and determination. She was tempted to sit down and take the young lady's hand. "Lady Charlotte," she said with a frank humility of manner unusual in one of her vivacity. "I shall confess something. There was a day or two when I really thought I could fall in love with Mr. Kirkland—he seemed to me the finest thing I had ever beheld and so very gentlemanly! But now I have met you, I tell you frankly, I should like to do anything in my power to help you see him again if that is what you wish."

Touched, Charlotte only nodded and whispered, "Thank you, dear Miss Brown!"

As Harry did not come in from his ride for twenty minutes, the young ladies had an opportunity to converse together, and this they did with genuine pleasure. By the time Mr. Brown strode into the room, they had confided a good many things, and each felt a little the better for having met the other. What's more, the crisis which had brought them together seemed to cement their mutual regard and to make of this quiet half-hour in the pretty pink sitting room, an interlude upon which each would look back with happiness in the years to come. For Charlotte, who had felt utterly alone for many months, it was a chance to speak openly to a disinterested but sympathetic female, and it gave her a feeling of warmth for which she was very grateful. As for Chastity, her admiration for the other grew with every word. Imagine looking so feminine and being so strong! She had never had an idol when she was a little girl—no older woman who inspired her desire to emulate or even to mimic; now this young woman, barely her own age, filled her with such a longing.

"Well Harry! said Chastity when her brother came in, "You've been an age! You've no idea who this is!"

Harry, who was a bit more reserved, said he did not.

"It is Lady Charlotte Harrington, the lady Mr. Kirkland jilt—er—was never engaged to, but who *meant* to be engaged to him, only she never was, if you see what I mean."

"I'm afraid I don't, Chastity."

"Don't you? Well you shall—"

"If I may be so bold, Mr. Brown," interrupted the quiet voice of Lady Charlotte, "I shall explain. You see, Gerald and I were planning to become engaged, but then learned that he was very poor, much poorer, even, than he had known before, and my father—well, it is a long story, but it appears we have all been deceived. Like you, I was led to believe his intentions were other than the best; but I have found out my error and I have come to let him know that I still love him if he will have me. It seems that his friend, Mr. Canterby, has been telling tales about him, so that you might think ill of him—"

"HA!" exclaimed Harry, "I never liked the little beast! What did I tell you, Chastity, eh? So, he had no intention of breaking his engagement!"

"No," Charlotte went on, despite the interruption, "for there was no engagement to break."

Harry's face, which had been so enlivened for an instant, now became grave again. "This is all very well

Lady Charlotte; but perhaps you do not know that Mr. Kirkland is suspected of doing us all a grave offence."

"I have heard the story," cut in Charlotte brusquely, "and I cannot credit it. Indeed, I am tempted to believe that it is yet another fabrication of some mind too idle, or too jealous to——" All at once she stopped, and her head went up to her mouth. The other two stared at her in bewilderment.

"Well, your ladyship, what is it?" demanded Harry, exasperated with all of this confusion.

"Fitzwilliam Canterby!" she muttered slowly, "Fitzwilliam, now I recollect!"

"What, oh what do you recollect?" cried Chastity, running to her.

But Charlotte remained silent, her eyes growing wider every second as she gazed off into the air. At last, having thoroughly frustrated her audience she inquired softly, "Will you help me, Mr. Brown. Pray, will you?"

Impressed by the quiet intensity of the question, impressed still more by the extraordinary loveliness of the questioner, Harry drew himself up. "In any honourable way that I can, ma'am, I should be more than obliged."

"Thank you!" she cried, jumping up and seizing his hands. "Oh, thank you!"

Chapter 22

Having hardly slept or eaten in five days, having lived much like an animal hiding in his hole and scarcely daring to show his face for fear that yet some other stroke of ill-fortune would crash down upon it, Gerald kept vigil in the shabby rooms he had taken in the town to which his weary legs had carried him after the scene with the Browns.

Hardly yet had he begun to grasp the meaning of it all. To have sunk in their eyes from a gentleman and friend, one to be treated with kindness and generosity, to a sort of beastly highway thief! He had been too astounded upon hearing the accusations laid out against him even to raise a hand in his own defense. How could he do so, after all? What proof had he, except his honour, that he had not done all he was accused of? And they, on the other hand, seemed to have reams of evidence! At first, too weary of the world which seemed never to tire of punishing him, he did not even consider how circumstances could have so arranged themselves that he was accused at all. In his own country he would have had his good name and familial standing to count upon. In England, even the heir to a poverty-struck baronetcy would not be lightly accused of a crime! But here in America, where titles were things to be poked fun at, what cared they for the fact that he would one day be 'Sir Gerald'? And what was his word, a stranger's, against that of one of the most respected families in the country?

Besides, his wits had been taken too much by surprise to

enable him to think clearly. Even the memory of that
small group awaiting his and Harry's return from Albany
in the library was too painful to contemplate. He remembered it all going terribly fast—the grim face of Mr.
Brown, that gentleman he had not even had the benefit of
knowing when he was not *persona non grata*; the worried
twitters of his wife, who seemed too anguished by having
such a scene in her own home to make any comprehensi-
ble remark; the triumphant look of Miss Chastity Brown,
for whom, it seemed, this occasion was a happy one; and
the appalled, horrified look of Harry as he heard the news.
He hardly remembered what had been said. The encounter
had not lasted long, certainly. Mr. Brown had uttered a few
terse sentences expounding his guilt; Harry had made an unsuccessful attempt to defend him; and he had remained
mostly silent. He believed he had said something about his
word as a gentleman and having no proof other than that
to defend himself, which seemed horribly paltry against
the facts laid out against him. He recollected holding out
his hand, offering to leave the house at once, and having
the offer accepted but not the hand. He recollected Harry
following him to the door but failing to meet his eye,
remembered something about being told his trunks would
be sent after him and recalled being driven by a silent
coachman to the dock.

But he had not taken ship, though there was a steamer
due at any time going to New York. Instead, he had
walked, walked until his legs were too weary to take another step and he had no idea where he was. He had sat
down behind a thicket by the roadside, unmindful of the
cold October wind, and there, at last, he had fallen asleep.
On the following day he had walked farther until he
reached another town bordering the Hudson, this one too
small even to boast a pier. He had found lodgings at a
place too humble to be called an inn, and there he had remained ever since.

Lying on the board that was distinguished by the name
of bed, walking to the window and back again, he had
passed the remaining days, too much in shock to contemplate the future. He had only the clothes upon his back,
for he had not yet sent word where his trunks could be
shipped. He had not the slightest idea what he should do.
All his hopes had been dashed in these last months. En-

gland was hopeless—he could not bear the notion of returning to the land where Charlotte was married to another. America, which had promised so much good, would not stomach him. No—he had not the slightest notion what he could do, nor where he could go. One thing only filled his mind: he must clear his name before he left. The country and the family which had welcomed him so warmly must not be left with this bitter recompense for their generosity. If he were never to see them again—and it seemed now that he would not—at least they would remember him as an honourable man and a gentleman.

Yet where to begin? That question revolved in his mind till the words were meaningless and only their echo sounded in his thoughts. Where to begin, indeed? He had no notion where Mr. Brown could have discovered any proof against him. That fellow, Caldwell—he had called off the agreement made in his own hearing. But why? With only this one idea to go upon, Gerald called for hot water and a razor and prepared to make a journey.

In the little town, called Emery, he discovered that it was possible to be taken by sloop to the nearest port of call of the steamers. He arranged with an ancient captain to be given a ride with a load of coal and by nightfall was in Poughkeepsie. Here he lodged for the night, and next morning at dawn he stepped aboard a steamer. And yet how different was this journey from the others he had taken upon these wonderful machines! Three times before he had travelled by steam, and always in the most pleasurable of circumstances. He remembered his first time, stepping on the *Arcadia* at New York when he had just met Harry and Miss Brown. And then, going up the Hudson, this same passage, not a month before, with Harry—how different had that been! His hopes had been high, his interest fervid, and Harry and he had cemented their friendship on that journey! And then, hardly a week ago, coming back from Albany eager to learn what offer his friend would make him—for Harry had talked of it a great deal, putting off only the actual pronouncement till he had consulted with his father. "How much you shall like each other!" he had said. And how little had his expectations been fulfilled!

Gerald stood at the railing of the steamer, his hat pulled over his eyes so that he would not be recognized, and watched the shoreline pass. That fellow Caldwell—well! He would see him, and perhaps get a clue. If only he could find the old man—what was his name? Ah, now he remembered—hadn't Harry said he was too faithful an old dog to be retired from the warehouse? And yet he had been bought off! After sixty years of faithful service and being treated like one of the family! There was no telling what a man would do if he needed money. And suddenly, staring at the shoreline, Gerald took a deep breath. Money! Could it be . . . ?

They approached Albany, his thoughts churning more fiercely than the water beneath the rudder blades. He glimpsed a large square house set back a little from the river and recognized it as Caldwell's place. Yes, well—that fellow could tell him something if only he were made to!

He stepped off the steamer at the same spot where he had stepped on another a week earlier and hastened into the town to make enquiries. An hour later, having break-fasted heartily on his first solid meal since leaving the Browns', he set off down the river road towards Caldwell's place.

"Mrs. Judkins," said Harry Brown, "I must see your husband!"

The ancient woman, huddled into her shawl, looked pet-rified. She glanced from the stern face of Mr. Brown to the worried one of the lady—a real lady, too, not just a regular one! Fancy, and standing in her own front par-lour!

"I ain't seen him these past days," she muttered for the second time. "T'ain't like Judkins to go off like that! I been with 'im these three and fifty years, nigh on, sir! 'E never once left me alone like this and with me legs so rheumy, too! 'Tis all I kin do to walk, ye know! I'm assured somethin' is amiss. D'you suppose he's gone and died?"

She stared at him with eyes wide from fright. It was ap-parent from the look of her, thought Harry, that she had not slept or eaten much since her husband's disappearance.

"No, I am sure that cannot be the case," he murmured reassuringly. "Perhaps you will give us some tea, ma'am, and then we shall talk it over calmly."

Mrs. Judkins bobbed and went off in search of her

kettle. She brewed the tea and shortly they were ensconced in the small but cozy room in front of a roaring fire.

"Now, Mrs. Judkins," commenced Harry once again, "tell us about the last time you saw your husband. Did he mention anything about a sum of money?"

"No, indeed!" exclaimed Mrs. Judkins. "Jest what he always gits come Friday. But it was a Thursday when he took off."

"Did he come home from work that evening?"

Mrs. Judkins' eyes widened, and she shook her head.

"Come now, Mrs. Judkins—tell the truth. No one will hurt you." There was silence while the old woman pressed her knotted hand over her eyes and breathed. "He never come home," she said stubbornly.

Harry glanced at the fire in the hearth. There were four great logs in it and two more standing ready beside.

"Now, Mrs. Judkins," he spoke gently, "I know you cannot have put those logs into the grate, nor yet stacked these others beside it. I know your husband is about somewhere. You must get him. You must believe that we shan't hurt you. You see, a man has been accused of a crime which we believe he did not commit, and your husband is the only one capable of telling us who the real culprit is. Go and get him, ma'am—I pray you!"

The old woman glanced at the young gentleman whose frame was leaning towards her in his eagerness and then into the young lady's face. It was those eyes that had done it, she thought later—she never could bear to see so much pain in one face! Still, she did not budge, her lips pressing together tightly and a heavy breathing issuing from her nostrils.

"'Twas my own doing!" she exclaimed at length with an incredible vehemence. "You must not blame Judkins. He's such an old fool, he couldna done anything to hurt you, sir! 'Twas I put 'im up to it, that day he came home with the strange tale of how a funny little man wanted to offer 'im gold, jest so's he'd hide hisself a while! 'E weren't goin' to do nothing, sir, till I made 'im, I swear it! 'Judkins,' says I, 'you been sweating out your poor old bones this age, an' never did see the likes of so much gold as you got in your fist now! What's the harm in hidin' yerself, a wee bit? Tain't as if you was to do anything wrong nor hurtful to Mister Brown and them. All ye got to do is hide yerself a wee bit to make yer fortune, an' then p'raps we kin have a girl to help us, an' p'raps a new coalstove, like what I seen. Nothing much, surely!' "

The old woman stopped, and before their eyes began to sniffle audibly. " 'Harriet,' 'e says, 'no good never come o' lying.' But 'e did it after all, when I begged 'im. See, Mister Brown—yer ladyship—I be that frightful bad in me hands and legs, an' poor Judkins, 'e kin hardly manage no more!"

Charlotte stared in dismay at the old woman and then glanced at Mr. Brown. She saw that he, too, was affected by the story.

"I never knew you were so badly off, Mrs. Judkins," said he now. "Indeed, I did not! But I promise you shall have a girl to help you, and the coalstove too, and anything else my father and I can do to help you out if you will go and fetch your husband."

Shaking her head—for she never had believed that good could fall out of the sky without your doing something to get it—the old woman hobbled off to the kitchen. They heard her scuffling about, the sound of a door opening and then her call. In a few minutes she returned, followed by Judkins, who, from the look of him, had been folded into a coalbin himself. He wore a very sheepish look and, hardly daring to meet Harry's eyes, sat down upon a stool before them.

"Now then, Peter," said Harry gently, "this lady and I have just heard from your wife that you were offered some money to hide yourself last week. I suppose you can't have heard what has gone on since you left the warehouse?"

The old man still with his eyes to the ground, shook his head. "No, sir."

"Well, then, I had better tell you that your hiding has helped to discredit an innocent man and that whoever offered you that gold is a villain. I must know who it was, Peter!"

The old man, too miserable to raise his head, kept shaking it, as if by doing so he might shake off his crime. " 'E was a little bit of a gent, sir—not 'alf so tall as you, nor 'alf so broad. 'E never tol' me 'is name, but said I might expect to 'ear from 'im when I might come out of 'iding.

'E gave me five dollars, sir, and told me I might have five more when 'e came back."

"And what were you to do, Judkins? How were you to explain yourself to me?"

The man looked even more miserable than before. " 'E said 'e'd make it all right with you, sir. Fact is, 'e told me 'e was a partner of yourn. I didna understand, sir, but I meant to ask you yourself, only you had already gone 'ome, sir."

"A partner of mine?" demanded Harry, thunderstruck. "Presumptuous bloke! But you didn't get his name?"

"No, sir. The worst part of it was, 'e made me give 'im my ledger sheets. The rest I didna mind so much—but I knowed you wouldn't want me giving them to anyone else, sir, without yer express permission."

Harry sighed, and stared into the fire. Having watched and listened in silence until now, Charlotte ventured to speak, "Excuse me, Mr. Judkins, but will you tell me something? This man who spoke to you and offered you money, was he—did he look a bit like the Devil? Pointed ears and curly dark hair?"

Evidently the idea struck old Peter with some force. Not an ignorant man, and very clever with numbers, he still possessed the fear of demons common among his Welsh ancestry. He trembled visibly.

"Was 'e the devil, ma'am? I though 'e might of been! Coming upon me like that tempting me!"

"No," said Charlotte kindly, "he wasn't the Devil, only a Devilish sort of man. Mr. Brown, I am quite sure I know who our villain is. It is Mr. Canterby."

Harry, who had been coming to the same conclusion himself, nodded slowly. "It seems so, Lady Charlotte. Fool that I was! I ought to have put two and two together! After hearing of one untruth he had perpetrated against his friend, why did I not realize he would not mind stooping to even worse antics?"

Charlotte smiled at the bewilderment in the eyes of Mr. and Mrs. Judkins, who both seemed extraordinarily relieved that their visitors' wrath was not directed at themselves.

"Well," said Harry, rising, "I shall take you back to Chastity in Bleaker Street, and then I have another bit of visiting to do. Peter, do go and bathe—you look a fright.

And I shall want you back at the warehouse as soon as you can get there—there is much cleaning up to do amongst the books!"

Judkins bowed, a comical maneuver, and grinned ear to ear.

"Yes, sir!" he exclaimed.

"And mind you don't accept any more money from strange men, eh? We shall see about your stove, Mrs. Judkins, and your servant. Good day!"

In their journey from the Judkins's little house to the lodgings at Bleaker Street, they had a few moment's hasty consultation.

"Poor things!" murmured Charlotte when they were in the carriage.

Harry grinned. "Poor things, indeed! Well, I shan't ask Judkins to give back that five pounds. If Canterby has lost them, it's a small price to pay! I shall leave you with Chastity, Lady Charlotte, if you don't mind. I am going to pay a call on Mr. Caldwell, our exofficio agent."

Charlotte did, in fact, mind. Having initiated this investigation, she wished to be a part of it all and not left in rooms with Chastity to gossip. But Harry Brown was vigorous in his protestations. Caldwell was a sly fellow. There might be trouble, though he hoped not. The ladies had better stay behind. "Besides," he said, "we have still to find Gerald. And then there is Canterby to think of—what shall we do to him?"

Charlotte could think of several things to do to that gentleman, but none which would become her as a lady to mention. The question of finding Gerald was now of much greater importance.

"Well, you may wrack your brains, the two of you, while I see Caldwell. He may be able to give us a clue about Canterby's whereabouts, if, in fact, it was Canterby made him forestall our agreement. But why on earth—? That is something I still cannot fathom!"

At that moment, as it happened, Gerald was in the process of beginning to fathom it himself.

He had gained admittance to the great square house on the river with some little degree of difficulty, for it appeared Mr. Caldwell did not receive people without appointments. At length, however, having assured the ungainly butler that his business was of the utmost urgency, he was reluctantly allowed to go in. In the upstairs hallway he passed a gentleman of vaguely familiar appearance who seemed to be on his way out. They bowed to each other, as strangers do meeting on unfamiliar territory, and passed on. It was only when Gerald's hand was already on the knob of Caldwell's study door that he recollected the face.

"Philipse!" he breathed and turned sharply around in time to see the other gentleman had done the same. Each caught out, they bowed again, and Gerald went into the room.

"Well, Mr. Kirkland, what an unexpected pleasure, to be sure!" exclaimed the huge man seated behind the desk. He heaved himself up and smiled what Gerald thought was not in the most genuine happiness.

"What brings you to my humble house, sir?"

"I think," said Gerald, taking the seat that he was motioned towards, "that perhaps you know already, Mr. Caldwell."

The bushy eyebrows shot up the weather-beaten brow, and Mr. Caldwell laughed.

"I think you give me more credit than you should, sir! I can't read minds, you know. What can I do for you?"

Gerald looked him square in the eye and thought he discerned in that direct but opaque gaze something like a challenge.

"I have come to find out why you cancelled the agreement you made the other day in my hearing with Mr. Brown's firm."

Again the weather-beaten face showed signs of mirth.

"Oh, ho!" exclaimed the fellow, slapping his leg. "And to whom do I have the honour to speak? An agent of Mr. Brown's?"

"A friend," said Gerald simply.

"A friend?" repeated Caldwell, grinning widely. "Well, sure and I never heard of so good a one! Fancy taking his troubles into your own hands. I suppose he knows you're here?"

Gerald was forced to shake his head.

"Ah! So he doesn't know, does he? And yet you consider yourself so trusted a *friend* that you think you can assume what he would like?"

Irked by the cocky manner of this great hulking beast, Gerald said stonily, "I consider myself intelligent enough to know that he has been cheated, sir. Why did you cancel?"

Suddenly the great red face was drained of laughter and the small eyes in their wide frame grew smaller. "Since you consider it your business, Mr. Kirkland, I shall tell you: because I had a better offer."

"Oh?" said Gerald, curiously. "But I thought you had many clients, Mr. Caldwell. Why should one good offer cancel out another? Cannot you do business with more than one party?"

Caldwell seemed caught, but only for an instant. "Now listen here, young man," he said fiercely, "my business is my own, even if yours ain't. If I make an agreement, I may break it, do you see? There was no contract, anyhow—nothing on paper."

"Only the word of a gentleman and a handshake," muttered Gerald. "Would you take it as lightly if Mr. Brown went back on *his* word? If, after your work was done, he decided he did not like doing business with you after all?"

"It's a different situation," said Caldwell. "Quite different. If you were a businessman, you'd know. I choose my business, and my partners. I have decided Mr. Brown is not to be my partner."

"Then who is?" demanded Gerald quickly, but not quickly enough.

A slow smile crept over Caldwell's face until it was a grin. "That, young feller, is none of your affair! Good day, sir. I'm a mightly busy man, and I have got a great deal to do."

"So have I," said Gerald, ignoring the great hand stretched over the desk at him and keeping his chair. "So have I, but I shan't do it till I have an answer from you."

The smile grew wider, and Caldwell seemed to purr.

"You won't, won't you? We'll see about that!" And he reached for the bellpull.

"It is Philipse, is it not?" inquired Gerald, smiling. "Mr. Henry Philipse, whom I saw just now in the hallway? Mr. Philipse, who is in the slave trade?"

"That's not what I'm in it for!" growled Caldwell, his hand still touching the velvet rope.

"No? Then why *are* you in it? Just to keep Brown out?

Is that it? Or have you made some other arrangement with the . . . estimable Mr. Philipse?"

Caldwell saw he had made one slip and was not about to make another. His eyes narrowed even more, and his hand dropped from the bell. He was silent.

"Well, never mind that, just now. Who made the agreement with you? Who made you a better offer? Philipse himself? Or was it an envoy of his?"

Caldwell had taken on the look of a maddened bull, not sure where to charge but about to nonetheless. "What's it to you? The deal with Brown is off, in any case!"

"I shall give him your gracious message, Caldwell," said Gerald with heavy irony. "But I wish to know with whom you dealt. It was not, by any chance, a compatriot of mine? A Mr. Fitzwilliam Canterby?"

The great jaw dropped slightly; the eyes bulged. "How did you know that?" demanded the agent, his eyes suspicious.

"Merely a fortunate guess," replied Gerald, standing up. "Thank you for your time, Mr. Caldwell. I shan't trouble you further."

He walked to the door but turned round, his hand upon the knob and a smile on his lips. "Oh yes, I had better tell you: I know this Canterby pretty well, have known him all my life. Don't trust a word he says. His promise is about as good as . . . as yours, sir!" And then he was out.

He felt a certain elation. At least he had bested that fellow, at least he knew it was Canterby who was behind all this! As he walked down the length of the great hallway, he reminded himself that there was more to do, however. If Mr. Philipse had made an arrangement with Canterby, then surely they were not up to any good. No doubt Fitz had smelt a golden opportunity to make his fortune and had not winced at discrediting his friend's name, nor even at doing business with a slave trader, a man generally hated in New York! Gerald would still have to find out what they were up to. It was the only way he could help Harry Brown. "Word," indeed! The fellow, who had seemed so charmingly rustic to him before, was a perfect lout!

His foot just ready to come down upon the first step, his hand reaching for the banister, something caught his eye. No more than a flash of colour beneath the stairway—but something live! He stopped suddenly and held his breath. Craning his neck about, he saw the great mass of a butler standing to attention at the door, Gerald's hat and cloak and walking stick in hand. He seemed unaware of any other presence in the entrance hall. But surely there had been—something. But what? He was very jumpy—probably it was nothing.

He took another step and then stopped cold. He saw the butler glance nervously at something beneath him. Was someone there? Had Philipse never left? Was he waiting to catch him? But what the devil for?

He made himself continue down the steps, slowly and deliberately. But when the blow came, he was ready.

Chapter 23

Chastity, sitting beside her new friend and facing her brother, was brilliant with excitement.

"Fancy thinking we'd stay at home, Harry, when things are just beginning to be interesting! Anyhow, I've always wanted to meet this Caldwell person. Rather a character, Papa says."

"A character is about right, Chastity. The man's the best there is when it comes to fur and dealing with the trappers, but somewhere along the way he must have picked up something of their savagery. He's only half civilized, if you take my meaning."

"Really?" demanded Chastity, who was thrilled. "As bad as all that? What does he do?"

"Well, you shall see, if you insist. He lives in a big house full of frippery and furniture, but he possesses not one iota of taste. He has a butler who is more of a bodyguard and footmen who might be a herd of wild animals, though they are dressed in livery. His speech is a combination of crudity and affected refinement—he slips between the two without blinking. And he is—well, I should say he is about as hungry for a dollar as any man I have ever known, though he'll work for it better than most and he has a great many already."

"*How* fascinating!'" cried Chastity, leaning back in the carriage. "I can hardly wait to meet him, can you, dear?"

Charlotte smiled slightly and nodded. Her head was still too full of Gerald to think of anything else. Now that she was certain of his innocence, she could not sit still until she found him. Certain! For there had been the tiniest shadow of a doubt, if she was perfectly honest. But now that was vanished, along with every other shadow, save the great one of not knowing where, nor how, he was.

"Hadn't you better wait in the carriage for me ladies?" Harry inquired, when they had drawn up before the big square house.

"Wait in the carriage, Harry? No such thing! I shan't be cheated out of my character!"

"Very well, then," said Harry in resignation.

"Come along, then. But I won't have you with me while we are talking business. This isn't a sideshow, you know!"

"Oh, we'll entertain ourselves, won't we, Charlotte?" demanded Chastity with a smile. "Only let us see him and we'll stand up in the hall if he won't let us have a chair."

Harry mumbled something and went to knock. No answer came for some little time, and Harry was just on the point of saying that perhaps Caldwell was not in when a step was heard.

The door opened about an inch, and a voice said, "Yes?"

"Open up, there!" remarked Harry irritably. "It is Harry Brown to see Mr. Caldwell."

The door stayed at about the same width of openness, and there was silence. Then, "Just a minute, sir." And the door closed!

Harry Brown turned around in astonishment. "Well, what the Devil!" he breathed. "The fellow has no breeding, but at least he has never shut the door in my face before!"

But then they all heard a strange murmur of muffled voices and sounds as if a large bag was being dragged across the floor. "One moment, sir!" came the voice through the door, and then, at last, it was opened.

"Well, I never!" said Harry, going in after the ladies. "Is this the way you entertain these days, Caldwell?" For the vast man was standing on the stairway.

"From time to time," said the vast fellow, as if it were an ordinary way of going. "Well, Brown, glad to see you! And are these your fine ladies?"

"Lady Charlotte Harrington, may I present Mr. Caldwell? Caldwell, you do not know my sister."

"Lady Charlotte!" boomed the agent, smiling all over

his face, "Well, I'm pleased to know you, ma'am, and you too, Miss Brown. Now, what can I do for you?"

"I wish to have a word with you, Caldwell, in private. The ladies shall be all right down here, I think. Will you offer them a chair?"

Mr. Caldwell was all affability. "Delighted, young fellow! Yes, indeed, they may wait in there. Bring some sherry for the ladies, will you?" The butler went off to get the sherry, and Caldwell escorted them into the drawing room. "I hope you won't be bored." said Caldwell. "I'm sure our business will only last a minute." Harry gave him a glance but said nothing, smiling at Lady Charlotte and his sister, who were taking chairs by the fire.

"Well!" said Chastity when the men had gone out. "What a place this is! Did you ever see such gaudy things? And that man! I thought perhaps we had stumbled into the forest when I saw him! Just like a bear!"

"Or a sea cow," said Charlotte with greater accuracy. "What an odd way that was to let us in!"

"You shall think we are all of us savages before long," smiled Chastity.

"No, not at all—I never was welcomed anywhere so warmly!" replied Charlotte with real feeling.

The butler brought in their sherry and, bowing, went out, closing the doors behind him.

"What a peculiar kind of butler!" giggled Chastity. "He reminds me of some character from a novel! He looks only half tame!"

Charlotte smiled and looked into the fire. She was thinking of Gerald and that she would not be calm again until she was with him.

Chastity commenced walking about the room, picking up books and pieces of bric-a-brac, finally coming to a halt before the window, which gave out onto the drive and gardens. Suddenly she gasped,

"Come here, Charlotte! Come at once!"

Charlotte hastened to her side. "What is it, Chastity?" But then she, too, gasped. For out of a side door, just visible from this vantage point, the butler was issuing. He was dragging behind him, as if it were a sack, a human being! Just then a cart drove round the bend from the stables, and Charlotte breathed, "Chastity! It's Gerald! I know it is he!"

Chastity gasped. "*Gerald*? What are we to do?"

But Charlotte didn't answer. She was staring at the figure, limp as a dead man, and her heart stopped. The man was being hoisted by the butler into the cart, and the driver was preparing to whip up his horse.

"Quick!" cried Charlotte, "while the butler is outside! Slip into the hall!"

Stealthily, they crept through the drawing room doors and, holding their breaths, across the marble floor to the front door. Chastity glanced questioningly at Charlotte, who nodded urgently, and they ran out into the drive.

The carriage was waiting where they had left it, the coachman leaning against the box. He jumped to when he saw them and swung the door of the carriage open.

"Hurry!" ordered Chastity in a low voice.

"Jump up and drive as fast as you can after that cart!" exclaimed Charlotte, nodding towards the little vehicle which was now coming around the corner of the house. The coachman, bewildered but obedient, did as he was told.

Jostled by the poor springs of the hired carriage, the two ladies had no time to think of their own comfort. They were each leaning against opposite windows trying to get a glimpse of the cart. It had a lead of a few minutes upon them, but the driver did not seem to know he was being followed. With their team of four, they overtook him quickly. Knocking on the carriage roof with the command stick, Chastity ordered the driver to pull over ahead of it. The driver of the cart, seeing them, looked frightened and stopped. The coachman jumped down and approached them just as Chastity and Charlotte descended.

"Where are you going?" demanded Charlotte with such authority that Chastity stared. "Whom do you have in that cart?"

"Why—nothing, mum!" exclaimed the driver. "Nothing but an old bag!"

"We'll see about that!" cried the coachman, jumping onto the cart.

"Miss Brown—the scoundrel has got a man here! A gentleman from the look of it. He's bound and gagged!"

The driver paused only long enough to glance back and forth between the coachman and the ladies before jumping into the bushes. He vanished from sight in a trice, but no one paid him any heed.

Charlotte, heedless of her gown, boots and stockings, clambered up beside the coachman and, looking into the cart, gasped.

"Gerald!" she cried, "What have they done to you?"

"It's awright, ma'am, I think," said the coachman, drawing a handkerchief out of Gerald's mouth and untying his hands and feet. "Wait till he can tell you hisself."

What Gerald said, as soon as his mouth was free to speak, was only three words:

"Charlotte, my angel!"

The moral of which, as pointed out somewhat obscurely by a very merry Chastity some hours later, was that one ought always to take one's sister's advice and never—but never—to undertake any dangerous situation without at least two good strong girls to help one.

"For you see," she said, laying down her napkin, "who knows what would have become of him if we had not come along."

"I think," said Harry, smiling at his sister, "that it might have come right in the end, after all. They would have dumped him by the road and eventually someone would have found him."

Charlotte gave a shudder, and Gerald grinned.

"Thanks awfully, old boy—it was all I needed to make my day a little brighter!"

They all smiled, for with relief had come a sort of unnatural jollity. Charlotte, however, whose hand was joined in Gerald's beneath the table, gave his a little squeeze.

"It was Chastity who saw you," she murmured.

"Yes—but Charlotte who had the idea of following," put in the other. "*I* should never have dared on my own!"

"Well, whatever the case, we have got you back," said Harry with great feeling. "I blame myself dreadfully. I should not have let them persuade me against my better judgement!"

Now it was Chastity's turn to look guilty. "Well, it was *I* who believed that dreadful Mr. Canterby!" she exclaimed. "Really, I don't know what can have possessed me! He always looked a perfect weasel!"

"I should like to know, however, what he had to gain

from all this," remarked Harry. "Aside from discrediting his friend, I mean."

"Well, I believe," said Gerald thoughtfully, "that I have figured it out. I believe he made an arrangement with Philipse, who, as you told me, is in the slave trade. It must have had something to do with that. Perhaps the running of slaves through Canada or some territory over which Caldwell has influence."

"Caldwell wouldn't agree to that," responded Harry. "Even he is above that sort of thing. No, it must have been furs they were after."

"Perhaps he didn't tell Caldwell it was slaves," suggested Gerald, and Harry looked struck.

"Well, we shall find out for certain soon enough. I have already written to my father and asked him to put out a watch for Canterby. As for now, I think we all had better have a decent night's rest if we are to return to Garrison in the morning."

Chastity yawned and patted her mouth. "Yes, I'm *awfully* sleepy, dear! But perhaps you and I should go off and let these two—er—friends have a bit of time together?"

Harry grunted and got up from the table.

"I don't know if we ought to leave them alone, Chastity. After all, it is a private dining room, and Lady Charlotte is unmarried."

At which Chastity clapped a hand on her brother's arm and whispered, "Oh, bosh, Harry! Now come along and hurry up!"

Harry grinned over his shoulder as he was dragged off, and Gerald answered with a heartfelt smile of gratitude.

There followed one of those interludes which are perhaps left best undetailed but to say words were less a part of it than long, deep looks, sighs, and murmurs. For nearly six months these two lived without each other, and now they were together, is not that enough? They managed, in the next two hours, to convey a little of what had gone on in each of their lives since they had parted, but the great majority of what they said and looked concerned not the past, but the present and future. They drank from each other's eyes and—yes, from each other's lips—what they had craved for so long, believing they would never again be quenched. For those who like Chastity, crave a moral to their story, it was perhaps best articulated by Gerald as he sat in the greatest contentment he had ever known with his lover's head resting against his shoulder.

"Well," he said at length, "it was your father's ruse that separated us and Canterby's ruse that nearly did the job for good, but it was your ruse, my darling, that put their ruses to shame."

"What's that, Gerald?" murmured Charlotte happily.

"Why, brought us back together again, of course—a miracle!"

"But what was my ruse? I never played any tricks!"

"That's it, you see, and that's why it worked the best. Your ruse was—simply love!"

"Oh, I see," murmured Charlotte, smiling.

"You don't, dear. You are too pure to see how tricks work. Kiss me!"

And she did.

Afterword

In later years when Sir Gerald Kirkland was required to give an account of how he had reached that pinnacle of success which he enjoyed in the world of trade, he liked to smile and make mysterious sounds, which some swore were "Charlotte's Ruse."

When asked to explain, he would give a somewhat expedited version of the story we have just heard, ending with the words, "My good friends and associates, the Browns, were kind enough to offer me a partnership in their concern in return for what they considered had been my help to them. Naturally, I could not accept so great a favour, but I did become a sort of go-between for them here in England and eventually opened a branch of their office in London, which is now known as Kirkland and Brown, Limited. My father was somewhat shocked when he discovered I had 'sold out to trade' as he put it, but astonishingly, my wife's grandfather, the then Duke of Keynes, was greatly impressed. He went so far as to go against half the laws in the land and to give my wife a dowry consisting of half his fortune. It allowed us to go into partnership in very good standing, and, as you know, we are now one of the largest international conveyors of merchandise, with offices in eight cities. I believe His Majesty, King George, has come round to my views, at last—that trade is the best thing which has happened to our nation since the Spanish Armada.

Trade was, indeed, the wave of the future for England, and Sir Gerald Kirkland, later Lord Kirkland, received countless honours from the Crown, as well as from the American government. In the year 1836, when he was forty-five, he was named Royal Emissary to that nation, and for six years he and his gracious wife, Lady Charlotte, were able to enjoy once more the society of the friends they had made there nearly twenty years before. Amongst them, Mrs. Horace Wellingsworth, born Chastity Brown, and her brother Harry, were their greatest intimates. At the end of their tour, they built a house in Garrison, New York, close to the old Brown Manor House, with a view of the Hudson they had both grown to love, as a promise of many future visits.

The Marquis of Beresford, deprived of the income he had counted upon, lived to a bitter old age and never married. His affair with the Duchess of Devonshire gave way to many others, each ending in boredom on one side or another. He held the title of Duke for fifty years, after which it passed to the nearest male relation, one of his nephews.

Fitzwilliam Canterby left America in disgrace and before many years were up disgraced himself in England. He spent the remainder of his days travelling from one continental resort to another and living upon his winnings at cards.

About the Author

Judith Harkness was born in San Jose, Costa Rica, the daughter of parents in the diplomatic service. After a childhood spent in eight countries in Europe and South America, she attended Brown University in Providence, Rhode Island, where she studied literature and theater. Six years as a starving actress and a successful fashion model led unexpectedly to a freelance career in journalism. She currently lives in Milton, Mass., where she divides her time between writing fiction and magazine profiles of artistic personalities.